HOLES IN WATER

Matsie Non

Copyright © 2024

All Rights Reserved

ISBNs: 978-1-7326453-8-7

I AM A TOWN
Words and Music by Mary Chapin Carpenter
Copyright © 1992 EMLI April Music Inc. and Getarealjob Music
All Rights Administered by Sony Music Publishing (US) LLC,

424 Church Street, Suite 1200, Nashville, TN 37219
International Copyright Secured All Rights Reserved
Reprinted by Permission of Hal Leonard LLC

For those granite mountain men and women who I came from

And who passed the stories on to me.

For those generations before who allowed my story to be.

I send my heartfelt thanks and prayers to thee.

In the canvas of life, as blessings unfold,

Let gratitude paint stories, brilliantly bold,

May every heartbeat, each breathe that we take,

Be a symphony of thanks for the blessings you make

Acknowledgments

So many who have helped along the way deserve thanks and praise.

My Father, who told me this story and steered my writing with his stark way of speaking. My darling husband, who was my first reader and gave me wonderful insight and a point of view. My other first readers who helped with questions and suggestions: Lisa P., Barbara H., Rob H., Sande G., and Deb O., I thank you all. My first professional editors; Roberta E. and Blaine R., thank-you for your clear directions and great suggestions to make parts of this novel more focused. Finally, I want to thank the managers at Amazon, Aaron Wilson, Sr. Book Consultant, and the editing staff for helping me get this apple polished and ready for publication. It does take a village to create wonderful things!

Letter to Reader

Dear Reader,

As in all historical fiction novels, there are elements of historical fact blended with fiction. I've taken a great deal of liberty with both. Some names are fictionalized from both past and present. Most of the historical facts here are the facts that have been recorded over the years by others.

This story was told to me by my own Father, who grew up across the river from Tobacco Garden. This novel is dedicated in honor of his memory and the man who was hired the morning that Grinnell was murdered. Ole Thorson would sit with my Grandfather, my Dad, and his brothers on the men's side of the Scandinavian Lutheran Church in Beaver Creek; he would hand my Dad a penny and tell him, "You and me Maylen, we're going places."

Many have dug in the area over the years, and now everyone wishes to have a piece of what treasure hunters uncover. It is important to know how the government itself has changed over the years and demands their full share of found items. Please note the list of buried treasure in North Dakota as well as the list of different rules and regulations for treasure seekers to follow. The treasures listed still have not been found, or at least if they have been found, someone, somewhere, is keeping a shiny secret.

I hope you enjoy reading this novel of a strong and spirited woman that quietly changed history in this nation. After reading, I would love to hear from you.

Be Aware! This novel is intended for an adult audience and contains scenes of graphic sex and abuse. A gentle reminder that historical fiction novels are intended to be read as both pieces of historical fact blended with fiction.

Sincerely,

Matsie Non

Kin-ni-kin-nick *(noun)*: A substance traditionally used by some North American Indian peoples as a substitute for tobacco. Typically consisting of dried sumac leaves and inner bark of willow or dogwood.

Contents

Foreword i

Chapter One Alpha and Omega 1

Chapter Two Moon of New Grass 17

Chapter Three Last Summer 27

Chapter Four Moon of Turning Grass 35

Chapter Five The Bell Tolls 46

Chapter Six Moon of Sky Water 54

Chapter Seven Ideas Born Again 64

Chapter Eight Iron Horse 74

Chapter Nine Coming Home 82

Chapter Ten Moon of Slow Water 96

Chapter Eleven Work Heals 112

Chapter Twelve Sturgeon Moon 132

Chapter Thirteen A New Start to Life 140

Chapter Fourteen Moon of Yellow Grass 151

Chapter Fifteen Ranch Rhythms 161

Chapter Sixteen Corn Moon 177

Chapter Seventeen Rest and Relaxation 189

Chapter Eighteen Berry Moon 201

Chapter Nineteen Rest, Ride, Relax 210

Chapter Twenty Ice Moon 221

Chapter Twenty-One Diving Deep 228

Chapter Twenty-Two Planting Moon 237

Chapter Twenty-Three Back Home 247

Chapter Twenty-Four Strawberry Moon 256

Chapter Twenty-Five Return Dive 267

Chapter Twenty-Six Thunder Moon 280

Chapter Twenty-Seven Water Rights 288

Chapter Twenty-Eight Cooking Moon 301

Chapter Twenty-Nine Golden Family 311

Epilogue 332

Bibliography 335

About The Author 339

Foreword

Nestling upriver from Tobacco Garden was a natural bowl-shaped coulee fed by a freshwater spring. Wandering tribes had been returning to this summer camp area for eons. Where the dust-gray clouds tumble from the bluffs into the slow-swirling river, the wild tobacco plants called kinnikinnick still cling precariously to life. Shadowy silver-green slender leaves hide the seed clusters in this plant. They ripen and turn black under the heat of the prairie sun and provide food for small animals and birds, as well as smoke for the tribes. Tribes would gather the kinnikinnick kernels from the plants so they could use them for smoke in the winter around the hearth fires. The smoke from the kernels would weave in and out with the stories they told as the smoke drifted up to the night sky.

Many nations would meet here as they hunted the area around Cuesik Springs to provide for each winter. Women and children would work the draws, plucking berries as the men and boys would run the game to ground and return to the camps with their daily rewards. As one season melded into another, the nomadic tribes would follow the path their food source would take.

The sweet berries of Tobacco Garden would be crushed with dried fat and meat and made into pemmican. Glimpses of the sun, heat, and dust would be pounded into thin strips of memory to be eaten during bitter cold, gray days of prairie winter when the land was no longer awash with the warmth of green, blue, and gold. Scrapping hides and turning them into leggings, breechcloths, tunics, and moccasins while cooking and gathering herbs and berries kept the entire tribe busy.

When the time was right and the preparations to ensure each nation's survival were filled, they would send men out to capture horses that roamed wild along the river banks. To capture and expand bands of horses, they used feats of unsurpassed daring. A man would tie a leather thong around his arm and 'ride along' beside the wild horse to keep it from running away after he looped the other end of the leather around the bottom lip of the horse.

Tobacco Garden really had her start with the bands of wild mustangs that would cross the river and clamber up the bluffs into the fertile Nesson Valley. Bits of dried plants, strips of rawhide, and scars barely visible under thick coats told stories of past adventures. Cherished by many, caught by few, and broken by even fewer strong men, these first four-legged travelers created a groundbreaking time for those who had the courage and strength to catch, tame, or steal them as they left their own brand on the west.

The native tribes that hunted and followed the animals were Salish, Mandan, Hidatsa, Teton Dakota, Arikara, Sioux (Lakota and Hunkpapa), Cree, and Assiniboine. These men and women wove history in the smoke as they told of brave captures made when the sun beat hot on the land. The ways of 'The People' were wild, rough, and savage to the white trappers that followed Lewis and Clark into this garden area of the river. In August of 1825, 'Moon When Buffalo Become Fat'; the military presence came with eight paddle power keelboats to accomplish two things; to overawe the Nations and to enforce the law stopping foreign traders from operating in U.S. territory. From this point on things would change forever for the Nations.

It was the promise of coins from 'easy to catch fur, gold, and mounts that led many men there. Later on, it would be the promise of flat rolling land to farm along with easy money to be made selling horses if the crops didn't come in. The added bonus of grazing land for beef would lure more into the promise of the garden area.

The town was given birth eons before her official calendar date of 1880 and her watery demise when the dam waters flooded her under in the 1940s. The truth behind the beauty of those years is not only that this inland town had no dusty roads for pioneers to reach her, but that she was a prairie garden and was told about in smoke stories much older than the calendar records.

This is the story my father told to me about the land he was born and raised on across the river, *'Holes in Water.'*

Chapter One
Apha and Omega

"It's always the droning of a fly trapped in a window that brings the memory back." Mort dry coughed as he said this. Wiping the blood from his mouth into a cloth, he inhaled deeply through his nose piece and continued, "Always think 'bout that day...and that penny."

Never one to miss an opportunity to hear another tale from his years growing up on a small ranch in the West, I would beg for more. My dad, as he would say, was getting ready to put his boots on for the last time. As Doc had said, "Your dad is dying."

"So, Dad, what does the sound of a trapped fly remind you of?" I gently urged him to tell me more.

"Well, it brings back the memory of a place, nope...not just a place, but a time and some people who changed me forever."

"Dad, you might be getting ready to meet your maker, but I would say you've been pretty solid for many years now. How could a place and some people have changed you at all?" Thinking back on what I said, I would come to realize later I would have been better off not asking that question.

My dad had changed from a very large man to a shrunken version of himself in the past three months since he had been diagnosed with his sickness. He once stood a solid 290 pounds at around six feet. Now he weighed in at 195 and was actually measuring five feet, ten inches according to his Oncologist. By the time he would pass on, three months from this conversation, he would weigh about 180 pounds and be around five feet, eight inches tall. It seems that cancer cared nothing for who you have been, only what it can take from you.

That was the night that set me off on this chase in the first place; this hidden treasure of money in a forgotten valley on a much-traveled river, sweetly sleeping under waves. This chase has changed my family as well; my brother and his conniving wife and two terrible children, and sad to say my own husband, children, their spouses, and children.

How could the sound of a fly droning in a hot window bring this all to just one family? The question really isn't how, but why? It involves the ever-present need for more in life of everything. More questions to ask and not enough time to get the answers. And then more money to spend on more things that are just things is really the dilemma behind this all. I guess this is all easy for me to write since others would love to have our problem.

For right now, my problem is contained in a simple bundle in the back of our weather-beaten work truck. How do you divide a fortune now held in a wrapped tarp in the back of my truck? Sitting here beside the muddy water watching the twisting eddies reminds me that the whole story is more interesting than just the ending and deserves to be told.

I should start with before he passed away when he told me that hot summer afternoon while a trapped fly brought back the memory of Tobacco Garden.

BEFORE

"Let me give you some of the before story," Dad said as he sat in the warm sun and took a small sip of cool water from the glass. I watched the glistening sweat beads and listened as the beads slowly slid down and left another wet ring mark on the already stained oak table. The stains were so uniform, at that point, they looked like an ancient Celtic map on the surface of his side table.

"Before my dad and his brother arrived on the Immigrant Train up in Nesson Valley, it was an even wilder place. The horses that were still wild would run up through the 'rez (for those not from around these parts, this is the way locals refer to reservation lands) and cross the river right in the bend across from Nesson Valley. This is the spot I'm talkin' about. Those horses, that I 'member seeing when I was a boy, were things of beauty. Wild manes and thick coats covered with burrs and bite marks on some would come up from the river bottom in groups of 30 to 50 head. They were amazing to watch, smell and listen to 'em call to each other."

He coughed again and sat quietly before he could continue.

"Yep, right there in Nesson Valley was the spot on the river where the Missouri took a turn and on the other side was Tobacco Garden. That was where the town was, the landlocked Prairie Queen. You could say she lifted her skirts for just about everyone, but that wouldn't even be close to the truth. She was a Queen long before our people came, and she will be long after we are gone." Dad took another small sip from the glass he held in his shaking hand.

"What exactly do you mean she 'lifted her skirts'? Are you saying she was a lawless town, filled with saloons and whorehouses?" I didn't mean to interrupt the meanderings of my dad as he was dying, but the way he started this story was already filling me with a sense of dreadful curiosity. I flipped my shoulder-length brown hair over my shoulders and had a strange sense of realization that the more I heard, the more I would want to know until I had uncovered some terrible secret about this town that had disappeared.

"Nope, not saying that at all, Missy. I'm telling you that Tobacco Garden was a town of The People before it became a white man's town. The People would travel there with the seasons as they followed the herds of animals. Don't tell me that you've forgotten all you learned about this." He looked at me and then winked.

Never before, and probably never again, will someone I know and love be on their deathbed and wink at men when they were dying before me.

"Dad, I haven't forgotten the place history, I'm just curious about how it ties back to you and a penny." I waited patiently for him to continue the story.

"I guess it isn't so much about the penny, but about the man who gave it to me in church that day and what it would mean to me after all these years." He continued in that dry raspy sounding voice more slowly as he remembered even more of that day. "It was hot, just like today. The church was hotter than this side of hell. Elgin, Cledith, and I were with Dad on the men's side and Ma and Harriet were right across from us on the women's side. I remember Ole looked like he was a hundred years old to me.

He came in right before the service started and sat beside Dad. He leaned over to me with his hat balanced on his knee and took out a brand-new penny and gave it to me and said, 'You and me kid, we're going places together.' I remember my dad smiling down at me because of this 'gift' from this big strange-looking man.

Dad leaned over to me and whispered, "Maylen, this one does not go in the offering plate or for candy in town, keep this one safe as long as you can. This penny is very special and will bring you great things."

"I still have it, you know, it's right over there on my dresser, Missy. Go get me that little wooden box on the top now, will you?" Dad coughed again into his ever-present cloth that grew with more and more stains of blood as the sun moved across the cloudless sky.

Moving across the sun porch and through the French doors into his bedroom area, I found the little wooden box that I had seen sitting on his dresser since I was a child. The same plain small box that was about the size of a small candy box. I remember he told me once that he had made it in high school when he noticed that his old baking soda tin looked like it was getting rusty. I cradled it in one palm and carried a pitcher of ice water in the other. This seemed to be the only thing that he could keep in his stomach these last few days.

"Here it is, Dad, just what you ordered." I smiled at him as I placed the small wooden box on his lap and refilled his water glass.

"Thanks, Missy, you're a good daughter...even if your older brother and his family think differently!" He gave a soft little cackle of a laugh that sent him into another round of coughing. "Guess I better stop with the jokes and finish my story, while I still have time."

"Dad, it's alright if you don't want to talk anymore, you don't have to. I'll just be here while you rest." I was worried he would die in my arms and worried that he was suffering as well.

"Nope, I'll have none of that nonsense now. You know what I say, plenty of time to rest when you're gone." He didn't laugh again, but just smiled at his own attempt at gallows humor.

"Where was I? Yes, the penny!" He gently lifted the lid from the box, and under some papers that he didn't show me, he brought up a penny that was dull with age, but in near-perfect condition. "I've kept it all these years, and just like Ole promised me, I have gone places." He passed the coin to me to look at, and I was startled.

"Dad, this penny is from 1925; you were only three then. How is it in such good condition? Were you really only three when Ole gave it to you? Who is Ole anyway? What does this have to do with Tobacco Garden?" My questions that weren't stated pushed behind the other ones that had already spilled out until I saw my Dad's face.

His brows, wispy white and almost gone along with the rest of his hair, were drawn together in a scowl, "Missy, you've always been more curious about things than you should be. I guess you're like your Mother that way! Same pretty brown hair, same warm brown eyes, and same sprinkle of freckles on your nose. Yup, you are your mother's girl in more than just looks, I guess. Let me finish now. Well, I was three when Ole gave me that very penny you're holding. I always listened to Pa, so I never spent that penny. I just kept it in my old baking soda tin Ma gave me, then this box I made in school. Now Ole was a man well known in the Valley and the Garden; he is a big piece of the treasure." Dad continued in his gentle, relaxed way.

"Treasure?" I'm not sure if I squeaked it or yelped it out at that point. I just know it was hard on his ears because he reached up and covered them with his hands.

"Treasure is what I said and treasure is what I meant, young lady!" Dad said more forcefully, "Look, I'm feeling tired right now; how 'bout I try some soup or something easy on my throat?"

"Promise me when I come back with the soup, after your nap, that you will tell me more?" I now was filled with dread that this amazing story I was about to hear would be lost for all time if my dad passed when I was in the kitchen, warming up soup.

"I promise Missy, just go heat something up and let me

rest a minute. I know better than to let you or this old story rile me up so quickly. I just need to relax and get settled before I share the rest." He shut his eyes then and appeared to be relaxing comfortably.

I handed Dad his penny back, and he nestled it carefully into the small box and handed it to me with one hand; the other motioned towards his dresser top. I returned it and smiled and said, "Be right back with some soup Dad."

I slipped down the back stairs in the ranch house to the kitchen in the back while he napped on the upstairs enclosed sun porch. The mountains in the distance beckoned me to walk, hike, ride, or jog up to them and breathe in the fill of pine-scented air to get the smell of the sick room out of my heart forever. Instead, I turned to the old electric stove and opened up a can of chicken noodle soup and warmed it on the stove. While it was warming, I called home.

My husband, Chuck, wasn't answering, so I left him a voice mail on his cell phone. I knew he was on yet another construction job. I also knew by the end of the day my voice mail would be answered with a call or a message. I told him how Dad was doing and said I had another amazing story to share with him. Even though Chuck enjoyed my dad's tales, he also told me that he thought Dad's stories were filled with imagination.

He really said, "Honey, your dad is filled with crap with those stories." I prefer the word imagination to crap since I'd heard stories from both my parents all my life and enjoyed them with the luster of imagination they stirred up inside of me.

Warm soup on a tray, some tempting fresh blueberries, and warm tea, I headed back up the stairs to Dad's domain. Placing a smile, I didn't feel on my lips and inhaling the sweet smell of the blueberries, to try and keep the sick room smell from myself, I walked into the room. "OK Dad, here is a little bite to eat."

"Had a good nap, Missy!" He opened one eye a little and sniffed at the tray, "MMM, smells just like your Momma would make me."

I had to laugh out loud, even though I didn't feel like it. "Mom never made decent homemade anything in her life, and you know it! If it hadn't been for Aunt Florence coming over, we probably would never have known that you could make your own anything!"

Dad just nodded his head and slurped his soup with his spoon; "Course you're right there, Missy, but it does make me smile just to think 'bout your mom as a real homemaker when she was around. I do miss that woman so..." His voice trailed off as he continued to slowly sip the soup.

I watched and waited patiently for him to continue his meal, and then when he pushed the tray away from his lap, I moved it to the bedside table to take the nearly empty tray back down before his next nap. I noticed he had eaten half the soup and finished off the cup of tea as well as half the blueberries. I took that as a good sign; at least he still had his appetite.

"You know your mom has been gone for fifteen years now, and I still like to think of what a great woman she was!" Dad smiled as he leaned back in his recliner.

"But I know you want to hear more about the penny, Ole, and the Garden than you do her. Let me think here about where I left off in my story."

I was almost biting my lip off at that point, not wanting to rush him but curious and filled with a sense of wonder about what treasure he was going to tell me.

"OK," he said more gently, "a little review of history first. When The People were owners of the Tobacco Garden area, they were freewheeling folks who followed the herds and the seasons. They thought nothing of befriending the white trappers, those who came looking for beaver first and giving their daughters to them for wives. The trappers were for the most part good men, with powerful medicine behind them, or so The People believed. Now this was before Lewis and Clark came into the picture, of course, and that means before the Civil War." I just nodded at this point since part of me was afraid to interrupt in case the story was never finished.

"So that means that the Hidatsa, Blackfoot, Crow, Sioux, and all the other Seven Nations Members were all present at one point or another over the seasons at Tobacco Garden. That also means they used that place for a time to tell stories, swap horses, marry off children, and collect tobacco plant parts for winter smokes. They used all other kinds of plants and berries that were present in that garden of a place." Dad glanced out the window and sighed, "Time to switch chairs, Missy, after I use the facilities."

I had never known a time when my dad didn't call the bathroom 'the facilities' and this statement alone brought small tears to the corners of my eyes as I watched him slowly stand with the aid of a walker and even more slowly walk to the attached bathroom. I was glad we; my husband, brother and I, had insisted on this luxury being installed for Mom before she passed away.

"Back to the story now," Dad stated as he switched his seat to Mom's older recliner so he could face west and watch the Sun start to drop over the mountains. "So, there they were, these wonderful first tribes in Tobacco Garden; lovin' and livin' life large and in-charge of their piece of the world and wham! What happens next is still hard to think about for some, even with all the time that has passed." He shook his bald head lightly, "I wonder how it was the first time they saw Lewis & Clark? Did they realize that their garden meeting spot was about to be run over with jackasses? Sometimes I think the really wise men and women of the tribes did know even back then."

"So, there they are meeting up with this group of men from 'another world,' and what happens next? Right not to answer daughter...I'll tell you nothing for quite a while until the Big Cats from the East start to think about taxes for the land, and the riches in supplies and the gold they hear is further up river! Yep, plain old-fashioned greed is what started a lot of this stuff, probably will end a lot of this stuff as well."

"Dad, do you mind if I sit in your chair for a while?" It was silly I suppose asking him for permission, but old habits of respect for parents are always in place in this part of the world.

He waved me into the recliner he had just moved from and took a sip of water as he waited for me to settle in to hear more of this tale; could the treasure part be coming soon?

"I know, I know…you've heard all this stuff at least a thousand times before. It doesn't really hurt to be reminded of how far we have come and how far we still have to go. So, where was I?" He threw the question to me.

"Dad. So far you made it up to Lewis & Clark and taxes and gold. Is this the treasure part?" To my own ears, I suddenly sounded like a spoiled child and had the decency to blush. "Sorry Dad."

"Right, well, they really didn't care much about the area until right about the end of the Civil War. That's when the treasure story really starts, and that's where a Civil War Veteran comes to the Garden, things start to really get wild in the river bottoms. But before the young bucks who fought in the War started to show up and work the bottoms as Wood Johnnies, other trappers were here first."

"I guess you need to understand how a young gal could get traded to an old man before we get to the treasure part." Dad sighed when he said this; he had always been a gentleman where ladies were concerned. He had a passion for his only Daughter and for his three Granddaughters as well. He believed in the old West code of treating women with decency and respect.

"So, this French trapper comes down and is trapping in

the Garden area right alongside the Seven Nations; must have been a fairly good man working for the Hudson Bay Company and all. He gets himself hitched to a Nation Woman and they have some children, girls. It seems since that is when the trouble starts. 'Bout this time the Civil War is ending, beaver pelts are doing alright, but they are trappin' out the areas so there really isn't much left. Well, the trapper and his wife are offered some money for one of their daughters, a pretty young thing by the name of 'All Goes Out'. She was given the English name of Josephine by the local priest AFTER he found her 'livin' in sin' with a man twenty years older than her. "Dad paused to take another sip of tea from his cup. "They thought nothing of trading their children off for supplies; they wanted to make sure their kids had someone to take care of them. If they were a first wife, they figured they'd have it easier later on. So, the way I figure it, the gal, Josephine, was about twelve or thirteen when Beaver Woman, her Ma, and her Hudson Bay French Trapper Dad, Charles Malnouri, married her off to Grinnell in the way of the tribe." Dad's voice was weary now and his head started to drop to one side. "Think I'll take a rest now, why don't you saddle up the mare and take her for a ride? Marian will be here and she can wake me up to poke at me if she needs to."

I bent over and kissed the top of Dad's almost bald head. "Sounds like a good idea, Dad. I'll just wait for Marian to get here, and then I'll go saddle up for a quick ride. I'm expecting a call from Chuck soon anyway. By the way, I need to say, 'I love you, Dad.'" I turned as I said this with the tray in my hands before stepping down the stairs, but he was already asleep and didn't hear me. With a worried glance at him and how quickly he was sliding in and out of sleep, I knew the end was on its way. I was downstairs cleaning up when I heard the sound of Marian's truck pull into the front yard.

"In the kitchen, Marian." I said in a loud clear voice. "Come on back!"

"Good to see some action back here." Marian greeted me with a chuckle and a hug. "I'm always teasing your dad about this big old kitchen going to waste with him just heating soup for himself! How are you doing?" She anxiously asked with the next breath.

"I think I'm okay. I'm worried that the end is coming too soon for him. He is falling in and out of sleep so quickly now I can barely keep track on the notepad you left me." I shuddered when I said this as I realized I had once again forgotten to write down the amount of time he slept this morning, when he fell asleep, and if he seemed disoriented or not when he woke up. "Sorry, Marian, I'm not a good nurse in place of you."

"No worries on that front, Missy. When I check him, I'll be able to tell you more about the timeframe we are looking at. Just remember what Doc said, 'strange things happen all the time, no one knows for sure when the end will come.' You just have to hang on and give him whatever comfort he will take." With her arm draped over my shoulder, she gave me another hug.

Marian had always been like another Aunt Florence in my life. You wouldn't know to look at her that this small gray-haired woman who was a retired nurse was a dynamo of strength, resilience, and energy. She always wore her hair cropped close in a 'Pixie Cut,' as she called it. I think it was because she was a true no-nonsense woman of the West that I felt very close to and was comforted by her being here.

You never smelled perfume on her, and she wore no makeup or jewelry, but she was an attractive woman who would light up a room with her smile and make you feel the heat of the summer sun with her laugh. Marian had been through much in her own life, married and buried three husbands, and lost two of her five children as well. Some in town thought she was crabby; I just thought she had a streak of independence a mile wide, and I wished I was even more like her.

"Thanks, Marian. I'll come upstairs after I wash up when I'm done riding." I picked up my cell phone and headed out to the barn to saddle up the mare. Some would think it was terrible that my dad and mom had never given their animals names; they just didn't think it was necessary. A horse was just that, a horse, and not a family member. It would be good to get away from the smell of death that seemed to linger like a cloud around my dad. Besides, the ride along the flats might help me be in a better frame of mind when Chuck called.

With as long strides as my five-foot six-inch body would let me take, I headed out to the barn and marveled again that the paint looked good even though it hadn't seen a new coat of paint for the last three years. The last time it had been painted was when Dad had fallen off the ladder and, during his recovery in the hospital from his broken arm, had been diagnosed with cancer. I was really looking forward to a different set of smells and a little sage hint on the wind as I saddled up the mare. With any luck, I might even make it to the hills and get my lungs filled with the sweet smell of Pine.

She took the bit in her mouth and waited patiently as I slung the blanket on her back, then the saddle, and gently cinched up so she wouldn't feel the pinch on her belly. She blew her nose out at me as if to let me know she was just as impatient to get away as I was. We headed out, two aging females, just looking for a sweet breeze to fill our lungs.

Chapter Two
Moon of New Grass

Strands of lush, silvery-green cottonwoods and gray-green elm trees towered on the river bend as they shadowed the thick underbrush of chokecherries, buffalo berries, and even wild small sweet strawberries. Here in the shady cool river bend, the bugs were thick, the dragonflies droned and hummed as they captured one mosquito after another, but the girl paid no attention to them. She walked silently to the edge of the water and dipped her hide bag into a clear spot. Her Father, a white trapper, was in a hurry to get a cool drink as usual. She smiled to herself as she heard the cry of the owl startled from its daytime nap by something moving through the brush about a hundred yards upstream.

"Comes At Night," she called to her younger sister in Hidatsa, "is that you?"

No answer came back to her except a small giggle that she instantly recognized. "Come out now and help me carry this back to the lodge before Father gets angry," she said to the bushes where she was sure her sister was hiding from her.

Comes At Night stepped from the shadows and said with

a surprised voice, "How did you know it was me tracking you?"

"You walk like a big raccoon carrying a dead fish," All Goes Out answered in an angry tone. "You know you were supposed to be helping Mother with the berries and crushing them, how did you get away from the lodge without her seeing you?"

Comes At Night's bottom lip trembled as she looked up at her older sister. "I do not walk like a big raccoon, do I?" She asked with tears at the corners of her eyes.

All Goes Out felt her heart move as she saw her younger sister's trembling lips, "No, I really did not hear you, Comes At Night. I did know your laughter right away; you really are not good at being quiet at all. Now, how did you get away from the lodge without Mother seeing?"

"Mother was called to the lodge by Father because the cool water was not there yet; he said he needs a drink badly," Comes At Night answered very quietly. Even though she was two years younger than her sister, both girls knew that the need for drink wasn't for water, but for the strong whiskey their Father drank when he was bothered.

Charles Malnouri was bothered lately, ever since he heard word from the other trappers on the river that the War was over and that more white people were coming to their little corner of the world. Malnouri had come across the blue waters from France to Canada and then down from Canada to try and establish his fortune. A short barrel-chested man with dark curly hair, snapping brown eyes, a wide smile, and a love of the bottle, he was a trusted trapper for the Hudson Bay Company. Alone in the upper breaks of the Missouri or, 'Holes in Water,' as the Nations Tribes called it. He had married a beautiful dancer from the Hidatsa tribe. He had a peaceful life on the river bottom for the last 13 years, trapping and living quietly with his wife and two daughters. The beavers had been trapped heavily for the last five years in this little part of paradise. Unfortunately, Charles knew what his wife, Beaver Woman, and his children, All Goes Out and Comes At Night, did not know.

Even though their lodge was on a small rise close to the top of the cliff, where the prairie breezes could cool them in the summer and keep the heat close in the deep winters with the rocks behind them, they still had no legal claim to the land their lodge was on. Charles was nervous, and the only thing that seemed to settle this was a nice pull on a bottle of whiskey.

"Woman, 'git yer hind end in here!" Charles's deep bass voice shook the clay colds packed between the ceiling poles. Dust filtered down on the crude wooden table and the man's shoulders as he pounded again and rattled the empty whiskey bottle beside him. His brown eyes, that were usually sparkling, had a dull luster to them and were surrounded by red lines that looked like deep scratches. His nose had a hint of blue on the end that hadn't been there three years ago when All Goes Out had seen her tenth summer.

"Father, I'm here with your water," All Goes Out spoke softly to the raging bull of a man that sat in despair at the table. "Let me pour some into the bottle." She spoke gently and stayed behind the man, out of reach and out of harm's way. Quickly and without spilling a drop, she poured the cool clean water into the empty whiskey bottle to see if this would quiet the surly man.

"Ah, 'bout time you showed up with a new bottle, you good-for-nothing piece of bone!" Charles muttered under his breath as a newly filled bottle appeared at his elbow. Not knowing the only whiskey he was filling himself with now was clear water, with just a hint of fire from the bottle dregs, appeared to be content after he drank deeply.

Charles sat at the table, brooding and muttering to himself over what to do about his house, his wife, and his two daughters. He could blame the problem on the greedy George Grinnell, he thought, but his wife and daughters were much easier targets, and Grinnell was a recent Civil War Veteran, tough as nails, and younger than Charles.

Grinnell had already earned himself a name for being tough as shoe leather in this part of the Missouri Breaks. The tall, steely blue-eyed man with chestnut brown hair had worked as a Wood Hawk three years in a row before taking off last year for Montana Territory to try and strike it rich in the gold fields. He returned with a sullen look on his face and stories of a slaughter he took part in, where he mounted heads of 'murdered savages' on pikes along a river bend. No one questioned his story, and no one asked about any gold. Since no one dared question a true Civil War Hero, as George had proven himself with the troop out of Minnesota at Gettysburg and again as a spy for General Sherman. He seemed pleasant enough around others but dangerous in a crafty way.

"Likes 'em younger," Sally said, Charles muttered to himself as he took another pull from the bottle. Charles waited for the burn down his throat; he only had a weak sensation on his tongue. He wasn't drunk enough to not notice the difference between water in an old whiskey bottle and the real whiskey that should have been in there. He turned and smashed the bottle against the door in front of All Goes Out and shouted, "You little bastard! I should have known that Woman would try something like this!" He moved quicker than what All Goes Out believed possible and grabbed her by the braids and threw her against the door and pushed her outside.

"You damn fool women, the lot of you!" He shouted at Beaver Woman and Comes At Night, who both came running when they heard All Goes Out scream. "You have no idea that we are about to lose our place here. Instead of helping me figure this out, you tried to cheat me! I'll have none of it or of you; I might as well shuck out right now as to stay and try to figure out how to keep our place!"

Charles was panting from the drink, bellowing, and the hot sun as he continued his tirade. Beaver Woman approached him with her planting stick that she had been using in her garden area to check the squash. She was not willing to be lodge-poled in front of her daughters; this was a man's right if a woman disobeyed in her tribe. Her man could strike her with a stick, but only when they were alone and not around family. She kept the stick between them and stood back away from Charles so he could not grab her.

"Big Beaver Man, why do you shout so? We can move our

lodge to another spot. You worry too much, I think. Come sit in the shade and cool yourself so the heat does not make you howl." Beaver Woman watched Big Beaver Man as she squinted against the Sun and tried to keep her distance.

"Beaver Woman, you know...NOTHING!" Charles shouted at her. "While you plant squash and get firewood, there are white men who own this land right now. We will have......NOTHING!" he shouted again at her. "We need to find something of value to trade to keep our place here, and we need to find it soon. Think, if you can, of more than plants and firewood!"

Very quickly in Hidatsa, Beaver Woman said to her two daughters, "Leave and go to the river and swim for a while. Do not come back until I speak with your father alone. Quick before he grabs you again, All Goes Out. Go now!"

"Do as Mother wishes," All Goes Out said to her younger sister, pushing her by the shoulders as Comes At Night seemed to only be able to stand and stare at the giant white man who was their father.

At thirteen, All Goes Out knew what was going to happen even if her younger sister did not yet understand. When they left, Big Beaver Man would either couple with Beaver Woman right on the ground or would beat her senseless depending on how much whiskey he already had burning in him. He might even do both; they would know when they came back from swimming in the river.

Both girls stripped off their hide dresses and leggings and waded into the murky brown water that swirled around in a little cove away from the main river. The Missouri, or 'Holes In Water' as the tribe called it, was flowing slowly, but with a mean undercurrent. All Goes Out had seen at least three animals, both wild horse and deer, be pulled under by that current and not make it to the other side.

She warned Comes At Night, "Stay here in the circle area where we can stand so the big water does not take you away." For once her younger sister listened and swam quietly back and forth. Both girls took breaks from swimming and lay on the bank and dried out in the Sun. Plucking a few berries from the undergrowth made their lunch, and they drank cool water from the river in a sandy area that washed away the mud.

They swam, dried off, and slipped their shifts and leggings on and played hide and seek in the cooler shade along the river bank. They shared and ate the berries they found in the undergrowth when they were hungry and laughed often together. All Goes Out saw a sage grouse and whispered to her sister in Hidatsa.

"Comes At Night, be still; I'm going to throw a rock at the grouse, and then we can surprise Father with meat for supper. Maybe Mother will let us have the feathers for a fan from the wings. Be still now; I'm going to throw the rock." All Goes Out kept whispering and whistling the bird song as she lifted her right arm slowly overhead and threw the rock expertly at the head of the bird.

Jumping up from her kneeling position with a quick squeal, she said, "Got it! Comes At Night, we will have meat tonight for supper!" She moved quietly between the brush and undergrowth along the river's edge and picked up the dead grouse by the feet. "Look," she said as she turned to show her younger sister. "The wings will be perfect for fans for us when it gets hotter."

Comes At Night took out the skinning knife from her belt that her Mother had given her. After chopping off the head, she left the grouse whole and would finish cleaning the bird back at the lodge. In case this one had eggs inside she hadn't laid yet, they would bury those in the ash of the fire and have them for breakfast if they were lucky. They would mount the wings on a stick in a spread-out fan shape so they could cool the air around their faces and keep the flies landing on them. The rest of the inside organs would not be wasted either but would be thrown in a pot of water and roots to make a meaty stew. The carcass of the bird would be roasted over the fire on sticks, and they would have some good eating from this one small bird.

When the sun started to drop towards the West in a blazing ball of orange light and the air started to cool, the two girls headed back to their dugout lodge. They walked silently beside each other; they were not sure what they would find. All Goes Out carried the bird by its feet between her and her sister. All Goes Out spoke in a normal voice that seemed almost like a shout when it sounded against the walls of the dugout lodge. "Mother?"

No response could be a good thing, but could also be a bad thing. Shod pony marks in the ground by the front of the lodge meant company. No response and no snoring meant no one was home, or someone was hurt inside. Gripping Comes At Night by the hand, All Goes Out slowly approached the hide flap of the dugout door.

"Mother?" She called in Hidatsa. No smells or sounds came from the lodge. Both girls ducked under the flap at the same time and breathed a sigh of relief. Nothing was thrown in the room but the bottle that had been broken by their father. Both girls bent down and picked up the broken pieces of glass and moved them to the side to use as cutting tools.

Not knowing where their parents were, All Goes Out and her sister set out to build the fire up and begin to cook the meat. She skinned the grouse and when removing the organs found three eggs the bird hand not laid. She handed them to her sister and said, "Bury these in the ashes on the side of the fire. When morning comes, we can eat them for breakfast."

After getting her sister busy with a stick, she kept a close watch on her as she buried the eggs in the ashes on the side of the fire. All Goes Out mounted the carcass of the grouse on two crossed pointed sticks to slowly roast the bird next to the flames. They would need to turn it every so often so it wouldn't burn; they would eat well tonight.

All Goes Out had experienced this before when her parents had traveled with the beaver skins to the Fort. When they returned three days later, they had both smelled of cheap whiskey and filth. She was afraid this was happening again, but she kept quiet so her sister would not be afraid and would have food to eat.

Taking the heavy iron pot, she suspended it on the hook on the other side of the fire and half-filled it with water from the skin. She threw in the inside organs from the grouse and the root vegetables her mother had placed in the corner. She only used three of them, so they would have food to roast for the next few days as needed.

The sun was down and the grouse was roasted when they sat to eat together. Picking the meat off the bones they quietly talked while they ate their fill. Nothing was wasted here, and the bones from the bird went into the pot to simmer with the internal organs and root vegetables. All Goes Out took the wings from the grouse and spread them out and showed Comes At Night how to wrap the ligaments from the legs of the bird around the joint onto a stick to hold their fans in place.

Finally, the fans were done and would hold and needed to dry out. They left them on the table by their father's chair, after adding more water to the pot they banked the fire. They lay down on the opposite side of the lodge from their parent's bed. They fell asleep holding hands and trusting that their parents would show up soon. All Goes Out knew they would return with glazed eyes, stinking breath, and filthy smells around them.

Chapter Three
Last Summer

The horse and I left the corral and swung into a lazy lope towards the hills; the air, scented with pine and sagebrush, filled my lungs and gave me a quiet sense of calm. I let the mare have her head and didn't even bother to tighten the reins when she would slow and bend her neck to reach towards the buffalo and timothy grass. I imagined the old gal felt like I did – good enough to enjoy the day and just lazy enough to fill her belly with something extra when she had the chance.

I knew Dad's death was coming, perhaps sooner than I was ready for it. I didn't look forward to having to sell this place of peace. I didn't look forward to the confrontations with my older brother and his shrew wife, nor the Generation X kids they raised.

My own husband and children caused me some concern as well. I knew my daughter and her husband were more concerned with making ends meet and raising their own twins than they were with keeping this land. I also knew my son was more concerned with completing college and moving on to med school than keeping the land. My husband, let me put you straight, thought that land was a 'burden' and that horses were nothing more than hay burners. His thoughts about cattle were not that of cash on the hoof but of steak on the plate.

As I moved in a quiet rhythm in the saddle that smelled sweetly of horse sweat and leather soap, I tried to ease my mind with the beauty before me. Gentle hills with the mountains about 100 miles away and in the distance, a sweet breeze that I was thankful for, and the murmur of cattle braying.

When I got to the pine grove, I turned the mare around and headed back to the house that sat up on a slight hill. The old house had a welcoming front porch that said, 'Get down and sit down, have a cool drink and talk.' Just the sight of that made my mouth turn into a smile that filled me with warmth.

At that point, I had not planned on any treasure hunts with my family, nor had I planned on thinking about the future of this working piece of land and how it was tied to who I was. My only plan was returning to the barn, taking care of the old girl with a good brush after I unsaddled her. Then getting fresh oats in her pail, fresh hay in the stall, fresh water in her bucket and after a check of the corrals, letting her eat and have the run of the barn and the corral. Then it would be my turn; fresh hot water for my shower, clean hair, clothes and clean sheets to sleep in my old room. I really didn't have a thought about tomorrow at that point, my family, more stories, or any concerns. I was just very tired and looking forward to a solid night of sleep.

The saying goes something like this; 'If you want to hear God laugh, tell him your plans.' I know I've heard this in a song somewhere and for the most part, I've discovered it to be the truth. So, as I climbed the wooden porch steps, I looked at Marian's clear blue eyes as she sat with a cup of black coffee in her hand, rocking and waiting for me.

"Well, let me hear it then." I started out the conversation point blank. I knew she would have something to tell me about Dad and I preferred to hear it straight out. She took a slow sip of her coffee, cleared her throat, and nodded looking toward my dusty boots.

'Scrape 'em off before you go up for your shower; supper's still warm on the stove for you. When you're done, then we'll talk." She went back to her slow rocking and watching the Sun begin its nightly journey toward the horizon as she sipped on her coffee again. Marion was just as no-nonsense as I was in most areas.

I headed inside and made sure not to let the screen door slam, since I knew it would wake my dad. I started to scrape off the muck from the corral and decided to just leave my boots by the door on the mat. They were scarred and had the beaten look of things that had seen better days, but I was just stubborn enough and cheap enough to continue to wear them out here on the land I called home.

Supper was a nice quick dish Aunt Florence, Marian, and perhaps hundreds of other rancher's wives would cook in a hurry; a simple goulash of macaroni, tomatoes, onions and cooked ground beef. It was filling, fast to cook, easy to reheat, simple to freeze, and transported out to fields in covered dishes. I filled my plate with garden greens and ate the salad slowly while the goulash reheated on the stove.

The shower took me exactly ten minutes and I knew this because I timed myself with the old wind-up alarm clock that still sat on my nightstand. Slightly overstuffed with supper, comfortable with a feeling of being warm and clean, I hurried back down the steps in stocking feet to get a cup of hot coffee and refill Marian's cup. I settled in the rocker beside her after filling her cup and offering her some creamer.

I blew off the top of my coffee, took a sweet, scalding sip, and then said quietly, "Well then, let's have the latest opinion."

"I'd say around a few months is all you've got left," Marian said as she continued to rock and watch the colors brew into a sweet orange popsicle glow in the West.

"You've never been one to spend much time on being soft and easy, have you?" I answered back as my rocking matched hers with every creak of the tandem rockers.

"Nope. Of course, you can always call Doc and get him out here again since I'm only a retired nurse and not a Doc. But you know, I wouldn't want you to get your hopes up; I've seen too much of this stuff, and I'm only telling you what I think of this." She answered and continued to sip and rock, sip and rock.

"Does Dad know? I mean, do you think he has an idea about how much time he has left? I guess I'm asking how to handle this over the next couple of months here." My eyes started to dampen, and one tear after another slowly leaked from behind my eyes and dripped into the coffee; I had stopped drinking as I watched the sun set on this ground of dreams.

Marian glanced up at me since I had stopped rocking; she looked from my coffee cup up to my damp cheeks in the growing darkness. "Grief and crying are alright, you know. This cancer is really not causing him any pain at this point; it's just hard to watch a loved one go this way, is all."

In a gentle Western woman's show of support, she took my free hand in hers, held it, and urged me with the motion of her rocker in the growing dark stillness to match her again. We continued to sip coffee as we looked for strength in the twinkling lights, and quiet strength we each held inside.

We didn't speak after that; the Milky Way glowed like a beacon that night, and the stars looked closer than I had ever seen them before. The ranch lights in the distance and the cattle moving in the fields all took on a dreamlike quality that night. I knew that peace would be a long time coming once I start calling family, the bank, the lawyer, the funeral home, and making arrangements. I was glad that Marian was here beside me in her quiet way, urging me to use a cup of coffee and a rocking chair to find my center of peaceful strength.

When Marian left to drive home, she simply patted my cheek, gave me a quick hug, handed me her empty cup, and walked determinedly down the steps to her truck. She didn't wave or honk, just drove off into the darkness towards her own spread. I knew she would return tomorrow, and tonight I would have the time I needed to ready myself for the end that was coming sooner than I wanted it to with my dad.

The next morning, I awoke to a buzzing phone lying beside my ear and a buzzing voice that filled my head with yet another layer of sadness.

"Honey, I miss you, and I need you with me on the job site. I'm hungry for your cooking and even hungrier for you in bed at night." Chuck whispered into my ear as I barely managed to get out a sleepy grunt in response.

"What kind of things has your dad got going on now with his health? He's been battling this cancer for so long now I know he'll make it at least another three days. Get your sweet ass in the truck and drive now. You'll get here by suppertime, and then we can have dinner and make love all night long. Please Kitty, I miss you like crazy woman!" This last pleading comment made me open one eye and glare at the clock; it was 4:50 A.M., and the sun wasn't even warming the sky yet.

"MMMMMMMMMMMM, I think you have lost your mind." I groggily answered. "Do you have any idea what time it is right now?"

"Ah, Kitty, I'm sorry. I woke up with a raging hard-on and needed you here. When I reached to your side I remembered where you were and had to call you right away!" Chuck lowered his deep voice another octave and started whispering.

I think he thought it was like sex talk with a company you pay to have someone on the other end say filthy things to you in the hopes they can make money from your loneliness.

"I bet you were out drinking last night, and now you're feeling guilty, right?" I pegged his night in one swift comment.

"Kitty, don't be bitchy; it isn't like you to say no to me. You know how you love to cuddle in the morning before I have to go to work. PLEEAASSEE, say you'll come here today." He drawled this out like a little boy hoping to get the bike he wanted for his birthday.

"Listen, I hate to disappoint you; I really need to find out from the Doc how safe it is for me to leave for even an overnighter with you. The current thought is that Dad has about a couple of months left, I need to get everything ready before the end here, can I call you later?"

I could just imagine the pout that came across the high-priced piece of technology I held in my hand. The snort of derision that echoed across the miles wasn't lost on me either; boy, did he have the guilt trip for me down pat or what?

I waited, counted to ten to myself, counted to ten again, and then softly said, "I know you're still on the line. I can hear you breathing, and I heard you snort. So that tells me you are more than disgusted with me right now for not caving into your demands. Honestly, death is right around the corner for Dad. Personally, I don't give a rat's ass if you care or not about him; he's my dad, and I'm staying."

I heard nothing more but a soft click and then the buzzing of the line tone. Well, round one to me this time. Standing up to someone who was only thinking of themselves felt really good. I'm not sure how many more times I'd have the grit to pull this off with him and his fine Irish temper, but I was certainly going to try!

Rolling out of bed, I threw the quilt my Grandma had made with the 'Around the World' pattern back over the sheets. Gram made it for me because when she first held me, she said I was the one family member who would go around the world. I let the feel of the wooden floor slowly cool my warm toes before I stepped across the rag rugs and turned on my shower to warm so my day would have a little luxury at the beginning.

After dressing in jeans, a long-sleeved, worn-out denim shirt and boots, I hit the stairs to go start the coffee, pancakes, and bacon. I was determined not to let one cantankerous husband spoil my day.

Chapter Four
Moon of Turning Grass

They did not speak to All Goes Out as they walked together as a family to the tree that stood on the edge of the river bank close to their dugout home. The little parade was led by the comely young girl, All Goes Out, who was dressed in a doeskin shift decorated with a band of teeth around the neck. In her hair was a small fluff of turkey feathers and she carried a prairie hen wing fan. She held her head high and smiled at her groom as she walked to greet him.

Charles stepped around his little family and extended his hand to George. The tall, dark-haired, blue-eyed man had a pleasant smile on his face that made All Goes Out relax and feel comfortable around. As her father spoke in quiet tones in English to George, her soon-to-be husband, she felt proud that the man known as George spoke so respectfully to her father.

George, however, did not dress up for the occasion and instead wore an older pair of pants and a clean shirt. When he looked at All Goes Out, he noticed she was tall for her age with a very pretty face. She was not thick around the middle yet like her Mother and sister, but shapely and having the look of high pointed breasts under her shift. George couldn't wait to get her to work in both his bed and on his ranch. He figured with a couple of good nights in bed with him teaching her how he liked to be pleased that she would be willing to do anything for him when he pointed.

If All Goes Out did not listen, he was familiar with 'lodge poling', a tribal tradition of the man's right to beat his wife if she did not follow his every command. His mouth started to moisten as he thought of all the positions he could tie her up to the bed frame and what his plans for her first night with him were. Yes, the old drunk of a Father of hers had no idea what he had traded his daughter into.

"I see that you are smiling at my oldest and special daughter. I know that she is worth more than just the land you have promised us to live on by the river. I see in your eyes that you already have made plans in your heart for many children with her, for she is not only beautiful to look upon but strong and will bear many fine children for you," Charles said all the words he himself had heard when he took Beaver Woman as a 'talking pillow'. The 'talking pillow' arrangements made with tribal fathers went well for both the tribe and the trapper since then, trappers would learn how to speak the language of the locals, ensure good passage across other tribal areas and continue to build strong families of mixed blood ties.

Charles knew that white men had a different value system when they arranged a tribal marriage. After all, he had a wife and another family that were white as well. Perhaps they thought he was dead; he really did not know or care at this point. All that he knew was that more whiskey would be his soon and that he would not have to worry about his house on the river anymore because this man had a large ranch and money.

George spoke to Charles then in a gentle voice he saved only when he hoped to impress people and relax them; "You would be right in saying that I smile because your daughter is very special. I see that she is strong, like a wild horse, and will bear many children for me to take pride in. I think she is worth more than just the land by the river and would like to give you one, no, I think two ponies, as well as a jug of the finest hot water I have to celebrate."

Charles smiled back at George and replied in a smooth voice, "I knew you would see the value of this oldest child of mine. I think she is worth at least two jugs of your hot water so that I will have one for today and one for tomorrow to celebrate this joining of families. What say you to this?"

Standing in the hot sun was making George sweat around his neck and begin to get irritated. Enough with the damn fool trade talk. He just wanted the young teenager tied up to the bedpost and doing his will. He saw All Goes Out shift on her feet under the hot sun as well and noticed her shift sticking to her breasts where she was sweating, the tips beckoning to him to be sucked on and sucked on hard. He tampered the rising desire in his groin so he wouldn't frighten her in front of her family. He smiled gently instead and said, "Let us come to an agreement then, tell me the English name All Goes Out is called by you, then when I call to my wife, she will come to know my language, and I will know hers."

Charles nodded and smiled and turned to the women, for he knew negotiations were over and that his hunger for the whiskey and George's hunger for his daughter were equal in lust. He pointed at All Goes Out and spoke her name in her native tongue for the last time. "All Goes Out, you will be called by your man as Josephine from now on, for now, you will become one with him and will no longer be in our lodge."

Josephine moved up to stand beside her Father, who smelled of the drink from yesterday. She waited patiently for her Father to take her hand and place it in George's as was the custom. When her Father stood there and did nothing, she lifted her hand and let George pick it up. George smiled and placed his lips in the center of her hand and licked it like a dog. What sort of man was this, she wondered?

George looked up at her face to see her curious expression and was delighted that she was totally unprepared for the first sexual moves he brought to her. He knew her mother had spoken to her about bed share and what to expect, but she was in for a wilder ride with him than any ancient wisdom shared could prepare her for.

The arranged marriage ceremony was complete, and George led Josephine to the ranch house, followed by her family. The log home sat low on a slight rise, with a few cottonwoods around it for shade. A porch with split rails across the front and a few chairs looked inviting. George motioned for everyone to sit down as he went in to get the jugs of whiskey for Charles. He ordered one of the ranch hands standing and watching to get him two 'sharp lookers' from the corral. The hand knew that 'sharp lookers' meant green-broke horses that really weren't safe to ride. He walked away with a knowing smile and wondered if George meant for the good-looking young woman he had taken as his own talking pillow to have her father killed on her wedding day.

Without a word, Jed Mcdoggell turned and headed to the corral to lasso up two ponies for Charles to take back to his squalid dugout on the river. George turned and clomped into the ranch house without scrapping the mud off his boots. He had a plan that involved Josephine on her knees wiping the floor up while she wiped him up with that pretty mouth. Now, just to rid of the hands for a couple of days so he could please her and beat her at will until she was his without question.

George got out two jugs of his rotgut whiskey to give to Charles and then poured four glasses, three small ones and one large one of his good whiskies for Charles, Beaver Woman, Josephine, and himself. He knew the old goat would be drunk before he got home, and with a little whiskey in her, Beaver Woman would be in a mood to do his bidding as well when they were back at their dugout. His plans for Josephine had her sacked out cold on his bed, stripped naked, tied up, and waking up with his cock in her mouth, rear and center. George carried the jugs out first and set them by Charles's dirty boots. "Now, before we take any of the bride price, we need to celebrate right here. I have poured some of my own hot water in glasses, and we will all toast to our families." He smiled at the family and felt the tingling start in his groin as he watched Josephine lick her lips.

Carrying out the glasses was a problem, so he decided to

start her training right then. "Josephine, come in and help carry out the drink," George said in a louder and friendly tone.

When Josephine heard her name spoken by her new man, she jumped, and her Mother motioned to her to go to him, she nodded and smiled and did not look worried at all. Josephine walked into the ranch house for the first time. She spoke in her native tongue to George asking him what he needed her for. His eyes flashed dark at first and then he just smiled and handed her a small glass of whiskey and motioned for her to drink it up in front of him. She held the glass and smelled the same thing her Father drank daily and did not want to drink this, but her man watched her. So, she sipped a little of it. He motioned again with his hand as he wanted her to drink it all. When she lifted the glass again, George stepped next to her and made her keep swallowing the hot water, she almost gagged on the warmth.

He stepped away from her to see what effect it was having. Josephine immediately began to get warm and started to fan herself with the feather fan and pull on the neck of her shift. George nodded to himself and poured her another glass, placed it in her hand, and carried the other three glasses in one hand, leading Josephine out with the other.

"Here we all are now, ready to toast the beginning of a fine time together," George spoke with a happy tone as he passed the glasses around to Charles and Beaver Woman.

Charles lifted his tumbler and smelled it, then smiled as if he had been granted a wish from the heavens. Beaver Woman smiled because she knew what even a little hot water would do for her. Josephine's sister, Comes At Night, sat on the boards and said nothing but watched with quiet eyes.

All them sipped slowly, simply enjoying the first sweet rush of the warmth spreading through their bodies. George did not want his head or body clouded for what was coming. He kept pretending to sip his glass, and when he lifted his glass, the other three followed his lead. Soon, Charles, Beaver Woman, and Josephine all had empty glasses, while George's glass was over half full.

Josephine had a wild rose flush on her cheeks and a vacant look in her eyes. George kept licking his lips and looking at the two jugs by his feet. Beaver Woman had a flush on her face and kept looking at the jugs as well. George knew it was time to get rid of them and his hands for his own wedding party to truly begin.

Jed walked up to the porch at that point, leading the two ponies he had lassoed. He made sure they were not the meanest looking nor the nicest looking in the bunch of mustangs. He did not want to be run off this place since the pay was good.

George nodded his approval from the porch and helped Beaver Woman and Charles stand. "Give the reins to Josephine's sister there and let her lead the horses back to their shack. I'm going to walk with these two for a while to get them headed in the right direction. When I come back, I'll give you the orders of where I want you to go for a couple of days."

Jed handed the ropes to the young girl standing in front of the porch and tipped his hat as custom dictated around any women or girls. He turned and left for the bunkhouse to get his bedroll and cook items. He had no idea how long the boss wanted him away, but since his bride was new to his ways, he couldn't blame him.

George led Charles with one jug to carry and Beaver Woman with another one to carry as Josephine's younger sister brought up the rear, leading the two ponies. Josephine stood on the porch, confused by the whiskey, hot all over, and curious about what she was supposed to do next. Maybe if she sat down, she would feel better if her head wasn't swimming so much. She sat in the chair and immediately passed out, just as George had planned. At the edge of the corral fence, George stopped and shook Charles's hand and said: "Today, we have made a good trade."

Charles already had the cork off the jug and, with a vacant look on his face, proceeded to walk back down the hill the two miles home, drinking the entire way. He was followed by Beaver Woman who also stole sips from her jug, and Comes At Night who was leading the two ponies.

As certain as night follows day, the next item for George Grinnell was to get rid of his ranch hands for a few days while he would follow his plan to break Josephine's spirit. He stepped away from the corral fence and headed down to where his hired hands were working the horses.

"OK, men, I need a little alone time with my new bride. Don't be back around here for a few days. Five days is perfect for me." He licked his lips and laughed as he grabbed the crotch of his trousers. "You get my drift fellows?"

The three men nodded in unison, not wanting to anger this quick-tempered boss today of all days. The oldest hand, Jed Mcdoggell, gave his boss one last look over his shoulder and said, "Be careful now. She's a young 'un."

Grinnell snorted at him and said, "Mind your own damn business Mcdoggell, or you'll be riding fence longer than five days, you hear?"

Jed nodded and swung his long legs astride his mustang without looking back. As he and the two younger men headed out, he quietly said to Chance Gainy and Lem Helding, "That young gal is in for a bad time with him. No good will come of this, mark my words."

As night follows day, the next five days on the ranch were filled with cries, pleas, and finally, broken spirit directions as Grinnell used to drink, sex, and violence on a young girl to bend and break her into a slave to his every whim. He was only gentle with her the first time he had her, and that was to make sure she was a virgin in every orifice of her body. As she was carried into the ranch house after all had left, George shut and barred the doors after he laid her on the bed. He stripped her naked and then slowly took off his own clothes and had one more shot whiskey, then bent down to start licking her pussy that was only just beginning to grow hair.

When he had the lips of her pussy really wet, then wet his fingers and sent them searching into the folds of her vagina, he readied his member and pushed home into Josephine for the first time as she lay in a drunken stupor. He slammed hard without a care as he pummeled her over and over with strength and raw need for her young body. He bent and suckled on her nipples and had them taut and hard as he finally released all his bent-up sperm into her. If she acted like she was coming around and waking, he would force more whiskey down her throat, and she would retreat into the land of drunken slumber once again.

He trained her to sit under the table at meal times as he ate the food she cooked and serviced him with her mouth. It took four meals to teach her to lick the length of his hardened shaft and twirl her tongue around the head. By the second meal, she was able to both lick and twirl her tongue. By the end of the third meal, when he lifted his hard shaft out of his trousers, she tried to slide away from him. He grabbed her by the hair, pulled her up, and bent her over the table onto the food. While grabbing her breasts with a hard hand, he fondled her peaks and pulled on them. He pulled her shift up and slammed into her rear, and pounded into her over and over as he said, "Suck the whole thing in your mouth, the whole length, or this happens over and over again." When he finally released his load, he would slap her ass checks hard until they were red with his now limp shaft still in her ass. If he could get hard again, he would continue this ride, saying the same thing over until he couldn't get hard.

By the third meal on the day after they were wed, he finally managed to come in her mouth, but she spit it on the floor and once again was pulled up and onto the table. If she would not drink with him when his needs were rough, he would force rot gut whiskey down her throat and then tie her naked to the bed and ride her mouth and force her to swallow every drop of his load.

When she did please him in bed, he would then take the time to 'pillow talk' with her and teach her English words for body parts and what he liked to do with them. Josephine was broken in the skills of a brothel madam by the time Charles was done with her during those five days. He was pleased with himself and Josephine was left wondering if this is what her own Mother went through.

Chapter Five
The Bell Tolls

Knocking on the bedroom door softly and waiting patiently for a response, I listened for the familiar sound of his hacking cough followed by the "What do you want?" Instead, I heard gentle snoring coming from the other side of the door.

Peeking inside I saw that Dad must have been up during the night because the curtains were opened to the East to see the rising sun, and his clothes were laid out on the rocker next to his bed. He must have gotten up and done those things and then gone back to sleep, tired out from moving those few light things around.

I stood and listened to make sure his breathing sounded as quiet as possible and then gently shut the door. I headed downstairs to continue making pancakes, then piled some on a glass pie plate to stay warm in the oven.

I ate slowly by myself that morning, waiting to hear the sounds of someone stirring upstairs. After washing dishes, moving items from shelves in the kitchen and scrubbing down things, I finally heard some noises upstairs. I started a fresh pot of coffee and then climbed the stairs to Mom and

Dad's bedroom.

Dad was sitting on the bed, dressed and ready to greet the day with his slow smile. Boy I would miss this part of our time together. Mornings with Dad were always the best. He would have time to visit, tease, and discuss things before the cares of the day would worry him away from us all. I smiled in return, "Well, good morning to you, Dad. I was up here earlier, and you were still snoring, so I thought I should let you sleep."

Chuckling at this, Dad's smile got even bigger, "No way! I never snore; when your Maw was alive, she would always say that she never needed an alarm clock because my buzzing would wake her up every morning around 5:30. Darned if I didn't dream about her last night again, she was sitting right here talking to me about what we were going to do next week together. Isn't that strange?"

"I don't know about strange Dad; I think it's a way to bring you comfort is all. Dreams are a healthy thing to have you know." I replied as gently as I could. "Do you want to try making it downstairs today and have breakfast in the kitchen with me?"

"You know, I think I will. I always did love your pancakes. I bet you already had your usual three of them, haven't you?" blue eyes twinkled as he said this to me.

Smiling in return, I answered, "Well, of course you're right. I could eat another one with you, though. I look forward to our morning visits, you know that, Dad."

I gently reached under his arms to help him stand. I

worried about the stairs, but he shook my hand off as he gingerly reached for his walker to make it to the stairs and then waited for me to follow him down. I took the stairs backwards, step by step, and he hung on to the railing and placed one foot painfully in front of the other as we headed down to the kitchen. It took almost ten minutes to reach the bottom of one flight and Dad was sweating by the time we reached the bottom.

A man of few complaints, Dad's only comment was; "Well now, I remember a time when an afternoon of throwing bales would make me sweat like. Getting old sure isn't for sissies, is it?"

When I finally had him seated at the kitchen table, and a cup of black coffee poured for him, I warmed a ham slice and pulled out a stack of 'flippers', dad's name for pancakes that were only good for flipping out to the chickens to peck apart.

Slowly lowering himself to the chair while gripping the edge of the table, Dad picked up his cup of coffee and took a slow sip then released a long, "Ahh, that made the trip downstairs worth the sweat I worked up to get here. Perfect with just a little sweet and milk added just the way I like it, Missy." His voice was weak, and I thought to myself about the portable oxygen tank hanging on the laundry room door. I thought I should go get it while he ate breakfast.

He slowly continued to eat his stack of pancakes with warm syrup swimming over the butter melting on top. At first glance he looked like he was eating a great deal, but he was only pushing the bites of pancake around in the syrup and had taken about three bites total.

Standing and moving to the laundry room door, I lifted the portable tank with the nose piece off the hook. I gently laid them on the table beside Dad, and without missing a beat, he picked up the nose piece, turned on the machine and hooked the hose over the tops of his ears. He sipped slowly on his coffee and lifted two more small bites of pancake to his mouth as he continued to watch me as I watched him.

He stretched his legs out beneath the table, cradled his coffee cup in his gnarled, weather-beaten hands and looked at me with his fierce blue stare before he commenced to speak.

"Well now Missy, I suppose this is the time to get as much of that old story 'bout my penny for you to hear. Do you think you're up to hearing about the sad story of Josephine and the treasure?"

Dad had me at first glance, so I willingly just nodded my head, sipped my coffee and continued to stare back at him. I waited and listened to the kitchen clock tick the time away as I waited patiently for Dad to pick up the story where he had left off.

"Let me see now. I think the last thing I told you about was how Josephine was traded as a young bride for the piece of land that Charles and his Indian wife, Beaver Woman, were camped on. Really not far from your Grandparent's Old Place. I'd say it was 'bout a couple of miles South and a bit West of there. Of course, this was before your Grandpa came on the Immigrant Train from Minnesota with his brother, Morten, and their load of cattle. But in the scheme of time, it was just a short hop."

He sipped his coffee, cleared his throat and leaned forward on the table with his elbows resting beside the plate. "How 'bout you start the dishes while I start the story? That way, we can get more than one thing done at a time."

Always searching for work and problem-solving, the best way to get things done, I didn't bother to argue with him and tell him I just wanted to listen. I just drained the coffee in my cup, picked up his plate and utensils and turned to the sink. While the warm water gurgled out of the faucet onto the soap-covered dishes, I watched the mountain of bubbles build before I turned the water off, turned to the stove and picked up the coffee pot with a pot holder. I refilled my cup and after a quick nod, refilled my dad's as well.

I turned back to the sink and waved my hand in the air as a signal for Dad to start.

"As a young teen Josephine was a very pretty woman, and soon, the fact that George had a very young, good-looking filly he was pillow talking with made the rumors start to fly. The first years of being together must have been very rough on her, for George was a mean drunk and heavy-handed as well. I know that this was about the time that the gold and silver mines in Montana really started to pay off. Miners looking to make it rich overnight were selling off and floating up river to get to the gold nuggets that they believed were a big as eggs and just lying on the ground to be picked up.

Now remember that old George was a smart Civil War Vet, a former spy, and a man who had spent his first two years after the war on this very river as a wood hawk. Those were the men who cut timber along the river bottoms, stacked the cord wood up for the steam boat captions to fuel the ships, and received pay for their work.

Well George, being George, after a few years of doing this back breakin' work, decided that he had to have an easier way to make money. So, he headed up to Montana Territory on one of those boats and spent part of a year panning for gold and fighting Indian tribes. When he came back the next year, it is said he was meaner than ever and drinking more. He told talks of a massacre he shot Indians in, cut off their heads and placed them on poles at the mouth of the Marias River. Now, I don't know if that was true or not since history doesn't have a record of all the fighting that went on between cultures. Personally, I think old George wasn't one to brag unless it was the truth.

So, he comes back to Tobacco Garden and starts to improve his ranch and spread out his property. He gets more cattle and even decides to build a roadhouse for the boat travelers headed to Montana Territory. George just seemed to luck out and have money to create all these things in the wilderness.

The roadhouse was really a saloon on the bottom with a house for 'ladies of the night' on the top part. Here, let me show you what I mean." Dad reached to the center of the table and took a paper napkin out, spread it on the table and proceeded to draw an almost octagon-looking shape with another shape on top at an angle to this.

"See Missy. This is what it looked like before the damn was built and they flooded that whole part. George had a nasty temper and a wicked sense of humor; he named the Saloon and Entertainment place 'The Blind Pig'. Some said he named it for one of the women who worked for him. Others said he named it for a pig he raised from being a runt and the pig was so old before he butchered it that the pig was blind.

No one knows to this day who that saloon was really named for, but as luck would have it when George was growing his little kingdom, along comes trapper Charles with his wife and two good-looking young girls and bed down by the river in an old sod shack. George was on the lookout for a woman to warm him when and where he wanted. It was said that no woman dared to say no to George."

Dad opened his mouth and let out a huge yawn and then slowly stretched his arms over his head and yawned again. "Well Missy, this breakfast and visit have just worn me out. I can't seem to get enough sleep lately since I feel like I'm always tired. I think I'll just creep out to the porch and sit down in the sun for a short nap. I promise I'll finish the story this afternoon when we finish lunch. Do you think you could make tuna casserole with those wide egg noodles and creamy mushroom soup in it?"

I had quietly finished washing, drying and stacking dishes and cutlery away as Dad was telling his story. I nodded and turned to offer my arm while he slowly stood up from the table. He waved my hand away, and with his cane, his portable oxygen tank over his shoulder and his sweat-stained work hat on his head he slowly leaned on his cane and headed out to the porch. His steps were measured and slow as one leg was clearly causing him to limp, and he moved with a snail-steady pace to the porch door.

I knew that Marian would be over in about an hour to make lunch and check up on Dad. So, I laid the package of egg noodles, can of tuna, can of mushroom soup and the salt and pepper beside the stove on the counter top. She would know by looking at what the request was.

I also had to talk to my brother and let him know the situation and get him out here if I could. I needed to check on my husband and make sure he wasn't feeling too sorry for himself and reassure him that I would be with him as soon as I could. I dug in my pocket and pulled out my lucky quarter and flipped it; heads for my husband and tails for my brother.

Flipping it in the air, I watched it spin in the light before catching it and flipping it onto the back of my hand; tails it is, this round goes to my brother. I reached into my shirt pocket and drug out my cell phone, pressed speed dial number four, and waited for either his voice or his weird 'record a message' voice.

"Hey weird-O, it's me. Call me back and let me know how soon you can get out here. Dad's slipping fast, and I know he'd love to see you and Barbette. Call me ASAP. Love you Stink Bomb." With both of the affectionate names we had for each other on his cell, I knew I'd hear from him in less than an hour. I decided it was time to do a little dirty work in the barn on my own. I left by the back porch door so Dad wouldn't feel the need to chew me out for doing more than I should on the spread.

Chapter Six

Moon of Sky Water

"Over here you dumb ass, over here," George shouted at his men as they pushed the remuda uphill toward the fenced-in area close to the river bank. The men had been rounding up as many of the stray horses and cattle as they could find. The plan was to send them down river by steam boat to the more populated areas of Minnesota and sell them for a profit. They started broom-tailing the horses together almost immediately in the pen and kept the cattle off to one side as they did this procedure. Broom tailing involved tying the horse's tails to the mane of a lead horse in front to create a triangle shape structure of moving wild horses in a group. This allowed the wranglers to control the horses more as they were being moved onto the flatboat for shipping. George only broom-tailed with no more than six horses at a time.

George had just come back from his year away in Montana Territory where he was hoping to have more gold and silver in his pocket. He had a great time fighting 'Injuns' and recently told his men over drinks about how he and some other miners that were left over from the Civil War had killed a few braves, beheaded them and placed their heads on poles at the mouth of the Marias River to warn others away. He didn't get as much gold as he had hoped for either. That required too much physical work. He wanted to spend more time with the bottle and the women in the brothels. He made his mark there on many 'soiled doves' with his bruises as he liked to rough up women before using them up physically.

The only thing he wasn't really pleased about was his young wife, Josephine. The year he was gone, she made friends with a noisy priest who had recently appeared in the area. Now she had religion, and damn, it was getting harder and harder to relieve his itches. It seemed to him that before he went to the Territory, he could walk into the ranch house, knock Josephine around when she wouldn't drink with him and then push her down on the table and mount her ass and listen to her squeal every day for lunch. He loved rutting her and drinking pulls from the bottle when she squealed. Just the thought of that made him hard and wanting her again that way.

He pulled his beloved watch from his rawhide thong out of his pocket to check the time. The watch comforted him since it was the only thing left from his father, who had died of influenza in Baltimore, and his mother, who had soon followed. His life of comfort had ended there, and he found himself sleeping on the streets behind a warm bakery as a young teen himself. George smiled to himself. Just about ten minutes to noon, perfect time for a nice drink and a squealing woman.

"Men, finish up here, then break for lunch. Chance, you

cook today; I'm having lunch by myself with the woman. Stay away from the house." Grinnell turned his sorrel to the house and, feeling himself harden, spurred the horse to get back to the ranch house quickly. Clods of prairie gumbo flew from the hooves as he spurred his mount faster.

"Damn that man's got a problem." Chance muttered under his breath. The men had come to like Josephine and her family. They had been around them most of the year that Grinnell was in Montana Territory and saw how hard she worked alongside her family. They didn't care for the way George abused her and had witnessed him chasing her on his horse when he was drunk. In the West, the code was to stand up and protect women at that time. Unfortunately, women of color were not included in the code. Women who were already 'soiled' were also not included in the code, even if they were white. The code only applied to young white women and married white women with or without children. It certainly didn't apply to a young teenaged Hidatsa given to a white man for trade and squatter's rights.

"Where are you, Josephine?" George shouted as he leaped off his sorrel, dropped the reins and let the horse start to graze close by. No sound came from the house, no noises from the kitchen range of coal being placed in the fire box, no sounds of iron pans being placed on the stove, no smell of biscuits baking or beans cooking met George's ears or nose. George walked as quietly as his muddy boots would allow him to see where she might be hiding. Josephine was just coming back from the outhouse when he spotted her. A plan formed in his mind how he could ride her in the mud that was slick under foot, and he smiled.

"Josephine," he called. She jumped with a startled glance in his direction.

"Yes," she answered and lowered her eyes as she had been taught.

"Come here to me now," George said as he lowered his trousers and his erection lifted up from his gumbo-stained pants. "Drink with me."

Josephine kneeled in front of George at the back of the ranch house and drank from his erection. He held her head tightly against him when he felt he would explode in her mouth and knew it wasn't enough. He pulled her away from him, panting hard, and smiled. "Now we really are gonna' drink."

George flipped her over in the mud and got down on his knees behind her. She started to sob quietly little noises since she knew what was coming. "Now I'm gonna' drink your rear into me and listen to your squeal. Next time, eats better be on the table with you on your knees, ready to drink me up." George pushed two fingers into her clit as he held her down with one hand, "You likey that? Speak up, or I'll slap you hard."

Josephine complied and answered, "Yes, please, give me your drink." For she knew that she would be lodge poled if she did not comply.

George was waiting just for that statement, "Drink all of it then, you little piece." He reached his fingers out of her clit and rubbed the moisture around her anus and positioned his head at the entrance and slammed into her up to his balls.

Josephine was expecting the pain of the quick entry but not the force of it and let loose with a squeal. George rutted a few times and then spent himself in her. With a satisfied smile, he dropped her dress and covered her, placed himself back into his trousers and stood as clumps of gumbo dropped around them.

"Get up, and get inside and make me something to eat now!" George found one of his bottles by the back door, grabbed it and started to drink. "Get going now!" He shouted.

Josephine picked herself up off the ground and brushed as much of the gumbo away as she could. She meekly stepped around George with her head lowered and her eyes on the ground and went inside to make this man she was given to in trade something to eat.

A week went by before the traveling priest, newly arrived in the young territory a few months before George came back from Montana, showed up at the ranch to visit both the husband and wife. He thought things were well between them until he saw the condition evident on Josephine's face and arms. She sported a bruise on her chin and bruises along her arms. The priest was upset since Josephine was a clear favorite of his, as was her younger sister, now named Mary.

He sat with George on the porch and took the measure of the man as he visited with him and sipped a glass of whiskey. The priest was from the East coast too and knew that George would not want any remaining family or friends from His Civil War decorated veteran times to realize he had bartered for an

Indian wife, who knew little English and had no social graces. He decided after the first meeting to send off a letter and remove this girl and send her to school out East to give her a better chance.

"Well then my son, I know George that you don't like to be called this by a priest who is your own age, but let's talk about what you hope the future will be like here on the beautiful ranch in God's country." Father Piedmont said firmly. "I know you imagine that you and Josephine will have strong sons and daughters that will work the ranch and create an empire for you." The priest waited quietly to see what this quick-tempered man would say.

"Father, you know I don't suffer fools gladly, nor do I want men sticking their noses into my business. I appreciate what you've said so far, but don't let it go much farther." George tapped his whip at his side. His experience with the whip was spoken of in hushed tones in this wild prairie. "Hope you know I don't mean no disrespect to a Priest and all. It's just that my wife here is my business."

Piedmont nodded and added. "Yes George, I understand what you are saying, but know that as a man of the cloth, I am responsible for all the sheep in my flock, even you, George." The priest smiled and took another sip of the bitter whiskey. "George, I'd like to make a suggestion. Have you ever thought about selling this fine whiskey? I imagine you could make a nice profit if you had a place where men could come and share stories and have a sip of something fine like this."

George turned his sharp blue eyes on the priest and smiled, "As a matter of fact, Father, I have been thinking about doing something like this. My hands go all the way over to the Fort to have a drink right now. I think about selling my whiskey right here to save myself some of the wages I'm paying. Glad you are thinking like a real man, Father. Just don't be getting any ideas about my woman there; she is a pretty piece, you know." George smiled into his glass to see if his comment would raise the Priest's temper a bit.

The priest was a Civil War Veteran himself and knew from his own past about carnal knowledge. He had made a decision during that bloody war to turn away from anger, lust, and greed. He turned from them for all the opposite reasons that George had turned toward those things. He had left them beside his own dying brother's body and realized that he needed to find a different path for his own soul's sake.

Piedmont said nothing in response, merely sipping his whiskey slowly and even holding the cloudy glass to the light as he swirled the amber liquid in the glass to see if any separation had occurred. Better to let George think and stew about what he had said than to continue his suggestions. Better still to let him think he could not hold his whiskey and knew nothing about carnal knowledge.

Both men sat on the log stumps on the small porch area outside the front door and said little more to each other as they sipped their whiskey. Piedmont made a show of stumbling slightly as he got up to take his leave. "My, that is some fine whiskey, George." He made sure to slur his words a bit at the end to leave the impression with George that he was getting drunk.

George stood with him and said, "No more fine words of

advice, Father? Want to say a prayer here for me and the wife?" Turning, he bellowed into the dark doorway behind him, "Josephine, get yer lazy ass out here. The priest wants to say goodbye."

George missed the narrowed eyes and puckered lips of Father Piedmont, who was angered even further by the way Grinnell spoke to this young woman. She was clearly just a child and should never have been traded off to a thirty-something Civil War Veteran, no matter how decorated he was.

Josephine appeared in the doorway with her bruises clearly visible on her face and arms. "Father Piedmont," she said and lifted her hand.

Piedmont played his drunken stupor to the hilt and hiccupped and said, "Now my dear, I'll say a little prayer for you and your husband, but you know I won't take your hand." The priest struggled to his knees on the porch and said a blessing prayer for them.

George didn't remove his hat but stood in shock, looking down at the priest. What kind of man was this fool anyway? He would have offered Josephine as a bed warmer if he had any thought the priest would take her for a night. He had even thought about going to the Fort himself, getting liquored up and visiting one of the women in the brothel who liked rough sex.

The priest made the sign of the cross, and Josephine followed suit. Never in his wildest dreams did George imagine he would witness this on his own front porch. The priest decided to make his prayer short and even included a few hiccups to continue the charade of a drunken priest for George. As he finished, he asked both of them to recite The Lord's Prayer with him. Josephine complied, but George only stood with that strange expression on his face.

The young priest stood swaying beside the couple and even belched into George's face as he said in a stage whisper, "Now, George, I imagine when you are ready, you will have your vows blessed in the church. That is, as soon as I can get one built around here."

George was never one to let grass grow under his feet and said to the priest, "You know, Piedmont I hear that some immigrants from the railroad are planning on settling across the river. The area is called Tobacco Garden because of the smoke that grows there. The different tribes hunt right along that area too. It just might be a perfect spot for your church."

George smiled lazily at the stupefied priest. Not willing to let the charade slip, the priest just nodded and continued to sway and smile in the bright sunlight. "Well George, that's fine now. I'll be visiting with you folks on my next time through." With that, he turned and stumbled down to his old sway-back mount that clearly had seen better days. The paint was in need of a good night's rest, fresh grass and a dip in the river; the priest mounted on his horse looked the same.

He trotted off and was heard humming a tune that had no rhyme or rhythm to it. George turned to Josephine, and it looked like he wanted to slap her again. "Git yer' lazy ass into the house and fix something to eat."

George stormed off the porch, headed to his sorrel, grabbed the reins and headed back to the pens beside the river. "McDoggell, if that good fer' nutin' priest shows up again, you let me know. And let me know if he comes sniffing around the woman." On that short note, he turned his horse West towards the fort and went hell-bent for election to make it before the waning daylight turned into an inky black night that was only lit by stars. He planned to get a snoot full of whiskey and have some fun at the brothel, and then he'd think about an idea for a partner to help him expand his ranch operation.

Father Piedmont was forming a plan too and as soon as he arrived at the fort, he went right to his room and penned a letter to the diocese out East. Josephine wasn't the only young woman he was troubled over. There were a few at the fort that he believed he could save if he could get them to a school and train them how to better fit in with white society. He believed it was Josephine's only hope. The letter went out by courier the next day in the military post bag. His hope was that he would receive an answer before the Fall and get Josephine and the others to one of the Indian Schools on the East Coast.

Chapter Seven
Ideas Born Again

Try as I might, I could not seem to stop myself and gaze out the window at the mountain peaks to the West every so often. I missed this sight of beauty that always reminded me of how small each of us is in the plan of the Divine. It was during a break like this, with sweat beading on my forehead and rivulets dripping down my shirt that was already plastered to my skin, that I heard the familiar ringtone in my pocket. I reached with one hand to retrieve my cell phone as I leaned the pitchfork against the stable wall with the other.

"Yup" I answered in a short reply. I didn't recognize the number on the other end and could only imagine what it could be.

"Ms. Fairchild?" A pleasant man's voice started, "You don't know who I am, but I'd like to introduce myself to you."

I figured that this was another pesky salesman and was about to set the phone on the top rail of the pen and just let the fool continue to yammer to the air while I finished mucking out the stalls. Before I could set the phone down, I heard a familiar name that made me stop what I was doing and continue to listen to the voice on the other end.

"I know this may come as a bit of a shock to you, Ma'am, but I'm the Vice President of the Bank here in Rock Port, Indiana, the one that holds your brother Jeth's mortgage. My name is Pete Welsh; you can just call me Pete. We have a bit of an issue here and I was wondering if you could provide some insight into the situation for us." He paused to see if I was still listening and if I would respond or swear at him and hang up.

"Let me get this straight, Pete, is it? You claim you are my brother's banker and you're calling out here to Montana to see if you can get information on my brother and his family. What kind of an idiot do you take me for anyway!" I could feel the sharp pain of a headache building behind my left eye and I lit into the man like a hungry hound after a raw steak. "If, and only if, I can prove this is a legitimate call, you won't get one speck of information from me. I'd like to know how the hell you got this number anyway! I was just about screaming at the end of this tirade. If there was one thing I couldn't stand, it was people calling with fake claims, like 'You've won a car and a million dollars. Go to Wal-Mart and send us a money card for only $499.00 to get your million.' Yeah right, I'd heard this crap before!

Pete was apparently expecting this from me and said calmly, "Your sister-in-law is right here and would like to speak to you."

"Ah, hello, it's me, Babs."

I heard the breathy, bleached blonde bombshell voice over

the line and was speechless. The last time I had directly spoken to my money-grubbing sister-in-law had been at my mother's funeral when she had the audacity to ask me if she would be getting anything from Mom's belongings that she could sell online. I lit into her then like there was no tomorrow. My brother literally had to step between us since I was ready to rip her head off in the churchyard.

"Hello to you again, Babs. What is it this time? You were wondering when Dad is going to keel over? Or are you calling to tell me about your latest manicure?" For some reason, I seemed to have no sense of social skills around my sister-in-law at all. The closest times we ever had were when Chuck and I had visited as the doting Aunt and Uncle after the birth of their two children. We had managed then to discuss husbands and raising children and even went shopping for baby things after the first daughter, Maggie, came home. Since Mom's death, it had been an uphill battle to be civil and even try and pretend to be polite to her. I stopped after the last comment and just waited, knowing I was about to hear her whining tone soon.

"Melissa, do you have to continue to be so mean to me? We, your brother and I, are having a difficult time right now. We need the family to support and help us, not speak to us as if we had no common sense." She was speaking in her breathy little sweet girl voice; I found myself wondering if this was for the benefit of the banker or me.

"Look, Babs, I don't know what the issue is right now. Can you just spit it out without the theatrics?" I answered with a tight, clenched voice.

"Melissa, I am not being theatrical when you hear..." And then the sobbing started.

At first, it was only a little sniff from the end of the phone, but then it turned into a gasp for air and more sniffing, followed by a loud sound of a nose being blown into a Kleenex. "Babs, can you just tell me what is going on, please?"

The banker, Mr. Welsh, took the phone away from Babs and stated simply: "I am sorry to have to inform you of this issue, but your brother and his family will be evicted from their home next month unless they come up with their back payment on their mortgage. Quite simply, Ms. Fairchild, if they can't come with the $22,489.96 they owe us, they will be out on the street by next month." Mr. Welsh wisely said nothing more as he waited for me to speak.

"Let me get this straight," I responded in a controlled voice that really had nothing to do with the rage building inside me at this point. "Out of the blue, my brother doesn't let me know about this issue, but my sister-in-law calls me from the bank, with the banker, to give me this information." Now, I waited for Mr. Welsh to respond.

"Umm, yes, I guess that is the correct way to understand this." He said firmly. "I don't know why your brother, Jeth, isn't here with Babs right now either. Perhaps you can try to speak to her again now that you know the reason behind this phone call." I could hear papers being shifted around as he handed Babs the phone one more time.

"Missy, (sniff, sniff), I know this is hard to understand, but Jeth and I are having a difficult time this year. Is there any way you can sell off some of your dad's cute cows and send us the money? (Sniff, sniff) We would be so grateful for the help, and then we wouldn't be out on the street with the kids." Babs paused without crying and waited.

"I need to talk to Jeth about this issue. I will not promise anything of Dad's to you at all. And by the way, why isn't he there with you at this appointment?" I was starting to feel my pulse beat faster, the color rising in my face and the desire to reach across electronic imaginary lines and literally choke my sister-in-law.

"Well, you see, I...ah...I...um." Babs stuttered.

"GOD!" I shouted when reality hit me. "You haven't told him a thing, have you?" Now I was screaming into the phone like a mad woman. "YOU IDIOT! How could you go for six months without paying your mortgage payments?"

I continued my rant and didn't let her get a word into the conversation, "Let me guess, you spent all the mortgage money on those darling outfits you've been wearing lately. I imagine you even needed your hair color redone to match those 'CUTE SHOES' that had to go with the outfit. How am I doing with this one, Babs?" I finally stopped and waited to hear the next lie out of her mouth.

Silence that seemed to stretch as long as a cold sunrise in January, complete with icicles, seemed to drift wirelessly across the line. I continued to wait in that cold environment until I could hear the whining voice start. Was I in for a surprise when she next spoke.

A clear and controlled woman's voice began speaking, and

if I wasn't aware of it, I would have sworn I was speaking to another individual entirely. "It's not just shopping anymore. I have a true gambling addiction, and I'm afraid I've gambled away most of our savings and the mortgage on the house. It is worse than I can explain. I've been going to Gambler's Anonymous meetings now for about two months, and this is part of my recovery that I need to begin."

You could have knocked me over easily at that point. I was unprepared for her honesty, unprepared for her quiet dignity as she admitted a serious problem my brother had hinted at years ago, and honestly unprepared for the lack of the breathy little girl's whiny tone. I was finally speaking to a woman on the path of adulthood, accepting responsibility for her actions and beginning to see the truth of all she had done.

"Babs, let me say this once more to you. Perhaps I've been harsh with you; I won't apologize over that since I have my own issues with my own family and husband I deal with daily. I will tell you I appreciate your attempt at honesty. I still need to talk to Jeth about all of this mess. Until then, you, Jeth and your banker buddy will just have to wait." I punched the off button on my cell with as loud of a hang-up as an older cell model would allow and stormed up to sit on the porch and cool my heels one more time.

Even with my phone off, as I stared at the horizon, I thought of my dad, napping once again on the sun porch, waiting for his final ride to his heavenly home. He had even joked about it last night, eating the tuna and noodle dish Marion cooked up, along with the comment, "Fish is good for your brains you know!"

It was then Dad replied, "Well, where I'm going, I'll have access to all the brain power I need." Then he launched into a now familiar tale of 'Flum Blum and Flora,' the two horses his parents had on the ranch in the Dakota's that he grew up riding. I had noticed that lately, even when he was awake, his stories had gotten funnier and included crips and clear memories, almost as if they had happened a few years ago instead of decades past.

I sat for a few moments on the porch, sadly trying to assure myself that an answer would come to me without disturbing Dad and without causing too much trouble with Jeth and Babs, who weren't already waiting to be hit like a stick against a nest of angry wasps. My clothes reeked of hay, sweat and manure. My boots were sticky with a mixture of those three fragrant barn smells and mud. I felt exhausted from the inside out. I sat for almost an hour, letting myself bathe in stink and sorrow, until I saw the glimmer of metal coming up the road. Not wanting to be caught smelling like this, looking like this and feeling like I looked and smelled, I headed for a quick shower inside.

I heard the screen door slam when I got upstairs and a familiar, "Hello house! Anyone stirring?" Marian's cheerful voice rang up the stairs.

I hopped out of the shower, cracked the door and yelled back, 'In the shower from the barn, down in a sec' Marian." I closed the door and tried to finish in record time. Clean jeans and sweatshirt on with my hair brushed and moisturizer on my face made me feel almost good enough to take on the task that was ahead of me.

Clumping down the stairs in my pair of hiking boots, I headed to the kitchen to pour a cup of freshly brewed coffee that smelled as close to perfect as I could imagine. Marian was sliding a meatloaf in a cast iron skillet along with four foil-wrapped baked potatoes.

She always believed in cooking more potatoes in case 'Company might show up.' Or her other reason, 'Spuds are good for hash browns at breakfast.' No one in our house ever disagreed with her since she was usually correct and didn't waste her breath.

Marian turned with a smile and looked at me as I sat sipping my coffee at the table. "What's going on now? Should I just guess?" she said. When I didn't reply, she grabbed a cup, poured herself some and sat down across from me.

"I know you're worried about the 'when' with your dad, but I'm thinking something else is brewing. Is that good-looking knot-headed husband of yours giving you grief?" When I didn't respond, she tried again, "Well then, it has to be your equally knot-headed brother and that excuse for a wife of his." When I raised my eyebrows a bit with that statement, she slapped her hands on the table, making the cream and sugar jump and said, "I knew something was up just as soon as I saw your face! Come on now, spill the beans before it bubbles up inside and comes out of your ears."

With a deep sigh, I told her about my recent phone call and what I should do to tell my brother and help and all the in-between nonsense with my own husband. Marian sat quietly and listened. Marian was a gem, and when she was ready to give advice, I would sit quietly and listen.

Her white eyebrows were furrowed across her forehead. Her eyes almost shut as she sat staring into her coffee cup after my rambling on about both my brother and his issues and my own.

Her tanned face had a few wrinkles around her clear blue eyes. Even the lenses of her glasses didn't hide the humor, love and intelligence that bubbled behind them. Only at this time they conveyed worry, concern and a hint of deep sadness. Her slight shoulders were hunched forward in a brightly colored purple plaid shirt. Her jean-encased legs were crossed at the ankles as she sat and carefully pondered all I had shared with her. I blew across my coffee and took a sip as I waited for the wisdom that was sure to come from her.

"Well now!" she blew across her own cup and took a large, noisy sip of coffee. "I almost don't know what to say 'bout this. Seems to me your brother is still the 'no attention to details man that he was when he was a kid. And that damn carpet-bagging wife of his should be shot, in my opinion! Your husband, well he needs his rear kicked by a good horse right above his shoulders! Mind you, and this is just my opinion for what it's worth!"

I sat with my wet hair dripping down the back of my sweatshirt, leaving little trickles, turning the light blue color into navy, and waited for more. Still sipping my coffee in the heat, I knew that some good ideas would come from this conversation. I stretched my legs out in front of me and mimicked Marian's pose. I crossed my ankles as I relaxed into the tall wooden chair back.

When Marian cooks up a meal, she usually cooks up ideas

right beside it! This meal was a gourmet delight on all sides. When she finished explaining her idea and outlining all the possibilities, from handling my husband's greed to that of my sister-in-law. I was even more amazed at the wisdom of older folks that is sometimes lost on the young. We talked and wrote lists for almost an hour as the smell of ketchup-covered meat-loaf, baked potatoes and carrots in the oven wrapped around us. When the meal was done, so was the list. Marian stood and raised her arms and stretched the kinks out of her small 5-foot frame.

"Well now!" She repeated her favorite phrase, which told me a page had been turned, and she was ready for the next event. "It smells ready to eat, and I just bet your dad will love this supper!" Off she went and prepared the tray with slices of hot meatloaf, a medium-sized baked potato wrapped in foil with a slice of onion in the middle, and a heaping spoon of small cooked carrots. She added a pat of butter to the spud, pepper on the meat and a squirt of ketchup on the side of the meatloaf. Pouring a cup of coffee and adding milk to it she arranged it all on a tray and turned to me and winked. "Think I'll be the one to harass your dad into eating tonight. You've got a lot to think about with our ideas there. Help yourself, and when I come back down, we'll shrink that list down into something workable." Off she went up the stairs to 'harass my dad into eating'.

Chapter Eight
Iron Horse

When the letter from the Diocese finally arrived, the local priest could hardly contain his delight. Not only had a full scholarship been provided for two women and their children they had also included Josephine Malnouri. Father Piedmont was beside himself with joy that John Southworth had provided full scholarships for the Hampton Institute at Hampton, VA, for all five of these lost souls as he had referred to them in his letter.

Two of the women had children, and thankfully, Josephine Malnouri did not have any. It was the Fall of 1877 when Father Piedmont received word of the scholarship and the women were expected at the Hampton Institute in the fall of 1878. Josephine would be gone for almost three years. She would return in September of 1881 and receive the church's blessing for her marriage to George at that time. She was almost 17 years old and had been a 'sleeping dictionary' for George since 1871. It was time to provide her with more choices, and the Priest was delighted to be getting her away from Grinnell for that length of time. George was 20 years her senior, and he personally saw nothing wrong in his actions, nor did most of the trappers and soldiers in the area, for Josephine was a Native and to them, that said it all.

The Hampton Institute in Virginia was an interesting place that was established and helped to come into existence by General Samuel Armstrong in 1868. The thought was to provide an intense 'Western Civilization' existence of moral training and practical industrial education for southern blacks. Care was taken to provide different forms of education to different races. Both Indian students and Black students took classes together, and some classes were just for Indian students who needed to learn to build English speaking skills. Most were fully changed upon arrival, with braids being trimmed, clothes being burned, strict enforcement of weekly bathing rituals, regular meals and total civilized clothing being enforced. Josephine was part of the end group at this Eastern boarding school.

The Priest decided the best course of action was to involve her parents first and went to see them. That cool fall day he rode comfortably on his horse over to the shanty where Charles, Beaver Woman and Mary lived. He yelled his, 'Hello the house!' as soon as he came into the yard before he even dismounted.

He had been here once before and Charles had come out of the house waving a rifle at him because he hadn't identified himself and called out. Father Piedmont was no stranger to weapons and carried one under his black robe tucked into the waistband of his pants. Not a tall man, Father Piedmont stood around 5' 11", and he was lean and muscular with hair that had turned gray during the War Between the States. He towered over the short French Trapper, who stood around 5' 4" and was barrel-shaped in build, had dark brown hair and dark small eyes. Piedmont was always uncomfortable being around him. He smelled of cheap whiskey and unwashed skin, and his beard was always crawling with some flies whenever he stopped to visit. The Priest thought about making sure to stay upwind of this quarrelsome drunk. Lucky for him, he had thought to bring along a bottle that just might appease the surly trapper when he started up the conversation about the upcoming civilization of his eldest daughter.

Charles stumbled out onto the porch and immediately planted his large rear onto a plank bench. "Father, what do you want?" he mumbled with no sense of warmth or courtesy in his voice. The Priest could tell that Charles had already been drinking and wondered how much time he had to actually discuss the plan for Josephine before he passed out.

Slowly at first, Piedmont began to speak, "Charles, are you not feeling well? I know some medicinal drink might help, but if you are really ill, I am afraid to give this to you."

Charles had been slowly lowering his eyes and squinting against the glare of the bright fall sun as he enjoyed the cooling breeze outside of the shanty. He opened one brown eye a tiny bit and glared at Piedmont, who towered above him. "Sit yer ass down so's I don't have to stare at you!" he growled.

Piedmont lowered himself to the plank porch beside the bench and made sure he was upwind of the foul-smelling trapper. "I have something important to talk to you about. It is about an opportunity for Josephine. I need your help to make sure that Grinnell agrees with it. I have a bottle for you if you agree to help me."

Piedmont said it simply and as straightforward as he could. No use making a big pitch to someone who couldn't think past the next bottle.

Malnouri straightened himself up on the bench and laughed loudly! "Haw, Haw, Haw. Had you going their Father, you thought I was drunk already, didn't you?"

Piedmont reared back in surprise. Of course, he had thought him drunk, wasn't he always? But here was a different side of this man altogether. "Charles, I'll admit I don't think I've ever seen you anything but tipsy during the day. Want to tell me what's going on here?"

"Well Father, you know since the incident by the Fort with that group of Injuns attacking that mackinaw, sinking it and stealing that gold last year?" Charles waited to see what the priest knew about this.

"Ah, no Charles, I'm not sure what you're talking about. Perhaps you should explain more to me." Piedmont said quietly.

Charles stood and looked to the left and right of his property, walked the short distance to the river and then walked back to the porch. "Well Father, I've been hearing some stories now and again when I take the fur to trade at the fort. I'm hearing about things, and I don't like everything I'm hearing."

Piedmont sat very still and listened to George for the next

two hours as the sun and temperature lowered and the wind picked up and blew gusts of dirt by their feet. The stories enthralled Piedmont, and he wasn't sure how much was the truth and how much had been made up by Charles since his memories might be hazy because of his drinking.

Charles started his story with the attack on the mackinaw: "Near as I can 'member, they said they had 21 people in that boat. They were a keeling down the river towards the big city. Then, later on, I heard they had 32 total since the woman and the kids didn't really count the first time." He nudged the priest at that point with his elbow and said with a wink, "If you get my drift."

"Well, that mackinaw was loaded with miners who come all the way from Idaho Territory. Total Injuns kilt was 91 after General Sully got hold of 'em. Heard tell that the miners had over one hundred thousand dollars in gold dust on 'em. Not all of it has been found, I hear. Well, George's good buddy from the fort, Fred Gerad, had some of those flea bag hangers from the fort go out and look. He heard that the warriors that attacked that ship thought the gunpowder had turned rotten. Hell Father, it wasn't no gunpowder at all. It was gold dust they had in the pouches around their waists! So old Fred shows those fleabags what gold dust looks like and tells them to head out towards Tobacco Garden and look at the attack site. They come back to the Fort, but first, they make a stop at George's place since they hear he has better whiskey than the fort does."

"No one knows for sure, but Red Blanket and Whistling Bear later told Joseph H. Taylor about this. They won't say how many pouches they took from the site. But I did hear George ended up with a coffee pot filled with gold dust from those miners that were butchered!" Charles sat back in his chair for a while and then went on.

"If it's true, what else I've heard about Grinnell? He was one mean son of a bitch, meaner than me when drunk, that is. Don't know if it's true, but I'm wondering if me and my woman made a good trade for her just to squat on this land and get whiskey every couple of weeks. You think you've got a way to make it easier for Josephine?" Charles stopped again and looked over at the Priest to take his measure of the story.

"I think I might, Charles, but you need to tell me more about George. I haven't been to their place in a while, but I hear he is building up his ranch. What's going on over there? Piedmont asked almost quietly since now the conversation had become even more serious.

"You know he's been a sellin' his whiskey to his men for a while now. Well, some jackass told him to open up a saloon and start selling to all. George up and starts building a big building with a second story on part of it. Mind you. This just started AFTER the massacre at Tobacco Garden with that their mackinaw. Don't know where he got his money all of a sudden, but he sure seems to have it now! I hear that he plans on having his own brothel upstairs of the saloon so he can have even more fun!" Charles was just sitting now and staring towards the river.

Piedmont shook his head in despair, "We really need to get Josephine away for a while before something really horrible happens. I think I know what we can do. I need you,

Charles, to pay a visit alone to George. Pretend you are half-looped. Maybe he'll listen and mull over your idea and decide it is his own then. The priest looked seriously at Charles, "Do you think you could do this?"

Charles nodded his head, "Father, that's a great plan. I know I could do this, but just what exactly am I talking to him about? I traded my girl fair and square for the rights to stay here by the river for as long as we need you know."

The priest nodded slowly and then quietly said, "I see what you are saying. Perhaps some others could be convinced first to send their daughters, and then George will follow suit, if he sees this action from someone he is comfortable with. Doesn't Fred Gerad have two daughters?"

Charles slapped his dirty leggings, and a cloud of dust motes rose in the air around him. "Well, I know just the man," he coughed and took a slurp from the bottle. "Yup, I know just the man! Mind you, Father, I'll be in touch in a few days and let you know what happens."

With that, Charles grabbed the bottle and hopped down from the porch with a swift movement that seemed impossible for the rotund little man. He went whistling off to the corral for his horse, and in a moment, he was mounted Native style with no saddle riding off towards the Fort.

The priest said in shocked wonder at this amazing turn of events: 'People murdered by Native Warriors, stolen gunpowder and gold, what next?' He slowly stood, brushed off his black frock, stepped down onto the dried slate gray gumbo and grabbed the reins. Swinging one leg over the horse, he was just ready to head out when Beaver Woman and Mary came onto the porch. The priest stopped his action, blessed them, and simply said, "Charles has gone to the Fort." With that, he turned and rode away from the sod shack that was more than filthy and reeked of stale whiskey from the house and the people in it.

Beaver Woman watched the Black Robe ride away and turning to her daughter Mary and said in Hidatsa, "When the time comes to find you a mate, we will make a better choice."

Chapter Nine
Coming Home

As Marian saw it, "It's simple, you see, you just call that idiot brother of yours first and tell it all, just like you told me. Your man now, he's a different sort of problem. First, he'll blame you for having such a worthless family who can't figure out how to come in from the rain. Then he'll switch it over and try to include you in his so-called 'reasoning'." At that point, in typical Marian style, she raised her arms above her head, quit rocking and using two fingers on each hand, proceeded to draw quote marks in the air.

I couldn't help myself with a slow chuckle deep inside the hollow where the gnawing feeling was nesting. Once it started, I couldn't seem to stop and just kept up the chuckle that seemed to grow louder with every rocking motion. By the time I stopped rocking to catch my breath, Marion was staring at me in a quizzical way over the top of her glasses.

"Well now, that was a long time coming out of that place, wasn't it? I really didn't know if you were gonna cry and make a blubbery mess over my shirt or not. Tell you true, I'm glad you went for the laughs about this instead." She stood in one swift motion, bent down, picked up her never-ending cup of coffee and spoke. "I'll start the meal. You get on that phone and come in the kitchen to call that knot head brother of yours. I'll be there for support and hollering if you need me."

True to herself and all things of nature, Marian was a comforting angel in disguise for me. I knew right then exactly what to say to my brother AND my husband. Picking up my own cup, I headed into the house, being careful not to slam the screen door since Dad was still asleep. I picked up my phone from the sofa table and headed into the kitchen down the hall. A tiny little bit of mischief was in my heart, and I knew in a twisted way I was going to have fun with both of these men in my life!

"Hello, Jeth? This is Missy, you know the one, your sister?" I grimaced my face into a pucker fish face and winked at Marion.

"Well, yes, it has been a long time since we've talked. No, Dad is still hanging on, getting weaker, but still hanging on. When are you planning on coming out here? I see; well, I bet you'll be here sooner than that little brother." And now I could not help myself as I started to laugh. I couldn't stop myself and being the chicken I am, I kept laughing and handed Marian the phone.

"Hello whipper snapper." Marian almost shouted into the cell phone. This only kept me laughing even harder since this nickname is one that Jeth has always hated and was given to him by Marian's husband after an incident with a whip, a bull and a smart-ass teenager who thought he knew everything and listened to no one. Marian just steamrolled the conversation, and Jeth was trapped, trapped within the truth of Dad's upcoming death, his wife's gambling problem, the house foreclosure, his bratty spoiled children and the fact that he was needed by family here and now.

Silent now and stern of face, Marian turned and handed the phone back to me. "Go out on the porch and have the conversation you need to have with your brother. That way, I can finish this meal and go wake up your dad."

I walked slowly down the hall and, even more slowly, placed the phone up to my ear. "Jeth, still there?" I said with as much calm as I could bring into my voice after my laughing fit. "Sorry that Marian had to be the one to tell you, but I just couldn't bring myself to let you know how serious both the situation here is and the one at your place too. Any thoughts on what you're planning on doing?" I listened quietly as my younger brother aged over the phone. If I had been beside him, I felt I would have seen his hair turn gray and his brilliant blue eyes glaze and freeze over with pain.

The workable plan to sell off most of the herd and some of the hay crop while we waited to see what the market prices would do with the wheat was easier to discuss then. How the rest of the summer would go for his city family was a different discussion. It turns out that Jeth had a real hidden streak of meanness when discussing his wife and twin kids.

I had waited to speak to him before purchasing the one-way plane tickets for the family to be absolutely certain they would all be on the plane and ready to work when they arrived here. It was becoming an ever-increasing and wider tornado of despair swirling on the horizon.

Jeth also told me they (meaning the twins and his wife) would not be allowed to pack 'mall clothes or fancy anything. Only plain shoes, long-sleeved shirts, pants, shirts, shorts, and swimwear would be allowed. He chuckled when he said, "That will eliminate about half of the luggage they seem to think they need on the ranch. Apparently, the twins have forgotten what lessons they learned years ago when they spent a week with Mom and Dad out there."

The memory pot bubbled in the back of my mind then, and I remembered how staying with Grandma and Grandpa for a month had quickly dissolved into a week only when the 'turning into snots' twins had realized that they had to help with everything. They were used to having someone clean and cook for them in the city and had no idea that you had to gather eggs BEFORE you could cook them and that you actually had to perform that task yourself if you wanted to eat.

Jeth then said, "Missy, you there? I swear you haven't even heard a word I've said in the last three minutes!"

"Nope, Jeth, you're right. I was just remembering the last time the twins were out here and the horrors of actually having to step into the chicken coop if you expected eggs to be cooked for breakfast. "Do you think they have grown up past the 'icky' comments over anything connected to animals?"

Jeth laughed just a little and said, "We'll see how they feel at 4:00 every morning when they come hungry to the table. I'll let Marian take over some of that with them. We'll be in Dickyville the day after tomorrow. Sis, for what it's worth, I really love you and Dad and appreciate all that is being done to help us out."

"OK, I'll drive to Dickyville to pick you up with one of the suburban's; Marion can take the other one so Babs, the twins, and the luggage can be brought out in that. Jeth, I don't know how nice I can be to her after all this, but your idea of making her work for this money and stopping all ability to gamble is a start. I know the twins are old enough to understand this issue with money. Even if you don't want my advice at this point, I'd say your idea to take away all cell phones and cancel all accounts first from all three of them is genius. They really will not have time for any playing when they get out here to work." I spoke in a reserved tone with this last piece of advice since I didn't know how well, or how poorly, Jeth would receive it.

"See you in three days little brother. Remember, I love you as much as the moon." With that family whispering around my head, I turned to go into the house and saw my dad standing on the other side of the screen door. He looked frailer than I have ever seen him as he struggled not to cry. "How much did you overhear, Dad?"

He stepped out on the porch and, grabbed the back of one of the rockers and slowly lowered himself into the one with the full cushion set and extra pillows. The one that had been my mother's favorite. "Heard it all." He replied with a gruff tone.

I knew I would hear no other comment from him about his daughter-in-law, his grandchildren, or Jeth. I also knew that his upcoming death was a topic he considered closed since we had talked about it once, and he didn't feel the need to discuss it over and over again. I attempted to lighten the mood and said something silly, "Well, those purple flowers look really nice with your blue plaid shirt."

He slowly stopped rocking, turned to me and said very evenly, "I think Marian needs help in the kitchen with the meal right now." I took my exit cue and headed back into the house, mentally preparing myself to call my husband next.

Carefully taking my boots off again, I considered switching to muck boots the entire time Babs was out here helping with the cattle, the cooking and the cleaning. I remembered the last time they were here, about 12 years ago, right before she got pregnant. Jeth was helping her dainty size 9 feet into the muck boots and explaining to Miss City how important it was to keep your feet dry around the cattle when mucking out the stalls. I also remember the grins on both Mom and Dad's faces as I winked and made a motion to dump a pitchfork load of manure-filled hay on her head.

Of course, I was so much younger then and filled with more mischief at the time. It was worth both the apology, the beauty parlor visits with her, and the laughter of my own husband and father of twins when I recall the look of horror that came over that manure-hay combo-streaked face and hair. I imagine it would have been better if I hadn't said, 'I hear they pay big money in the city for mud packs.'

But that was years ago and the laughter seemed to slowly leave this house and land that we had grown up on as a family. It was true that the Earth still turned daily in a circle around the Sun, and the sky in the Spring was a beautiful shade of turquoise and pale green on some mornings. The air swept clean with the winds that would rush singing down the slopes of the Rocky Mountain range, sometimes stinging with bits of brush and brambles and other times just a gentle caress across the face.

Summers were equally blessed with the warmth of growing things across the fields and the smell of ripening grain and grass. The slow, steady heat of the ground answered the call of the Sun as the parched areas called out for water. On these days, as my Gramps once told us that happened in the 1930s, the Missouri River truly had holes in the water. It was so dry you could walk across and see the fish stuck in the only water holes. Some days at the end of summer, the heat became the oven of the Earth, the door opened and blasted you from the moment you stepped from the shade and soaked your skin in the warmth of the Earth's response to the Sun. Tiny rivulets of sweat would trickle down in beads on your face and neck and join the sweat-soaked shirt you wore out working in the fields.

Fall was my favorite time for so many memory-building reasons. I learned to swim one late summer, early fall day when the heat was still lingering, but the Earth had already started to cool off for winter. Not in any city pool but right in the river where my darling brother and I had a shoving match close to a bank. The clumps of gumbo clay landed on me and around me, as I surfaced after my dive, made a push, and shouted, 'Help me! I'm drowning!' And this was accompanied by my brother's howling fit of laughter as he tried desperately to say between gasps of breath, "Stand up, you fool! It isn't deep enough to drown!"

The smell of hay being hauled into stacks and barns for winter also brought memories of my first kiss on a hay ride when a hired college kid snuck a kiss while hauling a load of sun-sweet hay back to the winter pasture. He was a looker, and I considered him a real dream boat in my stored-away memories. I saw him a few years ago on a visit back here, married and happy with a nice big keg belly, a swarm of kids, I think I counted seven, and a wife who just adores him. A good first kisser who made me glad I didn't get more involved with him than that!

I loved the fall best because of the colors; the golds, reds, oranges, which all slowly turned to brown while the leaves slowly drifted as they twirled from their branches. Some remained all winter on the trees as if they were super glued to spots picked just for them by the heavens. The smells at that time of the year competed with the amazing smells of each season in an over-the-top way. Fires burning, apple cider warming, stews slow cooking, hay being tossed, and even the smell of the water seemed to change. Local football games when we could arrange trips back to visit, and the ever-present church suppers with local dishes brought by amazing cooks whose skills with simple ingredients called one and all to come to communion with them.

I also loved the fall best because the roads were still passable, visiting was frequent, and lights could be seen across the land on ranches and farms. Help was really only a call away when needed. Calves were growing and didn't need so much constant care; harvesting was, for the most part done, and once in a great while, a gently cool fall rain would dampen the dust down and bring a smell that could not be duplicated in the finest department store perfume section.

The fall was also my favorite because of Thanksgiving. One of the best and most simple seasons that did not require gifts or declarations of love and adoration in the form of presents or candy. It simply required the age-old invitation to sit down at the table and eat. A sharing of cooking and the human need for your body to be fueled and your spirit to be fueled as well with warmth and compassion is the very core of Thanksgiving all year long.

Here I am, preparing once again for Winter, not only the winter of the land as it starts its yearly trip away from the sun but the winter of my heart as I prepare for the loss of another parent. Some winters are deeper with cold and frost than others. This one, or so it is told in the Farmer's Almanac, will be a mild winter, with winds from the chinooks melting snow and ice before they can stay for longer than a month. It will also be a winter of some late ice storms that the cattle that remain will need protection from.

Finally, this winter will be the season of rebirth and the celebration of new life that comes at the beginning of this cold season. Far from friends and in the cold on farms and ranches, families will gather together and bring warmth in the form of gifts and treats as they sing and gather to join in warmth. Our family will be missing a family member this year. Our warmth will be in the blessings of knowing we have kept a family member from losing a home, but the winter of ice will hang around us as we try and wade through the court system of inheritance taxes, land issues and trying to provide for all of our futures.

It is going to be an interesting season of blizzards and storms by the time another year is ready to start.

I headed into the circle of the yellow porch light and still clutching my phone, headed into the house to grab a cup of coffee and prepare for another call. This time, the ice is sure to be thick when I explain to my husband what we need to do as we prepare to sell off most of the herd to help Jeth and Babs. I can hear the snorts of derision even now as I clump up the steps to grab a quick shower before we eat.

We were in for a time when they all got here, and I had a plan in place about leaving and spending time with my husband out on the job site. That way, I could poke around that God-forsaken area of Tobacco Garden and see what the old timers had to say about the place. Maybe, just maybe, someone would know more than what Dad had told me.

As I laid plates around the table and started fresh coffee brewing I tried to angle my way around Marian. I realized what a comfortable rhythm life held when you let things beyond your control go. It was almost as if by releasing my tight grip on the ranch and Dad's death and giving to others in the family, I could breathe again and feel lighter-hearted.

The cheap melamine plates looked almost cheery with their faded yellow flowers that sported brown leaves to match the cups and saucers the set had come with. I was never sure why my Mother had picked them out. She hated the color brown with a passion. In the fall and winter, during the 'dead time', as she called it, she would complain in her less than sugary voice about 'waiting for a little green again'. As soon as she had made that comment she would look at Dad and raise her left eyebrow and wait for him to say something, anything back to her.

Dad never remarked in all the years I remembered setting these same plates on this same table. I stopped and turned to Marian. "Hey Marian, remember how Mom always complained about the brown dead time?"

Marian quickly turned her back to me and only nodded. My question seemed to shake her up and it got my curiosity aroused. "So, I could never figure out why she would pick these plates with the weird yellow flowers with the brown leaves on them when she hated the color brown so much. Do you know the rest of the story with these?"

It seemed a perfectly responsible question to ask of a dear friend of both my parents who were both widowed and who used to ranch, ride, party and celebrate together when their spouses were alive. I held my comments and gently went back to setting the table with those cheap plates, just waiting patiently for some additional remarks.

No remarks came from the kitchen range and all and Marion remained unusually silent and kept stirring and stirring the pot. Her shoulders slumped a little and I wasn't sure but I believed she was crying as I waited patiently for proof. In less than a minute it was there, she picked up her shirt sleeve and wiped both eyes with them and turned to find me staring at her.

"Well now, didn't know you were still here, Missy," Marian

said quickly with silent red-rimmed eyes.

"Marian, I'm sorry if my question upset you. I knew you and your husband were close to both Mom and Dad, I really didn't mean to upset you." I tried, fumbled and failed miserably to attempt an apology for upsetting her.

"Missy, you didn't upset me over that. I'll tell you straight out. That damn dish set was bought on purpose by your mom. It was her constant reminder of the mistake me and your dad made years ago. She would proudly set out those damn dishes every time we came over after she caught me with your dad in the barn one night. She and Herbert came out to find us after the dance in town, we all were lit up and having a good old time. That night in the barn got hot and heavy real fast with your dad and I." She paused and then looked me square in the face and said, "I was ashamed for a drunken mistake for a long time and your damn sainted Mother made sure I'd never forget it. Herbert forgave me because he understood, your dad finally forgave himself and me as well, but your mother, oh your mother!" With a slight huff Marian turned back to the stove and then whipped back around and shook the wooden spoon at me. "And don't you dare upset your dad by telling him about this! This conversation is over as far as I'm concerned!"

That night at the supper table with Dad, Marian and me seated around and eating a plain home cooked meal we were separated by land mines of yellow and brown cheap melamine dishes. To confused at that moment to do much more than eat politely I finally attempted conversation at the end of the meal.

"Thought I should tell you Dad that when Jeth, Babs, and the twins arrive here I'm going to take some time off to go see Chuck and spend time at the site. Maybe I'll even poke around Tobacco Garden." I slowly blew on my coffee in that ugly brown cup.

I looked at the dishes and made a decision that I knew would make me proud even years later. Those dishes, those damned dishes were one key to unlock one door of the past; resolve it and then prop open the door and let the winds of forgiveness blow clean and straight though to release bitterness, shame, sorrow, and leave behind only the pungent smell of sage and grasses.

I stood and walked to the stove and quietly picked up the small saucer and set the weary brown melamine cup on top of the faded brown and yellow sunflowers. Filling the cup with a richer shade of brown coffee I gently added one teaspoon of sugar, stirred it and moved across the kitchen to set it at my dad's place.

He glanced up and said, "Well now daughter, thank-you."

I decided not to beat around the bush; "Dad, I'm curious. Mom always hated brown, so what exactly did these," and I tapped the saucer then, "mean?"

Dad set his cup on the saucer after only one long sip and a pleased 'ahh' that escaped his lips.

Marian looked at me and started to stand. I waved her to sit and held my hand to see that I meant for her to be included in this conversation.

He cleared his throat and looked me square in the eyes;

faded, blue, older eyes pierced mine. "I screwed up one night with another woman, and your mother and the woman's husband caught us. We all had a little meeting," and he thumped the table with his fist, "Right here, at this here table."

"Ok Dad," I laid my hand on top of his. "I didn't mean to upset you; I was just curious based on Marian's response tonight."

"Yeah," Dad almost snarled and looked across the table, "what did Saint Marian have to say about these damn brown dishes?"

"She told me the truth Dad. About mistakes and forgiveness and learning from the past. I also realized something about Mom, she never did learn how to really forgive, even herself."

Dad nodded and stood; "Don't know why these dishes are still here then. Your mom's been gone quite a few years. Think it might be time to clean up a few things before your brother, his citified wife and those bratty kids of theirs arrive."

He slowly moved from the table and with his cane went to the pantry. He emerged moments later with a small cardboard box. He picked up his cup of half-finished coffee and in one gulp swallowed it down. As soon as he was done, he wiped his lips on his sleeve nodded at Marian and said; "We'll start with these." Then he threw the cup and saucer into the box.

Chapter Ten
Moon of Slow Water

George stood back away from the dust, smoke and ash the engine was spewing as he watched his young talking pillow partner being helped up the ramp into the river boat with the other women, girls and boys being sent back East to boarding school.

He was in a silent rage and felt the rip cord muscles in his arms clench and unclench with the slow rolling anger he usually felt before he mounted Josephine and then roughed her up a bit so she would always do his bidding.

He had been tricked into signing the papers by that misbegotten son of the devil priest himself. The whiskey he had brought to the house was smooth as silk as he remembered that oaky, charred hint in the Kentucky bourbon. His saliva built into his mouth as he thought of the half bottle left on the kitchen table.

The sun shimmered in heat waves and matched the keening noises some of the women and girls were making. The boys looked afraid but remained rock like; silent, sturdy and strong in quiet fear of what waited for them ahead on this journey.

Indians were allowed to ride in the back of the boat. The smoke and ash would fall on them if no breeze swept it away. If they were lucky, they would be fed and given water once a day. To protect these uncivilized new converts the church had also requested they be 'kept away' on the way to school to protect them. They would transfer to a train to head east when they arrived down river in BisMan.

George wasn't sure who was being protected from whom. He stood still and let the whiskey sweat bead up on his forehead and trickle down his neck. He really stunk badly after the bender with the priest two days ago. He exploded again just yesterday when he was trying to sober up and saw the paper on the table and picked it up and read what he had signed. The rage built and he grabbed for the full bottle that magically appeared as he cussed and raged against the church, the priest, Josephine and life in general. That rage was filled with sexual frustration and only did satisfaction come after he released his rage on Josephine with the release of his sperm and his fists.

He stood in the beating sun with only his hat for shade and watched as Josephine turned her bruised face towards the crowd searching for any familiar face. Her parents and sister were not anywhere near but surely had heard of her being sent back East to the Hampton Institute in Virginia to be 'properly educated'. She finally saw him standing back away from the cluster of people by the wooden planks. When she saw him, she lowered her eyes and covered her head with her thick cotton shawl.

George waited in the dust away from the cluster of 'fort fools' as he called them. The Union boys in blue, the trappers, and the head of the fort in his heavy woolen coat he wore to impress others along with a few remnants of once great warrior nations; Arrikara, Lakota, Assiniboine, Hidatsa, Hunkpapa, Mandan and even some of the honored rearguard Sioux. The entire group appeared to be led by the priest who asked them all to bow their heads in prayer.

It was then he started his lengthy blessing asking his God, or who he thought to be the God of all, to watch over those headed to the Hampton Institute to receive a great education provided by the Pope himself and the Great White Father in Washington, D.C.

That made George's decision to head to Lil's sooner instead of waiting for the boat to pull out from the little post beside the muddy waters of the Missouri. The native name for this river has always been, holes in water, because of all the treacherous whirlpools that lurked beneath the murky and seemingly quiet surface. Many had lost their lives because of these holes, at the moment George felt his power over Josephine slipping away as if it too was being sucked under the surface to never return again. He was in a boiling rage inside thinking about the years of labor and on demand sexual release he had lost because of that damned paper he had signed!

As soon as he got to Lil's he knew the three thing he wanted right away. His thick dirty fingers closed around the leather pouch of gold dust in his pocket. The dust was courtesy of one of the miners who had come from near the

Rockies and he had been fleeced by George well in a game of cards. This pouch was going to provide George with some release after all and he planned on spending the entire pouch on himself. It would provide clean clothes, sex, a hot bath, sex, a shave, sex, whiskey and more sex in any tumbled order he wanted them for a few days of enjoyment.

Small puffs of dusty gumbo whispered out in gray clouds around his knee-high leather boots as he whiskey weary walked towards the clapboard tent saloon and brothel. The blue sky was building clouds in the West and it had a smell to the air like sweet water with no hint of mud.

He had to stop and wipe his brow with his sleeve when he was only half way to the tented building. His sleeve was turning a grayish brown from the elbows down from using his homespun shirt to wipe the whiskey sweat away. His clothes were a combination of creases and stains from the last two days of excess with drinking and whoring. Frustration and sexual tension whirled in ripples around him like holes in the river water, with every step he took he reminded himself of what he would miss for the time when she was gone.

His hat and boots were about the only items of clothing that wasn't stained and smelling beyond salvation. That hat, his boots and his leather watch fob with the watch connected to it were almost important religious items that George valued. The hat had seen a great deal of wear and was angled up in the back from him falling asleep many times with his saddle as his pillow as it shaded his face from the brutal elements. His knee-high buffalo leather boots were so comfortable they felt like thick socks to walk in. Those boots also had a knife sheath in them and carried his two favorite knives to use on a moment's notice.

Of these three the most important item to George, one he considered even more valuable than the other two was the watch that had been passed down, and the braided leather watch fob. The watch had gone to his father when his grandfather passed away, and not 3 months later with the passing of his father on to him. There were no molasses sweet sentiments attached to these two items, instead they represented an entirely different story than just a family to George. They represented memories of how he was trained, how he became a Civil War Veteran and a spy for General Sherman on the 'March to the Sea' and how George had learned his sexual preferences from his grandfather himself.

When he held the watch in his hand, he had two particular memories that would whirl to the surface for himself; the front of the watch with the hands ticking always reminded him of Mauve, his Grandfather and the greenhouse episode that happened a month before his Grandfather died of the fever that took all of his family from Baltimore. The back engraved side of the watch with his Grandfather's name almost totally rubbed off reminded him of Annie, the upstairs maid, and having his first three-way experience with his Grandfather directing it all two years before he had passed away.

George had come from a privileged background and was born into a wealthy and well-educated family that consisted of his Maternal Grandparents, Parents and a younger sister that was greatly expanded on with his own mid-sized estate and the larger estate of his Grandparents. It was there that the 'rear' of the watch opened the doors to George. Time and disease had a strange way of taking away family and innocence as it invaded family ranks. When the fever first hit it started out by the docks in a world miles away from where George lived and a few miles away from where his grandparents estate was. His favorite sweet Nana had been the first to go from the fever.

The hushed voices and discussion at this Grandparents house where Nana lay in her open casket had the young teen of 15 hearing that 'she didn't suffer' as others had since she was elderly. Confusion seemed to reign as his own mother was inconsolable and his father and grandfather were stoic and steady during such a time of grief at the passing of a normal and healthy woman. His parents and younger sister took their leave of the house the next day and left George in charge of 'helping his Grandfather adjust to life without Nana'. That week-end George became a man in the worldly sense with his grandfather's direction and manipulation.

His grandfather arranged for one of his favorite upstairs maids, Annie, to teach George everything she could about a wild romp of 'slap and tickle'. Grandfather told him later that Annie had always been his favorite of all the maids he tumbled. He had spent time with each woman in the house that way. His reason was that she liked it rough and could handle more than any of the others when he lost himself in the games.

He felt more like a man in his own right around his grandfather, and on the third day in the house after his parents left during his second sexual lesson from Annie, his grandfather came up to the third floor in hopes of catching George in the middle of a 'lesson' so he could join in.

The more George rubbed the watch back the more memories of that time came back to him. It started with the slow tread on the stairs with George embedded up to his testicles in Annie's rear and her shouting 'Harder in Georgie and if you can't thump it harder than slap me ass hard this time.'

His grandfather walked into the room, closed and locked the door, turned and, lifting his monocle to his eye, peered at the scene. Annie bent over the chaise lounge with exposed breasts that had bite marks on them and nipples that were taut and swollen looking. George had slowed his pace of stroking in and out of her rear as he still held her hips hard and puffed out, 'Ah, Grandfather.'

"Well, what have we here?" Grandfather said, peering over his monocle. "Lessons? I love to learn. Let me join you." With that, he proceeded to drop his trousers in front of George, and for the first time, George saw the full stiff rod of a grown man with large testicles covered in swirls of black and gray hair. Grandfather stepped out of his trousers, laid them on the bed and proceeded to close the distance to the front of Annie.

George was frozen in place with his young, smaller, hard rod buried up to his balls in Annie's rear. Annie turned and said, "Oh sir, I've tried to teach him exactly like you wanted me to. I'm afraid he doesn't get all the fine points yet." With that, she wiggled her ass again and said firmly, "Again, Georgie, pound the butt hole and slap my ass hard this time."

George grabbed her hips again and started to pound as he had been directed and slapped the right cheek and the left cheek, leaving bright red marks on her lovely peach-colored bottom. Grandpa had been stroking his rod up and down as he watched George follow Annie's instructions. And he stepped closer to Annie at that time and said, "Now George, you seem to be doing fine banging her bunghole, but let me show you how together we can really fill this lass with fun!"

With that, Grandpa took off his coat and tie but left his shirt on and stepped directly up to Annie. Annie had been licking her lips in anticipation of this part of Georgie's lesson. She swirled her tongue over her full top and bottom lips and said, "I could have a drink, Sire. I'm feeling parched."

Grandpa stepped up to her, and Annie easily slid his entire rod down her throat, both sucking and lapping around the length and tip as Grandpa held her head and pushed in and out of her mouth. "Now George, keep up with my rhythm here. Just like the jumps on a horse. In and out, in and out, in and out." Grandpa stopped talking and started pulling on Annie's hair hard and making her squeal.

Every time she let out a squeal when he pulled her hair, he would shove his rod deeper into her throat, and she would gag. "Oh, Annie, that's it, gal, your throat muscles are squeezing me hard when you gag. More of that gal, more I say!" Grandpa started pumping her mouth deep and hard and long. He would barely pull out to let her catch a breath until he grabbed her hair and slammed his full rod deep into her mouth until he could feel her tighten around him.

He picked up his pace and continued to pump her as fast

and as hard as he could. George kept pace as long as he could but eventually spilled himself into Annie's bunghole. His Grandfather released himself into her mouth with a roar only a few strokes behind George.

His 'lessons' with Grandfather and Annie continued on for almost two solid weeks, and during that time, George had his mind, mannerisms and general handling of women in place firmly before his 18th year. During his 2 years of visiting and spending quality time with his Grandfather during the summers, his parents had no idea of the education their son was receiving. He grew before their eyes and seemed to them to be more like a grown man. Before his Grandfather passed away from the fever, George received his last 'lesson' in carnal knowledge in the greenhouse of that estate.

As George flipped the watch over to check the time on this weary, dusty walk to Lil's, he was reminded of the last time he received a 'lesson' that his grandfather had directed with Mauve, the downstairs maid, who liked to be ridden hard as well. He stopped walking, blew the dust away from the watch face, and turned as the boat whistle blew. He watched as his talking pillow partner was taken away for a few years.

Rage still shimmered under the surface that he needed to release in the way he was trained as he watched the boat pull away. He thought of Mauve and how powerful he had been with her.

He was the one who had walked in on Mauve and Grandfather in the greenhouse. The butler had said with a smile and a wink, "Young Mr. George, your Grandfather has requested you join him in the greenhouse for some afternoon tea. He said to remind you to lock the door from the house and into the greenhouse with your key to make sure you are not interrupted." And under his breath, he had murmured low to George, 'Stick it to her hard and then throw in a slap for me since she is an uppity one."

George stepped outside in back and locked the door to the back with his key so no one from the house could interrupt his tea. He walked up to the glass door of the greenhouse and could see images and hear his grandfather shout, 'Move faster, Mauve, move left and right!'

Not knowing what he would see, George already felt his rod stiffen in his trousers in anticipation of another lesson of 'slap and tickle'. He walked in, turned and locked the door into the humid warmth of the greenhouse. As he walked and turned the corner on the gravel path, he saw his grandfather riding Mauve from the rear with a short riding crop in one hand and the other holding his watch fob that was around her neck as he pulled on the 'reins' and slapped her rear with the crop. He paused, turned to George, and said, "Step up front and fill the lass with fun, George!"

George complied with his grandfather's directions and dropped his trousers, kicked out of them and grabbed Mauve by the hair as he slid his rod deep into her throat. Both of them filled Mauve from either end, and George lost his load before his grandfather. He stepped back and watched his grandfather finally release. Both stood panting slightly as Mauve laid her head down and finally relaxed on top of her bunched-up skirts. Grandfather threw a damp towel to George, washed himself with another one and then laid the third towel on top of Mauve's slightly red rear.

As George wiped himself, he started to harden again as he looked over at the plumb bare checks still bent over and quivering with need. Grandfather nodded toward Mauve and said, "Sometimes young men need a little longer in the saddle to reach satisfaction. Let me help Mauve get ready for another round." He stepped up to the front of Mauve and proceeded to help her sit up as he sucked and fondled both breasts. He then proceeded to stick three fingers deep into her and get her satisfied from the front, and when her juices flowed around his fingers, he wiped them slick into her bung so she would be ready for round two.

George needed no more invitation than that and grabbed the crop and the watch chain still nestled around her neck, flipped her over as Grandfather kept his fingers inside her front and said, "Now George, let me keep her motivated here a while longer. I do so love the slick feel of this juice." He proceeded to lick one finger and then stuck it deep into Mauve as he sat beside her on the bench.

Wasting no time and ready to ride, George mounted her from the rear and plunged deep into her. Mauve squealed a little as she had been trained to do, and George jerked the chain and swatted with the crop as he had seen his grandfather do. George was stronger with his swats and harder with his jerks as he rode himself into dropping another load. By the time both men were done, Mauve was well and truly spent, and every part of her was exhausted with use. Bite marks appeared on her breasts as Grandfather sucked, pulled and bit on her nipples and kept as many fingers inside of her that he could bury as he fingered her to climax after climax. All the while, George stroked her from the rear as he rode her hard, reined her left and right, and swatted her with the crop to keep her moving.

After this episode, Mauve took to her bed for almost a week and informed Grandfather he could fire her, but she would no longer have any 'slap and tickle time' with George.

When George left with the promise of another summer with Grandfather in the back of his mind for the next year, he had no idea that within two months, his grandfather would be dead from the fever that slowly was invading households in Baltimore. Two years ago, his Nana had been lucky to the one of the first to pass from the fever. The new maid they hired to replace Annie came to the house directly from the boat. She was not as clean as Annie and brought the fever directly into all who came and visited at the house.

His Father, Mother and younger sister had been coming to the house when he was away at school that fall and contracted the fever as well. When they had all passed away within weeks of each other, the lawyers arrived to settle the estates and were able to strip George of both of his inheritances. George left Maryland soon after all of the sadness and bitterness happened. When the dust settled from reading the wills and time in court, he realized nothing was left of the family funds. All would be sold to settle outstanding debts, the largest being the lawyers' fee.

George headed out of town and joined up with a group of travelers headed west to Minnesota. His plan was to start over with his stallion and the two mares he literally stole from the stables. He believed they were the least of his birthright. These three things, along with his Grandfather's watch and gold watch fob, were all he really cared about. The watch and chain brought back memories of his grandfather and his lessons. When he felt frisky, he would continue to find satisfaction in riding the doves in the same way.

He jerked back to the heat and dust that swirled around him as the boat let out a long and lonely whistle as it gathered speed on the journey to Virginia. Now here he was, a Civil War veteran who had fought with the Minnesota 'Regulars' at Gettysburg and almost lost his life. He had managed to escape and went to work for General Sherman soon after as a spy for the Boys in Blue. He was involved in Sherman's March to the Sea, and if the real stories were told, he would have spent time in the brig for some of the things he did in the South. George took off his hat and held it in the air, and with one single wave, he settled it on his head and strode to Lil's for some important and uninterrupted fun.

Two days later, when George was headed toward a more sober state, he decided on a plan for when his 'pillow talker' was away at school. He was going to open up his own saloon and upstairs brothel. He had even picked out a name and had a favorite soiled dove lined up to run the place. It would be called 'The Blind Pig' in honor of his favorite dove that he had struck too hard too many times and was left almost totally blind. She would make a perfect Madame of the house. George could either run the saloon or get one of his ranch hands to pour whiskey for the miners. They had been coming both upriver to the gold fields in Montana and floating back downriver with their little pouches of gold with a great deal more frequency.

As he headed back to Tobacco Garden with a wagon with three girls in the back and some barrels of rotgut whiskey, he was whistling and smiling as he hadn't done in a while. The rolling hills were covered in brush with only a few blades of grass covering the prairie since it was August. The summer heat was in full boil, and the ground was parched as if waiting for fall rain and winter snow. George quietly thought his plan out in his head as the girls slept under the shade of the canvas cover.

Once they arrived at the ranch house George immediately rang the bell on the porch for the men to come to the house to see him. When they got there, they ogled the women who were dressed in corsets and bloomers with light shawls over their shoulders. George shouted, "Don't just stand there. Help these gals into the barn. We are going to turn that place into a saloon and a regular cat house upstairs! Now git to work and carry their trunks up the ladder first!"

He whirled with that and looked toward Bertie, the new Madame, "Well, Bertie, here is your place now named in your honor. The Blind Pig! I'll get you some buckets of water you can heat up in the stove in the corner of the barn, and you all will start to clean it out. When you get that done, me and they boys will have a set of stairs built to that loft, you can divide into cribs for you and the gals to earn your keep. Now you gals, git to work as well!"

George headed outside to pick up his saw, hammer and a small keg of nails leaning against the side of the octagon-shaped barn, soon to become the 'Blind Pig Saloon'. All he had to do was point at the pile of lumber, and his hired hands moved quickly over and started picking up the lumber to create the stairs to the hayloft and replace the ladders currently in use. As they sweated through the day the smell of hot, soapy water and an iron Dutch oven filled with beans bubbling on the stove filled the barn with smells that mingled with the smell of the hay and animal sweat.

George let the men and women stop for a mid-day meal of plates of beans and biscuits served with coffee strong enough to remove facial hair. As soon as everyone was done eating and the sun was making the ground even warmer, he pushed even harder on the entire group to get the whole place scrubbed down and the stairs and simple plank bar completed.

By the end of the second day, the women were upstairs in make-due rooms created with a cloth hung across the loft on ropes until more solid walls could be built. The plank bar had some glasses with a few bottles of whiskey and beer on the shelves. Those glasses would be used over and over again until more glassware showed up on the next boat floating in. The women washed and hung laundry outside to dry and clean in the hot sun as they washed themselves and rinsed their hair with flax water to get the shiny, healthy look they wanted.

All was ready to fleece the next group of miners that happened to float by here and stop before they got to the fort. And the Blind Pig was set to go with a lucrative business venture. With all that in place and the ranch hands working, George set off for the gold fields in Montana himself. He wanted to experience the rush of panning and getting gold nuggets for himself while still fleecing unsuspecting miners headed to the gold fields and those headed home. He had a few years before Josephine would come back from school, and the church would insist on a proper wedding ceremony for the two of them.

George had big plans for himself, and that year almost saw an early end to him with the gold field and fighting he got into. Josephine, on the other hand, had almost three years of being taught to speak and write in English, cook and sew like a young woman was supposed to by reading and praying for her own 'heathen soul' as the Nuns taught her.

Josephine struggled because the more she learned, the more she discovered how evil her life had been when she was given for land in the trade to George. She and some of the other 'pillow talkers' were not allowed to speak in their native language but managed a few whispered conversations when they could get away with them. She promised herself she would not become sad, for she was returning back to the prairie where the wind blew the smell of smoke away, and it did not cling to the clothes as it did here in this eastern city in Virginia.

Chapter Eleven
Work Heals

Following Marian to the airport in Dickyville was easy since Marian was a steady and solid driver of all rigs, whether she was hauling cattle, water tanks, hay, or humans. Our little caravan slowly merged from the quiet two-lane back highway onto the interstate where the speed and ignorance seemed to pick up pace with each other. We headed quickly to Dickyville and turned into the airport parking lot, short-term area, and headed together to the waiting room.

Not much really happened at this airport that all the locals weren't aware of. We waved to the local Security Guard who knew both of us by name. He stepped to the other side of the metal detector and said, "Who's flying in to meet you two good-looking gals?"

Only in the West would a man somewhere between my age and Marian's age dare to address women as 'gals' unless they knew them personally. Walter knew both of us well between our trips and our family's interaction in the western part of the state.

"Hey Walt," Marian chuckled, "are you really talking to the

two of us? Cripes, I'm old enough to be your aunt or maybe even your mom, you old fart you!" With that rejoinder, both Marian and Walt chuckled aloud, which left me to answer his question.

"Hey Walt!" I smiled and said, "It's my brother Jeth, wife Beth, and the twins; Marlow and Nylee. Do you remember them at all?"

Walt's face crumbled from a smile to almost a sneer, "Oh yeah, how could I forget that Queen of Sheba? I remember how she called me 'Boy' and pointed to her luggage expecting me to carry it for her. That little witch sure got a mouthful from me back then, and she'll get another if she thinks I'm her porter!"

Keeping my voice low and my face serious, I replied, "Walt, this isn't a pleasure trip at all for the family. My Dad is in really tough shape, and this might be the end of the road for all of us with him. If you could just ignore her, I'd really appreciate it."

Marian provided backup by nodding her agreement when I said this, Walt looked from me to her and back again, then he cleared his throat, turned around, and didn't say another word to either of us.

Our wait proved to be short and sweet after that when the plane touched down minutes later. Out here passengers have to walk down the steps and into the terminal, no cover provided in any weather, it truly is a smaller airport.

We saw Jeth walking quickly toward the terminal trailed by his teen-aged kids, while bringing up the rear was Beth, who told everyone, including strangers, she preferred to be called 'Babs'. She looked haggard and thinner in a very unhealthy way. The twins were scowling, had no earbuds in place, and no cell phones were visible at all on any of them. My first thought was 'Great, step one in place already!'

I waited as patiently as I could for my brother to come striding through the walkway short hall. "Jeth," I hooted, "God, it's so good to see you again little bro-bro." I couldn't help myself as the nickname from childhood slipped from my lips. "I know you never liked that name, but I've missed your smiling mug a lot!"

With a bear hug that was familiar but without the smiling eyes that came along with it, I just hugged him in return. When he saw Marian standing there patiently waiting her turn, it was his turn to hoot! "Marian, you wonder! I'm so glad to see you again! I've missed your smiling mug a lot!

He swooped Marian up in a bear hug with his 6'5" frame and spun the little gray-haired woman around and around. It seemed to me that he didn't want to let her go since she had become a second Mom to us since our own Mom had passed away. Marian was so busy returning the hug, and I was so busy watching the exchange that neither of us noticed the haggard-looking woman silently approach us from the rear. Carrying a backpack, wearing plain blue jeans, and an ordinary tee shirt with no message or bling on it, and feet encased in plain blue tennis shoes, the former 'Queen of Sheba' approached us warily.

I took one look at Beth's face that had no makeup on it, hair that looked like it hadn't seen a brush in days, red-rimmed eyes quivering mouth and my resolve to be the worst sister-in-law on the planet crumbled. I hated to see Beth trying to lord it over others when she was all 'gussied up,' as Marian would say. I hated to see her fading into the background as if she had become sub-human because of her mistakes.

I silently walked up to her and wrapped her in my embrace, swaying back and forth slightly, and that is when Queen Beth began to sob. "I am so sorry, sorry, sorry." The words went into a whisper as she sobbed into my shoulder with embarrassment and defeat.

"Beth, Beth, Beth." I responded and did not drop my arms from around her. "That is what family is really all about; support and love. Never giving up together and fixing things when they are broken." I gently held her in one arm and dropped the other and encircled Jeth with it. I looked over at Marlow and Nylee, who were gaping like carp out of water at the four of us.

"Family is more than just those that are under one roof. It is neighbors who become part of who you are with their support and belief in you as well. Marian is family as well, just like your grandmother; she is a part of who we all are together. This problem is one we all have, and we are all responsible to fix this together. I know you, Marlow," I nodded toward the lanky boy with his brown hair hanging in his hazel eyes, "you just want to be with your friends this summer; just hanging out, playing games, riding your skateboard, and eating junk. I know you, Nylee," I nodded toward his petite twin sister with the purple and blue streaked hair and the matching hazel eyes, "you just want to be with your friends; cruising the mall, shopping for pretty clothes, complaining about 'weird girls' and texting all night. News flash that I'm sure your Dad has already told you, your summer will be one of working to help the family make sure your house isn't lost and that you have time left with Grandpa before he passes." The deer in the headlights stares told me that they realized I knew a great deal more than they thought I did. I imagined that dropping the family 'secret' in the open area of the airport lounge had gone far enough. So, I dropped both arms from around Jeth and Beth and said with a phony smile, "Time to saddle up and get to the ranch, let's go get your luggage."

As I walked towards the luggage area where another old acquaintance was working, I imagined the tales that would be spun now that the family secret was out in the open. I really could care less about the whispers that would come when the twins or my brother and his beautiful wife had to go to town for supplies or hauling things. They would be well deserved for the nonsense they had dealt the family with the hands they had played. I was feeling out of sorts, missing my own family and grown kids. Dealing with Dad and his lingering death had started to take a toll on me. I had dropped 10 pounds, which really didn't hurt, but I had also discovered that sleeping wasn't easy unless I was exhausted from the daily ranch chores. I really hoped that the returning 'family' would be able to ease some of the burden.

I had braided my hair that morning in anticipation of heat, frustration, and the ability to look a little more 'together,' as

Beth would say. Now it really seemed a waste since she was a wreck and I looked more like a fashion plate in my torn jeans, green, yellow, blue plaid pearl snapped shirt tucked into the waist with a thin leather belt and a sweet agate belt buckle, along with my brown leather boots that my jeans covered. I kept my focus as my boots made a sweet clumping sound on the tile as I headed to the portable metal racks stacked with luggage and looked for name tags. Sweet Jesus, I thought, there were 8 carts loaded to the top with multiple luggage styles. They could not be just for this family, could it?

When I think back on it now, I realize I must have had the glint of murder in my eyes when I turned and glared at the family because Marian even stopped short when she saw my face. "Let me guess," I started out with a hint of steel usually reserved only for my husband. "ALL of this," and I waved both my arms to encompass the eight stacked carts, "is yours?"

I tapped my toe as I waited for an answer from one of the 'city family members.' Oh, I was now royally pissed off as I struggled to imagine how this would all fit into two vehicles with six of us being transported.

Jeth stepped up to me and laid his tanned, calloused hand on my shoulder, "Look Sis, we had to take everything out of the house that we didn't sell at the garage sale. I mean everything." He had a somber look on his face as he leaned close to me, brown piercing eyes like Mom's, into my eyes like Dad's and said, "You need to know we were two days away from getting evicted and losing everything. Without Babs calling you from the bank, it would be much worse. I'm sorry we have a load of luggage here, but I think we are going to be at the ranch longer than we imagined after I reviewed all the bills and tax information with the accountant yesterday. The bills are staggering, and we might just have to sell the house to get back on our feet at least a little bit.

I grabbed his hand off my shoulder, still annoyed with him and his wife because of these problems and tried to rein in my anger. "OK, I get the tough spot; I really do. I'm just pissed I didn't bring a trailer to haul all this. I didn't even think to bring straps to place all this on the roof. What the hell are we going to do with loading this all and getting back home?" Then the asshole smiled and started to giggle, ruining my bad mood permanently!

"God, how I've missed your cut-to-the-chase sassy attitude, Sis!" Jeth continued to giggle and soon had me laughing with him at how ridiculous this situation was becoming. "I have a great idea!" he said. "In one of these pieces of luggage, it's gray with a red strip; I have luggage nets and bungee cords. I sort of anticipated this issue when I saw how much Beth and the kids had managed to hang on to after the garage sale."

I merely nodded at this hidden logic that was coming to life in my brother. "I have another great idea; it just came to me right now, Flash!" I used my hands with fingers splayed to demonstrate an explosion. "Let's put your kids to work right now! They can haul everything out to the vehicles and start learning to follow packing directions!"

Jeth laughed his deep belly laugh and said, "Auntie M rides again. I always did tell my friends you were brilliant!" He turned on his heel and headed toward the group of four that had been staring wonder-eyed at us the entire time. "Guess what group? You are all going to work, kids! Head over to the carts, and everyone grab at least one. I'm in charge of the first lesson of the West: packing and stacking so you don't lose anything precious that might save your bacon later on. Head 'em up, move 'em out!" He threw his hands up in the air and raced towards the twins and picked up his son and daughter, spun them around once, set them on the floor, and swatted their rear ends. "Head over and pick a cart, kids, the first lesson is usually the hardest!"

Marian and Beth each headed toward a cart and started to push without any comment. I grabbed one to push and one to pull as Jeth did. We deliberately picked the carts with the smallest load and left Marlow and Nylee to grab the last ones left, which had the fullest loads on them. It was working like a charm until we actually got outside to the parking lot where the wind had started to howl.

A prairie wind is nothing to take lightly, for the gusts from the mountains to the West can easily gust from 50 to 80 miles per hour depending on the weather front being blown in. We were in for a whopper of a storm being blown in that day since it was gusting hard and had a chill behind the wind. Marian and Beth made it to her vehicle just fine, and Beth was following Marian's directions about loading the roof first with the heavier larger suitcases and the smaller pieces going inside the back. It was when the real 'greenhorns', Marlow and Nylee, got outside and the wind hit them that the slapstick comedy really started.

First one out the door pushing her large loaded cart was

Nylee. Being the smaller twin, she was hit with the gust hard since it also carried dust and rocks from the unswept parking lot. She bent down and started hollering, "Ouch, Crap, Ouch, Crap!" and let go of her cart that the wind decided to push down the street in front of the terminal. As she rubbed her eyes and tried to turn her back to the wind, the cart was merrily being pushed by the wind down the road. It headed to the run-off ditch that was filled with water and a few mud ducks that had sadly decided it was a perfect nesting spot. The slight hill let the cart really pick up speed as it careened left to right down the road. It missed the pick-up truck coming into the terminal area as it veered to the left; the silver pickup narrowly missed the front bumper being torn off. The truck slammed to a stop, and a man and his son got out of the truck and proceeded to try and chase the cart down while laughing loudly. At this point, Nylee stopped rubbing her eyes and hollering as she realized she had lost her cart. She started to run down the little hill towards the cart.

Imagine a picture in your mind of three little pigs; the older, larger one with a cowboy hat in the lead, the 2nd, a tall lanky boy with a baseball cap on backward, and the 3rd little pig with streaming blond, purple, blue hair flying behind her like a flag all racing to capture the runaway cart loaded with luggage. It wasn't even five minutes into leaving the terminal, and I felt like a kid watching the circus. The shit really hit the fan when the dad from the pick-up took a last gallant leap and tried to grab the cart and fell with it into the run-off ditch. He landed into the duck nest and the water. He came up sputtering with broken duck eggs dripping from his hat brim and a look of thunder in his eyes.

His son wasn't far behind him and tried to put the brakes on but slipped on the gravel and headed face first into the run-off ditch filled with water as his right shoulder hit the luggage and his left splashed into the filled ditch. Nylee wasn't far behind since she was lean and fast on her feet. Unfortunately, she wasn't fast enough to make her sneakers stop on a dime. She went into a slide and tried to stop by plopping her rear end on the gravel without success. She hit the water right next to baseball cap boy with a full splash; it reminded me of a belly flop in a pool.

Even more amusing than watching this was seeing the two 'gentlemen' of the West try to climb up the muddy slope of the ditch and try to assist Nylee in getting out of the water. After multiple attempts by the two of them and hearing swear words floating up to us between wind gusts, Marian and I headed down to the bottom with a few bungee cords to see if we could help out.

We tried really hard not to laugh at the situation, but that was a total loss when we got to the drainage ditch and really smelled what had happened. Barb had stayed at Marian's SUV and stood on the back area floor, watching the entire show with a look of bewilderment on her face. She saw exactly what we saw but didn't really smell it all until later on the ride home. Some of the eggs on George's hat were rotten ones that would never have hatched. And the green slime that was mixed with them didn't have a fresh herb scent either. George's son, Bart, hadn't taken his eyes off Nylee's soaked shirt because she didn't have a bra on, and her nipples were sticking out like sore thumbs. Nylee was furious, swearing like an old sailor, had lost a shoe in the ditch, and all three of them smelled like stagnant pond water.

Finally, a reason to have one up on both Nylee and Marlow, I chuckled with glee aloud. Marian, bless her, said in a quiet voice as she walked down and stood next to Nylee, "Dear, I want you to put my sweater on right now; that young man is staring at your chest and can't seem to stop swallowing. I'm afraid if you don't cover up, he'll swallow his tongue." Marian proceeded to hand her blue sweater to Nylee, who immediately stopped cussing and put the sweater on.

The young man, Bart, stopped staring once she was covered up and turned a bright fire engine red. His father slapped his shoulder, laughed, took off his hat and shook the weeds and eggs from it, and brushed it off with his shirt sleeve. George spoke up, "Marian, nice to see you looking so good, Ma'am. Sorry we couldn't grab that cart quick enough, but Bart and I will be happy to help you get this cart and wet bags up to your outfit." With that being said, he grabbed the cart and proceeded to yank it out of the mud as he pointed to Bart and said, "Son, grab some of them wet bags there, and we'll load this back up and push it up the hill for these ladies here."

Bart found the floating shoe further down the ditch and stayed in the water to cool down as he waded down to get Nylee's lost shoe. He tried to be a true knight, but when he climbed up out of the ditch, he slipped in the muck and ended up flat on his face, his entire body head to toe covered in putrid muddy ditch water. The only saving grace was his hat didn't have a drop of mud or water on it.

He approached Nylee, and no one knew if he was blushing red under the mud or not but said in a sweet flirting tone, "Miss, sorry I don't know your name yet, but I promise you I will. Here's your shoe back; want me to help you get it back on?"

Nylee grabbed his shirt with one hand, not caring about the mud at all, and said, "I'm not 'Miss' anything, bud, too bad you couldn't catch this cart though 'cause trust me, I'll never live this down with my family. Name's Nylee, and don't forget it." With that, she grabbed her shoe, let go of his shirt, and gave him a little shove, and he slipped back down the bank right back into the water. This time his hat wasn't so lucky; he came up smiling covered in weeds and grinning from ear to ear.

"Not forgetting your name, Nylee. Not forgetting you and your wild cart either!" And then he and his dad roared with laughter. They both went right to work and pulled the luggage out of the water and heaped all bags and luggage, wet, dry, and covered in wet mud, on the cart and started up the hill laughing together.

I could hear Bart's Dad's voice carrying through the howling wind up the hill. "Boy, you sure did pick one filled with spunk and sass! And just as pretty as a little prairie chicken she is! Better hang on to that one before school starts; she is liable to make all those other young bucks come arunnin'!" And George let out another deep belly laugh as he and his son pushed the overloaded cart back up the hill.

Dripping wet with muddy slough water and covered in dark green weeds, they looked a sorry sight as they laughed and talked their way up the hill to my suburban. By that time, Jeth had finished loading and strapping down most of the luggage on top of Marian's suburban and was headed over to mine. He stopped short, looked at his son Marlow, who had practically been killed when his luggage fell off the cart onto the gravel and tipped over sideways. He had caught his arm with some flyaway luggage and was staring at the road rash left on his right arm when he had tried to stop the car and luggage from tipping and falling over.

"Um, Dad, I could use some help here. I seem to have tipped this cart over." Marlow said to the air since Jeth had just left him standing there and went to help George and Bart finish pushing the cart up the hill. George recognized him right away since Jeth and George were old high school classmates from back in the day. I could see the handshake and smiles and the back thumping and the rumble of low men's voices.

Marlow still looked like a lost sheep and stared at the luggage and his arm, the luggage and his arm, as if he didn't have a clue what he should be doing. When Nylee finally made it up the hill with squeaking shoes and dripping hair, she shook a finger at him and exclaimed, "Not ONE DAMN WORD, or I'll rip your throat out!" Being the younger and smaller twin had made her incredibly feisty at times.

Marlow stood and looked from her to his arm and to the luggage and back again until he finally stopped holding his arm and said, "Hey Nylee, help me out, please. My arm is starting to throb, and I've got to restack all of these to get to Auntie 'M's' Burb so she doesn't bite my head off. Come on and help me out."

Nylee stopped short of my 'Burb' as they called it, and all I did was take my shades off and point at her brother and the luggage on the ground. She spun around on her wet squeaky heel and muttered under her breath back to where her seemingly invalid brother waited for someone to help him. I could hear her comments from where I was, and they were laced with a few choice words.

I certainly heard 'jackass, stupid, damned old aunt, damned ranch, and the cherry on top was 'this fuckin' wind is enough to drive you crazy!' I had to turn to hide my smile since I knew exactly how she felt. I heard the rumble of the deep men's voices carrying up the hill as George, Jeth, and Bart chatted as they pushed and carried the luggage to the ranch 'Burb'. I guess I'd have to rename the old gal something fitting for the city kids, something like 'Betty Burb' since that would be close enough to their mom's name to just about freak them both out. I turned my 100-watt smile on to both George and Bart and walked over to shake their hands. I saw Nylee stop what she was doing, helping Marlow, and stare at me as she tried to listen over the wind noise to what I was saying.

"We can't thank you enough for your help with all this. It sure looked like a three-ring circus from up here with what we saw. Can we please get you some supper?" I knew that was the least I was going to offer both George and his son.

Jeth chimed in, "Where the hell have my manners gone to? Yup, let us at the very least buy you supper before we all head to our places." Jeth knew George had a ranch/farm outfit about 30 miles from our place and that he and Bart would have to eat before leaving town. George just smiled and shook more of the weeds and eggshells from his hat.

"Well, some of us aren't ready to sit and eat right now since we do smell like slough water, but I'd appreciate a hot burger once we get our tractor part picked up and loaded." He smiled at Marian again and said, "Wife ordered it online from BisMan and they flew it on the plane this morning, speedy work for us."

Bart had already wandered over to the cart that still lay on its side, and I could hear his voice quietly talking to Marlow. Then Marlow reached down with his unscraped arm, and Bart, who seemed to be taking the full weight of the load, grabbed the other side and pushed as Marlow pulled. They right the cart with some of the luggage still on it. I saw Bart nod and heard him say, "Just a matter of physics, you'll learn that right quick when you start working with those bulls your family has at your spread." He tipped his hat to Nylee again and proceeded to push the cart over to 'Betty Burb,' and I decided then and there that I really liked this young man!

"OK, let's load up 'Betty Burb'! I giggled as I said this and saw Nylee make a spinning circle beside her head to Marlow to see if he thought I was crazy as well. Marlow just held his arm and came over to Marian and me. Marian had the ever-present first aid kit that is carried in every working ranch vehicle; she didn't say a word to him as she wiped his arm down with an antiseptic wipe and proceeded to pick out gravel with tweezers.

"No point getting an infection in this, Marlow. Just hold

on and I'll get this all cleaned up and get some crème on it and wrap it up. You'll be as good as new!" Marlow turned white as a sheet and started to keel over; if it hadn't been for Bart, he would have landed on his face in the gravel and skinned up even more of his exposed skin. "Hold on, Bart, and just set him right there on the driver's seat so I can finish this arm up. Good thing you caught him or I'd be scrubbing his face off as well!"

Nylee came running over with no luggage in her hands to check on her twin. Bart looked at her, and then looked back to the luggage and said, "Seems to me you wasted some steps coming over here. I'm sure he won't appreciate your seeing this. How 'bout I help you carry the rest of the bags and we'll let Marian and your aunt fuss over Marlow?" Bart grabbed Nylee's arm, spun her around, and gave her a little push over towards the cart. I didn't know if I should laugh or cry at that point. One passed-out injured teen, one scared teen, and one frightened Mom who had not said one word but sat in Marian's 'Burb' and watched the entire process silently. I was just thankful that Jeth hadn't made a big fuss about his arm as well. That would have put me right over the top of the butte!

With bungee cords in place and nets over most of the wet smelly luggage on top of 'B.B,' we arranged with George and Bart to meet them at the local 'Mickey D's' drive-through for a meal for the road. They both headed into the terminal to pick up their parts with a touch of fingers to the edge of their hats; they headed in, talking in low tones as they went.

Marian said she would take both Marlow and Babs in her

outfit, and I would take Jeth and Nylee in mine. I pointed to the backseat and said, "Nylee, that entire space left is all yours. You just need to share it with some of the fragrant luggage coming back to the ranch with us." I managed to even smile when I said this and received an eye roll, a flip of wet hair, and a squeaky heel turn with a 'whatever' comment in return.

Jeth held out his hand to me and said, "Keys please? I feel like a kid asking this, but can I please drive?" I smiled at the sorrowful pleading look he was using.

"I'll let you take it from the drive-through when we get the food all paid for, ok? I think you might be surprised at how much has changed around here. I know you won't get lost, but I just want to get there and get some chow. Oh yeah, by the way, you don't need to ask for permission to drive around here. It belongs to the family, you know." With that reminder, and since I really wasn't ready to release the chains of command with this small part of life, I hopped into the driver's seat and started the engine.

Nylee was already in the back seat staring out the window and looking glum as her hair dripped with a steady plop onto her shirt. Jeth buckled himself in, and the next part of the adventure was ready to start. With a steady push of the gas pedal, I shifted into first then second gear, and a perfect comment from the backseat reminded me how much my 'citified' family was missing in their life.

"Geez, you don't even have automatic transmissions here?" Nylee said in an incredulous tone.

Jeth replied even before I could respond; "Nope, and if you want to drive, you'll have to learn how to drive old school. This isn't uptown anything, it's a working ranch."

Conversation came to a dead stop after that remark as we made our way to 'Mickey D's' to get our chow.

With all three vehicles parked beside each other and orders written down, Marian, Babs, and I went in to use the restroom and get some chow before we headed out. Nylee followed us reluctantly and decided she would attempt to wash some of the slough water out of her hair in the sink with the foamy hand soap. It wasn't a perfect solution, but I admired her attempt at trying to be a little cleaner and less smelly for the rest of the ride home.

We carried the bags out to the vehicles, and Marian handed the bags for George and Bart to Nylee along with their drinks and said, "Nylee, take these over to George and Bart and mind your manners. I haven't heard thanks from your mouth yet for all the help they've given all of us. Trash talk I've heard, but I need to hear some sweetness as well coming from your lips."

Marian was a regular tough, no-nonsense Western woman, and no one argued with her, until Nylee tried. "Do it yourself then." She said with a sneer and turned to walk away from her. Jeth was checking straps on the back of 'B.B.,' and overheard his daughter.

He turned and grabbed her arm as she was walking away and said; "No one, and I mean NO ONE speaks to their elders like that young lady! You will apologize to Marian right now and then take the damn bags and deliver them and the drinks to George and Bart with a thank you and a smile on your smart-ass little face! I mean it right now!" He gave her a little shove towards Marian and stood with his arms folded across his chest as he glared at her.

Nylee headed over to Marian and said something to her in a whisper. Marian then took it upon herself to hug the young girl tightly and leaned over and whispered something in her ear. Nylee wiped the tears from her eyes and nodded then took the bags and drinks and headed over to George and Bart.

Once the food was delivered and we all stood outside the vehicles eating and chatting I realized that Marlow and Babs were still sitting in Marian's burb and eating and drinking. I went over the side doors and opened both of them up and said; "Both of you outside right now!" They were stunned and looked like deer in the headlights.

"Why, Auntie M?" Marlow said. "We're comfortable right here, why do we need to get out?"

"No one in this part of the country eats alone. Another crusty old school thing, companionship is just as important as food for the soul. Get out and talk to George, Bart, Marian, Nylee, and me, eat while you talk. It's going to be a long ride to the ranch and this will give you some time to stretch your legs and move since you'll be cramped for a while on the ride. You could even race your sister down to the street and back again. Just move around a bit." I opened the doors even further and stared at both of them until they started to get out of the vehicle.

I shook my head as I sadly walked around the vehicle and picked up the rest of my chicken sandwich from the rear bumper and proceeded to chew on it before I could make another negative comment aloud about how sadly they were missing basic social skills. I just smiled as Jeth nodded towards me and then turned to look at his wife and kids who were now clumsily trying to eat and talk with Marian, George, and Bart as those three engaged them in a lively story about a bull gone 'wild' from a neighbor's place.

Perhaps things would be alright.

Chapter Twelve
Sturgeon Moon

Westerners needed guts and toughness to handle their lives, and the men and women who forged paths for other immigrants to follow had that in abundance. Trail drivers, wood hawks, gold seekers, soldiers, ranchers, homesteaders, and the other individuals looking for a quick and easy life all were a part of this history.

While in the East at Hampton Institute, Josephine needed that same toughness to get through the years of education she was facing. She arrived, like the rest of the students, ridiculed, blamed, and jeered at by whites as they traveled across states to arrive in Virginia at the Hampton Institute where scrubbing, haircuts, 'civilized' clothes, and immediate punishment awaited them all if they dared to speak in their tribal languages.

Josephine was no different than many of the women who were 'pillow talkers' and had been taken as women of convenience by the men they lived with. Alignments for trapping areas were a part of that contract, and the child brides were just that, part of an alignment to try and keep the peace. Josephine arrived with the knowledge of a courtesan in her well-trained body, but little common knowledge and language to survive among the white culture. She kept quiet, followed every direction given, quieted the children who kept weeping, and by the end of her first week became a favorite of the teachers, nuns, and priests who worked with these 'savages'.

It was exactly one month into her two scheduled years at the Hampton Institute that Josephine had her first glimpse of what people thought of her based on outside appearances only. Those who had no knowledge of her life back in the Territory where she lived along Holes in Water with her George.

Mother Superior came up the stairs to the landing where Josephine was sitting on a bench and quietly sounding out words as she tried to read a prayer of the Church in a small missal. She was following with her finger as she quietly as possible mouthed the words to the prayer that she had heard Father Piedmont say when he arrived at the ranch and when he left. At that point in time Josephine had no idea that this common prayer was known throughout the world as, "The Lord's Prayer".

She had her hair neatly braided in long braids on each side of her head and wore a common dark blue dress with a lighter blue apron over the top for when it was time to go to the kitchen and learn more about bread making. Her white stockings itched her legs that were used to being bare and the black leather button high top shoes made her feet sweat. She was swinging them back and forth, but they did not want to cool down the way moccasins did.

She heard the quiet steps on the stairs coming up from the first-floor squeak but didn't look up. She knew from the quiet tread that it was one of the sisters, but didn't know if it was one of the older and meaner ones or one of the younger and gentle ones. She did not recognize the other firm slide of a boot on the stair tread, but knew it was a boot from the sounds it made.

Lightly the hairs at the back of her neck stood up as she had a terrible thought that maybe it was George come to visit and take her away from this peace and quiet that had buffered her abuse and replaced it with learning. She wanted to look up in the worst way but kept her eyes down on the page and her finger tracing the words as she silently tried to follow the sounds that were in her head.

Gently a black sleeve with a wrinkled and liver-spotted hand at the end reached forward and tapped Josephine on the shoulder, with a quiet voice Mother Superior said, "Josephine, would you look up from your studies please, for a moment?"

Relaxing inside and with a quiet breath, the doe brown eyes looked up into Mother Superior's faded hazel eyes and said in broken English, "Ya~na, Mother?"

Even after a month calling this elderly white woman 'Mother' seemed strange to Josephine. Her real Mother was Beaver Woman, a short and rounded version of Josephine. It was true her mother had lost most of her beauty due to the lodge poling her Father Charles gave her along with the drinking they did, but still, this white woman seemed a strange version of her true spirit. She always started each conversation with the reminder of who her mother truly was.

Mother Superior smiled gently and said in English to the older man standing beside her, "You see, this one has not even been here a month and already she desires to learn and is respectful. She is the perfect candidate to take pictures of because of her youth and beauty. The pictures will show Washington that we are doing great things with these savages to bring them to civilization and respect for the great United States Government.

Josephine, of course, could not follow the rapid response the older man gave to Mother Superior but kept his eyes locked on hers when he spoke in his drawling Southern voice that was thick with hidden insults. "How do we know, Mother Superior, for certain, that this one is a virgin as we intend to represent her to get the rest of the funding? She looks wary and possibly older than you think she is. Have you determined her age for certain?"

Mother Superior said nothing to the strange man with the gray and black hair, twirling mustache, and hair on his chin that came to a point. His hat remained in his hand as he spoke and turned away from Josephine totally, as if dismissing her with no more thought than a horse he was buying. His eyes were kept in a squint as if the shaded and cool entryway were something he wasn't used to. He was waiting impatiently for Mother Superior to speak and kept brushing his hat against his leg as he stood with one booted foot on the step below Josephine and one on the step even with Mother Superior.

He was very tall because he could look Josephine straight

in the eyes, as he did when he was first introduced to her. Josephine remained very quiet and waited for Mother Superior to speak. When she did, it was a bold move with someone who seemed to be in charge of her. Josephine knew what men wanted, and it didn't appear a pillow trade was going with them but something else.

Sweeping her right hand towards the dormitory where Josephine slept, the black billowing sleeve followed the motion of her hand, and Mother Superior pointed to the dormitory area and motioned as she said, "Josephine, go up and wash your hands, place a clean apron on and meet us in the kitchen to begin your bread making lesson." As she said this, she pantomimed everything with her hands, touching the strap around Josephine's neck from her apron and pretended to lift it off, place it in a basket and get a clean apron.

Nodding her ascent, Josephine stood and curtsied to Mother Superior and then turned and curtsied to the strange man with the hat. She picked up her missal and lightly climbed the stairs to the dormitory to wash her hands, place a clean apron on, and then head to the kitchen area. She did not expect what was to come next at all.

As she washed in the bowl so her hands were clean and removed her apron that wasn't even dirty and replaced it with the 'kitchen white' apron required when working with food here she thought about how strange these white eyes were. Rules for this, change into this, do not talk, men must cut their hair, men should shave their faces if they could, women should not be dirty in body or clothing, and the rules went on and on.

How would these people survive in her world of nature she wondered in her mind? Would they speak to the Earth, listen to the sounds and smells the wind brought to let them know when certain berries were ready, or if a storm was coming? She smiled when she looked into the small, chipped mirror above the pitcher and bowl for washing. She looked clean, but she still was 'All Goes Out' daughter of Beaver Woman and Bear Charles Malnouri, even with her name changed to white Josephine, and her experience as a 'pillow talker'.

She headed down to the kitchen for the bread-making lesson, kept her head lowered, but had learned how to look ahead for others that might be in her path so she could move around them quickly to avoid contact if possible. Some students had not learned the lesson of not speaking in tongue aloud yet, they were always punished when they did so, and Josephine had felt enough lashes to last her a lifetime and wanted no more.

When she opened the door that led into the kitchen she was surprised to see both Mother Superior and the man with the hat waiting beside another man with a large black box set up on three slender wooden legs. The man standing beside the box looked up at her and smiled, Josephine made sure that she did not look at either man but looked at Mother Superior only.

The large black sleeves and gnarled hands went into motion as soon as she saw Josephine. She motioned to the counter opposite the black box that had a mound of dough already rising in the large tan ceramic bowl. She came to Josephine and rolled up her sleeves and placed her hands into the dough to demonstrate how to knead the bread dough. Then she pantomimed for Josephine to do the same. Turning to the man with the black box, she said rapidly in English, "Take the picture without her looking up at you. We will use this one to demonstrate how rapidly our students are progressing with learning domestic skills."

Josephine kept kneading the bread dough until it was smooth and silky and then started to lift it onto the counter so it could be made into loaves of hearty bread for breakfast and lunch the next day at school. Carefully she began to pinch off the dough into the correct size for the loaves and place them in the pans.

She was not aware of the photographer taking pictures at that time. He made a few plates of Josephine working in the kitchen, and with the man in the hat, they shook Mother Superior's hands after she blessed them and promised to say prayers for them in Mass. The men picked up their supplies and quietly left as Josephine continued to measure out the dough for the bread to rise again, then bake.

Such a strange world that white eyes had, she thought to herself, as she kept at her kitchen chores in the warm and clean-smelling area. When she completed loading all bread pans with dough, she glanced up and was surprised to see that all three had left. She was in the room with other students who were working at their chores as well; cleaning vegetables, cooking meat to be placed into large pots, and washing pans and cutlery at the large sinks. Nor did she imagine they would follow her back to Dakota Territory to check up on her after she returned. She could not imagine that her speech, given to the entire school before she left, would have been written down and repeated over the years.

Lovingly and with grace, Josephine would continue her next years at the school and become an even better and more favored student. She learned English in some ways and became better at writing and speaking, but never achieved the perfection the nuns hoped she would accomplish. Her blended language, for she kept her conversations in her native tongue secret, helped her reach out to others when she was homesick.

When she would step back onto the prairie soil after her years in Virginia, she would again become George Grinnell's property, but this time with the blessing of the church as a marriage ceremony was demanded by the Hampton Institute, Father John, and the White Father Government in Washington since George was a decorated Civil War Veteran.

Chapter Thirteen
A New Start to Life

Pulling into the ranch yard in the late afternoon, the sun making dust motes swirl and sparkle in the wind seemed just about fitting with the way the day had started. Both Marlow and Nylee had slept like they were exhausted from the luggage race, and as I drove, I imagined Beth was sound asleep as well. Jeth didn't say much but occasionally would make a comment about the weather, the price of grain, the current price of box beef, or some other thing that was on his mind in connection with the home place.

I knew he was trying not to nod off without appearing to need sleep, so I poked him in the left shoulder and said, "Look, both the luggage twins are asleep, just shut your eyes and nod off. I've got this until we get back to the house. You can 'man-up' there and be in charge of luggage round-up and clothes washing/showering times, ok?" Jeth nodded and shut his eyes, almost immediately falling asleep.

With the radio low on my favorite station, because the driver always gets to pick, I nudged the older suburban along behind Marian and Beth, making sure to watch for any straps flapping or acting like a piece of luggage might shift and let go suddenly. No events happened all the way back, and I was filled with gratitude for a lack of entertainment at that point.

With both vehicles parked on either side of the steps leading up to the porch and that wonderful old oak door with the stained-glass arch at the top that always seemed like a welcome smile, I just rolled down all the windows, unlatched my seat belt, and stretched my back and arms out before pulling the key and swinging my legs out to jump to the ground.

When I shut my door as hard as I could, I never said a word to rouse the three sleepers in 'B.B.'! Marian was of the same mind, limbering herself out of her vehicle and stretching; her windows were all open wide, and Babs was sound asleep in the passenger seat. Marian met me at the base of the porch steps, and we both locked arms and climbed the steps to see how my dad was doing.

Calmly remarking, "Well, I'll just fix up some slush burgers and salad since I have a feeling all of those slickers will be hungry and not have a clue what to do for chow," Marian chuckled low to herself as she said this.

"Good thinking Marian, I don't imagine that anyone of those four have thought beyond the nearest fast food or fancy eating place in years!" I agreed as we opened the door to the cool and dark hallway and removed our boots beside the old oak hall tree. Marian headed directly to the kitchen, and I headed up the steps to check on Dad. Almost like a pair of synchronized swimmers in motion with hardly any spoken words between us.

As I reached the landing to turn into the master bedroom suite, I saw that dad was asleep in the rocking chair looking out the window to the Western hills. Those hills seemed to beckon him with beauty more each day as he spent a great deal of time just gazing out the sun porch windows and watching the seasons merge daily into dusk, then twilight.

Quietly I entered and went behind him and gently circled his shoulders with my arms so he wouldn't startle awake but feel a hug gently from behind. He was snoring lightly with his mouth open and a little drool coming off the corner of his mouth; I almost didn't want to wake him but knew he wanted to greet Jeth and his family in the best possible light that he could. Squeezing his shoulders lightly I said in a normal tone, "Dad, time to wake up. Jeth and his crew are here and Marian is making slush burgers and salads for supper. I think there is chocolate cake with ice cream for dessert if we can interest you in that as well."

Slowly opening one clear hazel eye, he nodded and said, "Done alright today then? I guess you have or you wouldn't be here would you now."

He slowly stretched the kinks out of his arms and legs mimicking Marian and myself before we left our rides. He stood and grabbed for his cane and ignored the walker. Winking he said, "can't have Jeth thinking I'm older and sicker than I really am."

I reached for his arm and steadied him, and when he seemed sturdy, I let go of his arm and deliberately grabbed the walker and smiled as I said, "This is just backup, you know, right?"

We headed for the stairs, and I secretly wondered just how much longer it would be before the first-floor office area needed to be his bedroom to avoid the stairs. I held on to the back of his belt with one hand and with the other held the folded walker as we bumped down the steps one at a time.

When we arrived in the kitchen, Marian was busy at the stove stirring the slush burger mix. The table was enlarged and set for seven, with paper towel napkins, mismatched plates, cutlery, and glasses set around the old scarred kitchen table. She turned as she stirred the big pot and said, "Figured I'd better make a double batch since I don't know if those kids will like it or not. You can freeze it or make spaghetti tomorrow with the sauce for lunch; it'll stretch."

"Marian, where are you off to then if not here tomorrow?" Dad asked as he settled himself into his favorite spot.

Marian blew out a breath that sounded like, 'Humph!' and didn't say another word.

I didn't know if Babs had been in the house or not at that point, or if anyone had even thought about supper. Marian pointed to the front yard with her non-stirring hand and did not say another word. Suddenly, we heard the clamoring going on from the front yard.

"You've got to be kidding me!" That sounded like Marlow, or maybe Nylee, I couldn't be sure. Then a moment later, I heard the low rumble of my brother's voice, and then Babs' pleading tone.

"Good grief Jeth, you can't expect us to do all that BEFORE we shower and eat, can you?"

I looked at Dad to see what he wanted to suggest in the worst way, and he just smiled and continued to blow and sip on his coffee as if nothing in the world about the brewing storm out front bothered him at all.

"Ah, maybe I should..." I started and regretted it immediately.

Both Marian and Dad glared at me and in unison said, "NO, leave it to Jeth!"

So, I left the room assignments and carrying the entire luggage pieces by themselves upstairs to their part of the house; three bedrooms on the East side where the sun would heat them up and force them to become early risers. I kept hearing muttered oaths mingled with swear words that appeared to be: "Get that bitch...she'll pay...crap I hate this stink hole already...I bet Grandpa isn't even sick...where are the hired hands on this ranch anyway...move out of the way brat..." and that was just from my sweet niece and nephew!

Thumping and bumping continued up and down the stairs with doors slamming and windows opening along with the continued muttered curses, and then finally, a silence not interrupted by anything other than the breeze gently blowing down the back steps into the kitchen. No noise for a wonderfully still moment, and then the sound of the shower and Jeth's voice ringing out loudly; "I'm timing everyone in the shower and shutting off the valve in the hallway if you go over your ten-minute time in the bathroom!"

Solidly warm Babs' voice carried down the hallway from their bedroom, where she was putting clothes away, and it curled itself down the steps into the kitchen, "Dad's not kidding about the time limits and the shut-off valve, kids! The first time I was here, your dear Auntie pulled that on me, and I thought she was joking about the time limit; it left me with a head full of shampoo, no messing around in the shower, kids."

More muttered curses floated from behind the closed bathroom and one of the bedroom doors. An amazing thing happened immediately following that; adult laughter. One of the sweeter sounds this old ranch house had heard in years; Jeth and Babs giggling together over the twin's predicament of timed showers.

Since Nylee was first because of the stench of her body and clothing, she went exactly one minute over the ten minutes and was blasted with cold water for only twenty seconds and then no water. I'm sure her squeals were heard all the way to the state line. The entire house erupted into laughter at that point, sad in one way that it was at her expense, but she had been warned.

A rumbling voice was heard above the kitchen ceiling; "I'll give you three more minutes Nylee to get the soap out and get your buns out of the shower so your brother has time. Get dressed and get downstairs to the kitchen table a.s.a.p.!" Jeth's voice contained no laughter at that point and sounded much like a drill sergeant.

About twenty minutes later, give or take a few minutes, the entire family was herded down the steps with Nylee leading the pack to the table. Smiling like the sun, both Jeth and Babs followed the twins and launched themselves at

Marian. "Thank you, thank you, thank you for thinking of us being hungry and cooking for us!" they both exclaimed in unison.

Marlow headed over to Marian and reached out as if to shake her hand, and she grabbed him in a bear hug instead. "Um, yeah, um thanks Marian for not having to cook tonight. Guess I didn't even think about this, sure smells good in here." Marlow muttered into Marian's shoulder.

Marian unfolded her arms from around Marlow and said, "The last time I got to feed you in this kitchen you were about half as tall as you are now and full of questions; and you were interested in everything. It'll be nice to see that young man back again."

Marian didn't wait for Nylee to move from her spot on the other side of the table and relax her grip from the back of the chair. She skirted herself away from the stove and around the table and clasped both arms around Nylee and hugged her tightly. "Don't let it be harder than it needs to be Nylee. You were always the straight shooter, even when you were younger. Let yourself be loved by this family and this land and it will love you right back."

Nylee slowly lifted her arms from the chair and hugged Marian back just as tightly and let out a deep sigh. "Marian, I forgot how wonderful it was to be hugged by you."

With those tender moments over, Dad thumped the table and said with tears glistening at the corner of his eyes; "Enough of this tender-hearted stuff, let's sit, say grace and then eat."

Dad didn't get exactly what he wanted at that point because instead of anyone listening to him, they surrounded him in a group hug with tender smooches on his neck from his Grandbabies, and a gentle clasp and hair rub from his daughter-in-law, and just a quiet hand across the shoulders from his son with a gentle hand laid on top of his.

It gave the appearance of a Norman Rockwell painting, except the truth behind that compassionate warmth was an ugly and selfish need for more self-centered behavior that had almost split this family in pieces and left a dying man with a broken heart along with his broken body.

I tried to clear my throat as I wiped my eyes and said, "Alright, enough of this crap folks, plenty of time for hugs and all this nonsense. We need to eat and start making a chores list out as we eat so we don't forget anything."

Jeth lifted his tear-soaked eyes and looked at me and winked, "Yup, smart-ass sassy sister returns full-blown! Imagine me thinking she had really changed!" He silently mouthed 'Thank-You for the reprieve from thinking and actually realizing how sick dad is.'

Finally, with all of us seated, we let Dad say grace; his was short and sweet like he usually was; "Bless this family and this food, build bridges to tomorrow and lead us in light. Amen." With that, we passed buns, the bowl of slush burger sauce, the salad bowl already smothered in ranch dressing, and a dish of dill pickles. Words were few until we finished eating.

The arid mountain air had a way of increasing appetites and the need for sleep until your body became accustomed to it. Jeth, Babs, Marlow, and Nylee were yawning by the end of the meal before the chocolate cake and whipped cream were taken out of the fridge and passed around. Marian pulled out a pad of paper, pen, and quietly went around filling cups with coffee for everyone at the table as she said, "The list starts now, coffee will keep you up for a few more hours to finish some of the chores, then it's bed for all you slickers. Tomorrow will bring a full day and you best be ready for it."

As she sat down and picked up her cup of coffee for a sip and then dug into the cake with her left hand, she set her coffee down, picked up the pen, and wrote down the words Dish Detail: Nylee, Marlow, Babs, Jeth, Missy, and Marian. The next heading was Cooking Detail: and the list was reversed and started with Marian and ended with Nylee. The next heading was Bathroom Detail: with the words ALL FOUR underlined behind it: and the list was reversed again. It kept going until the only thing left was Mucking Detail.

Nylee and Marlow kept gulping coffee and eating cake as they listened to all the chores entailed around the ranch. They included all the normal household chores one thought of in the city, but additional ranch chores were added; weeding garden, gathering eggs, feeding chickens, canning, feeding cattle, riding fence, cleaning saddles (leather cleaner), currying horses, checking horse hooves, and the list went on and on.

Just when we thought the list was done, Marian tapped the pen to her chin as she paused and said to Dad, "Didn't you mention something about painting the house and barn and checking the shingles?"

Dad nodded an affirmative and kept slowly eating small bites of cake between his sips of coffee without making any response.

Then bright-eyed Marian said, "I'll add that one as a group project along with the window washing and replacing the screens with the winter storm windows. We'll start that along the bottom first as we paint just so that is out of the way."

I just kept nodding when she would glance my way since she truly was taking the bull by the horns with the slickers at the table. I really didn't want to be the one doing the chores list; she proved to be a master at this with what she was accomplishing in such a short amount of time.

So, the chores list was set after some stony glances my way for not saying a word and some eye-popping stares from both the niece and nephew when they heard the extent of all the things that were not only done daily both inside the house and out, but the weekly list of chores as well. The seasonal work was a little different since it involved checking on the cattle, cutting hay and baling it along with moving the cattle from the summer pasture to the winter pasture closer to the house. Jeth knew and kept nodding his head at the list and at one point added a few items that Marian had blissfully forgotten about.

Finally, Dad raised his head and said with a smile; "So tomorrow it starts, it'll be nice to get those storm windows painted and ready before the fall winds come. Even when it's warm and dry, the weather tends to turn on a dime out here, and the cold can settle into this house right quick!"

He stood slowly then and placed his arm on Jeth's shoulders, "Son, I can't thank you enough for coming to help your sister out here. She's been doing a fine job, but she also has a family to tend to and needs a break sometimes as well."

Dad motioned to me then and I grabbed his walker that was still folded in the corner as he took his cane and slowly preceded up the stairs to his bedroom with me bumping along behind him.

Chapter Fourteen
Moon of Yellow Grass

Across Holes in Water from Tobacco Garden lay a little settlement called 'Beaver Creek.' Emerging from the dense river bottom that was covered in berry bushes, trees, and shrubs would set you on a sand hill about 300 feet high.

This was where Red Mike had crossed three nights before with three of the horses he had rustled from Grinnell. Mike was from the mid-west somewhere and had been working his way west to the gold fields for the last four years. A shady character with a shock of red hair, he had learned from others on the cow trail how to pick up a few horses or cattle along the way to provide funds for his journey.

His problem was that he never seemed to be able to hang onto his funds from one job to the next. Whether a job as a ranch hand or a rustler he liked to play cards, drink, and spend time with soiled doves. Between those three past times and getting new boots, hat and clothes when he had the funds, he was always on the lookout for the next big deal.

He had settled in the gently rolling hills about three miles from the river in a protected gulch. This area was filled with other rustlers and thieves as well and he hadn't seen anyone riding past this area. His plan was to take one of the horses to the Fort and sell it. If no one recognized it he would get top dollar for a well-trained cow horse.

His other plan had him thinking aloud as he sat by the campfire waiting for the coffee to boil. "I'll jest tell 'em I found this here horse a 'wandering down by the river and show 'em this here broken strap." Nodding to himself he added, "Yep, that's a perfect plan, no one will wonder 'bout that."

Reaching for the pot with his gloved hand he poured himself a cup and set it down beside his saddle bag. He decided a little shot of courage wouldn't hurt either so he reached into the bag and poured some whiskey into his cup to add some flavor to his morning.

Turning his freckled face to the sun just rising he sent up a prayer of silent thanks for his find of those three horses. He figured if he played his cards right he could rustle a few more and that money could get him to the gold fields in Montana Territory where he had heard the pickings were easy.

He saddled up after placing the lid on his little iron pan filled with beans and water and burying the entire pot in the coals. His beans would simmer and soak all day and all night until he returned. He'd have a hot meal and be minus one of the three horses.

He unhobbled all four horses and took them down to the river for a drink. He hobbled two and left them in the shade in the coulee beside the water. Then he eliminated all traces that lead back to his campsite.

With the sun at his back, he headed into the Fort to get some funds. Then he planned on going to the post for some flour, coffee and baking soda to make biscuits. He had both plans of what to say in case anyone knew the horse he was leading.

He returned two days later with some funds left over and a small pouch of flour, baking soda and coffee. He had enjoyed a bath, drinks and a soled dove and felt good about the money left over. Now to get a few more horses, sell them off and he'd be ready to head to the gold fields in Montana Territory.

As he sat beside the fire that night scooping up the last of his beans, he felt proud he had a sold a good cow horse to the Army for a fair price. He had made a promise to return with a few more.

Red Mike had told the Fort commander that he had broken the horse and trained him. When a soldier threw a saddle on him and mounted up he had no problem cutting another horse in the corral and roping him. Coming back to camp he was careful and had crossed the river back and forth two times to eliminate his trail. He figured only a really great tracker would pick up his trace further down river.

The next morning, he was up before the sun and had a quick breakfast of beans, biscuits and coffee before dousing the small fire and heading out. He headed Northeast, away from Grinnell's place and spotted some nice-looking horses on August Mattson's place. He waited behind a hill after hobbling his horse and slowly approached the two horses grazing.

He was successful getting his lasso around one, but each one meant money in his pocket. He led the roan around the hill to where his horse was silently cropping the prairie grass. He headed back to camp and carefully crossed back and forth over the river to erase all traces of his being there.

The next morning marked a week he had been at camp site and saw a change in him. He woke up before the sun and as he stretched he gave a quiet thought about staying around here. He imagined he could build a sod house against the bank and prove up the land here. Shaking his head, no, to himself, he shrugged it off and reached for the pot of coffee. He might have headed out to Montana that evening if he had any idea what the next few days would bring him.

He led his new horses down to the coulee and hobbled them in the shade where they could easily reach the river and still eat. He headed out Northwest away from Mattson and Grinnell's places. He landed on Ole' Thorston's land and spent his time scouting out the small herd of cattle and horses.

Ole' Thorston was a big Swede who, along with his wife, was raising a large family. They were raising all the children to be God fearing and hardworking. His eldest son, named Ole', after his father, was destined to take over the ranch one day. He was learning all about ranching from his Pa and the neighbors.

After two days of observing and scouting around the herd, Red Mike approached the herd of cows and horses and his plan was to cut out one or two nice cow ponies and head out with them. That same day, young Ole' was out doing a count for his Pa and he saw Red Mike approach the herd from the north. Red Mike saw the boy looking his way and acted as if he belonged there and the kid didn't.

Ole' watched as the man expertly separated a horse from the herd, lassoed it and led it off in the opposite direction of the house. He headed northwest over a hill leading the horse behind the perfectly good horse he was riding. The boy was unaware that he had just witnessed an act of rustling, but decided he'd just continue counting the new calves and ask his Pa about it when he went in to eat.

He puzzled over it once more when he had finished his count and sat down on a rock to eat the biscuit with a slap of pork in it for lunch. Ma had even given him another biscuit with jelly on it as well because she always said, "You're a growing boy and need a little more to eat than 'yer Pa." He shrugged off the sense of strange behavior and just figured his Pa would know what to do.

At supper that night while the family waited for the prayer to end, he nervously cleared his throat and said, "Pa, before we pass the plates, I've got something to ask you." His Pa just nodded and started to pass the plates around the table after he and Ma filled them for the children.

Young Ole' then told of what had happened right before noon and right before he had finished his count of the new calf crop. Pa froze passing the plates and said clearly, "Son, you ever seen that man before? Tell me again what his horse looked like and what he looked like."

He repeated everything he had noticed about the man and

his horse, along with the important information about when the man had taken his hat off and revealed his red hair. His Pa ate in silence that night when usually he would tease Ma and the other children. His face was very serious looking and he said to Ma when he was done. "I'll have to go tonight and see August and maybe we'll have to check with others around here tomorrow. I'll be back as soon as I can. Ole' you help Ma get the young ones to bed tonight. I'll check the barn when I get back." With a kiss on Ma's check and rubbing the young ones on the head he reached for his coat and hat on the peg by the door and out he went into the night with stars to guide him over to August Mattson's ranch.

Over five miles away nestled up in a coulee Red Mike had settled in for a quiet night and the only thoughts in his head were about the funds he would get for the extra two horses he had picked up along the trail. He had convinced himself that what he was doing was right to be able to fund his travels and that no one was the wiser in this area. His plan was to leave this place after one more day of scouting and head to the fort. He would never make it out of Dakota Territory.

The next morning Ole' once again left his house to go and get August and head over to another neighbor that had horses and cattle as well. After visiting with him and determining that he had lost no horses, while they both had lost one they decided to head over to Grinnell's to see if any mail had come in and find out if he had lost any horses as well.

Grinnell was at his usual place in the saloon drinking when the two men headed in. They both had a beer and went over to stand by Grinnell. Ole' started the conversation,

"Grinnell, how you holding up here?" He didn't wait for a response but just started in with what his oldest boy had seen two days before and the fact that he had lost a really well-trained cow horse.

August was next and added to the story, "He's not the only one Grinnell, I went out and did a count and lost a good strawberry roan myself. We was wondering if you've lost any horses over here. We know you have more than we do but we figured you might know if anyone else has complained about losing any horses or cattle. We think we've got a right smart rustler around here. None of us can afford to have someone taking our animals. Would you be willing to check with your men?"

Grinnell straightened up from leaning on the bar and said, "No one's said anything about any animals missing. Let's go out together and we'll check right now." He downed his drink in one swallow and led the way out the door into the mid-morning sunshine.

Outside by the corral Grinnell gave a whistle to Jeth McDoggell and had Ole' and August tell him what Ole's boy had seen. Grinnell went through the gate and got his horse, saddled it up and headed over to the other corral to do a count of the horses there.

He was plain mad and that was worse than when he was drunk mad. He dismounted beside the fence and said to Jeth, Ole' and August, "Looks like we've lost three head, all nice trained cow horses. Damn it, we've got a rustler here. We need to find him and fix him good before he rustles anymore head."

The men agreed to all look for tracks from the rustler and any traces they could find that day. The next day, they would meet at Grinnell's place and, share the information, and decide where to head next. The next day was the day Red Mike would head to the fort with his four stolen mounts.

By the time August and Ole' returned to their ranches it was mid-afternoon and they had scouted the draws and both sides of the river with some of Grinnell's hands. Ole' told them all that he would head out from where his herd was grazing to see if he could find any trace of the man leading one of his horses away from the herd. He'd tell them all what he found at Grinnell's place the next morning.

As night follows day Ole' was able to pick up the man's trail about two miles away from his herd. The man with the red hair had done a fair job of crossing and doubling back on his back on his tracks but Ole' managed to stay on a northwest line and soon picked up his trail. He figured the man was bedded down early with the horses and might light out in the early morning. He headed over to let August know to come over before the sun was up the next day. That way they could catch the thief in the act before he made it out of the area.

The next morning before the sun rose and started to warm the land the two friends headed over to Grinnell's and crossed Holes in Water with their news. Grinnell was waiting in the saloon for the news. He grabbed his whip, drank a shot of whiskey and said to the two men, "Let's get that son of a bitch!"

Out the door the three men went and mounted up. They

crossed the river and rode hard without speaking in the general direction of north until they picked up the trail that Ole' had found the day before. "Think he's picked up and gone yet?" August said in a whisper.

"Maybe." Was the only whispered reply back from Ole'.

They dismounted and the horses stood still as the men crouched and silently slow walked to the crest of a hill. They saw the still-smoking remnants of a fire and an obvious trail of tracks leading down to the river. "Bet we just missed him," Grinnell muttered.

"I've had enough. Let's run that son of a bitch down and get our horses back." Grinnell walked at a faster pace, picked up his horse's reins and mounted him quickly. "Come on August and Ole' let's move fast."

The other two mounted their horses quickly and let the horses have their heads as they made a beeline for the river bottom. Within three miles they spotted Red Mike with the string of horses; two of Grinnell's, one of August's and one of Ole's. They kept riding until they were almost on him and Grinnell threw the lasso around his shoulders promptly followed by one from August and one from Ole'.

Grinnell did the talking since he had lost the most horses. "What's yer name mister?"

Red Mike replied by lifting his hat and saying, "Name's Red Mike since I got red hair. You men taking me to the fort?"

"Nope. We'll take care to get our horses back right here. Then we'll deal with you." Grinnell replied.

Holes in Water

Ole' dismounted and handed the end of his lasso to August and walked up to Red Mike and took the lead ropes out of his hand and took his gun from him. "Stupid mistake mister, this will cost you dearly."

Grinnell nodded and said, "No tree to string you up here. We just have to get rid of you some other way. Seems like a dragging party is in order."

Once that was said, the other two men simply nodded. They proceeded to hobble the horses with the lead ropes and, remounted their horses and jerked Red Mike out of his saddle to the ground. He said, "Someone asks about me, tell 'em my name and where I ended."

The three mounted men headed north, dragging Red Mike to death. They stopped when they reached the hill that rose around thirty feet up from the river. To this day, no one, except a few, remembers Red Mike, but the named the hill after him in case someone asked about him.

Chapter Fifteen
Ranch Rhythms

With the dust motes dancing around the porch steps, the sun rose bright and early and started to warm up the old house quickly. The sheer curtains on the east side of the house only partially blocked the bright morning rays lighting up the bedrooms where Jeth and his family slept.

Missy was already up and having her second cup of coffee and chatting on her cell phone with her husband when she heard the first comments bounce and come filtering down the stairs.

Marlow was first, "Oh God, someone turns off the damn light!"

Then Nylee's voice, more sleep-drenched than awake, was heard, "Just shut up, will you! You snored all night and I hardly got any sleep at all."

Finally, I heard Jeth, "Get up, kids. Your mom and I are already dressed. You need to get up and head downstairs, chores start now and then you come back to eat. Get a move on!"

I could hardly contain my laughter as I repeated what was floating downstairs to my husband. He joined me in the laugh over the city slickers' trouble with being up with a late spring sunrise that promised more warmth and heat during the day.

Jeth was first to enter the kitchen and grab a cup of coffee followed on his heels by Bab. He had a baseball cap on his head, ordinary jeans, a plain older denim shirt, and a pair of boots on his feet with gloves tucked into his back pocket.

Bab, not to be outdone by her husband, was dressed almost identically with a few exceptions. Her jeans, shirt, and baseball cap had a great deal of bling on them. It left Missy wondering how she would manage to clean the manure off the bling that was sure to get on to all of them at some point today.

"Morning, hope you slept well," Missy said to both of them with a smirk on her face. "I know I did. Are you ready to start the day?"

Bab turned to Missy and said, "I guess we all are. I need to say, "Thanks for making the coffee first of all." We really appreciate having the help with all of this mess I've gotten this family into."

Missy just nodded, said goodbye to her husband, turned the phone to vibrate, and headed to the sink to rinse her cup out. "OK then, I'll see you out by the barn. I'm headed out on my horse to ride the fence this morning before it gets too hot and check on that late heifer that is ready to calf. I'll be back around lunch time and Marian should be here to make something up for all of us. I've already checked on Dad and gave him his medicine. Just call me if you need me."

Jeth nodded and said, "I'll check on him when I'm done taking off the storm windows and getting the screens ready to go up. See you later Sis!"

Missy heard the twins coming down the stairs to the kitchen as she exited the house out the front door and headed to the barn. Thoughts spun in her head about what the plan was to feed both surly teens breakfast after they were done with their morning chores. Marian had blessedly left the list clearly on the table in the kitchen for each of the four family visitors and Missy hadn't touched it but left it there center stage, so nothing was left to chance.

As she opened the doors and let the sun shine into the barn, she inhaled the sweet and musty odor of animal sweat, leather and hay and thought the only smell closer to heaven than that was of water from a creek or river flowing on a warm day. She headed over to her horse and rubbed her down before shaking out the blanket and hefting the saddle up and over her comfortable back. The filly munched on oats and patiently waited for the cinch strap to tighten. Missy knew her trick of holding her breathe and then letting it out after she thought the straps were tight. She snugged them up and then waited until the mare blew out her nostrils, and she tightened the cinch just a little more to make sure the saddle wouldn't slide.

She waited until the mare was done with the small amount of oats she had given her and then placed the snaffle bit in her mouth and, lopped the bridle over her ears and backed her out of the stall. Missy waited until she was out of the barn before checking her hoofs and making sure her shoes looked good and not rocks were in the center that would make her limp. In one swift move, she mounted the mare and turned to head out and ride the fence line with the sun.

The entire process took her maybe ten minutes tops and all the while both Marlow and Nylee had observed her from the front porch. They both remained silent as they watched their aunt ride out to do the work of more people than they knew even existed.

Marlow turned to Nylee and said quickly, "Dips on getting the eggs for breakfast!" and headed toward the coop area attached to the side of the barn.

Nylee simply continued to sip the coffee and cream from her cup and just smiled to herself. Just let her brother get pecked by those chickens once, and she would have that job tomorrow morning as opposed to helping dad get up on the ladder and take the storm windows off and put the screens up.

When Marlow returned from the coop with a container of fresh eggs for breakfast, he just looked at her from under his hat and said, "Better get to work on your first chore. Mine is already checked off!"

Nylee swore at him, dumped her coffee over the rail, and left her cup sitting there. She didn't give a thought about the sparrows that were nested in the bush by the porch or the fact that they might perch and poop into that same cup, but it was another lesson she would discover that day.

Missy continued riding at an easy pace, grateful that she

had remembered to place a full water bottle and some protein bars along with a can opener and a can of carnation milk in case the calf needed a boost of nourishment.

As she rode further east, she thought about her husband and the fact that she was missing out on some quiet time with him, fishing with him, diving time with him along the big lake and river that fed it, and most of all, just missing time being with him. She was glad she had made the decision to leave the ranch for a few weeks and spend time with him back in Dakota. Maybe she'd even have time to poke around the old fort and see what else she could discover about the missing reassures that were still buried back there. She fixed two areas where the wire was down, stapled them back to the posts, and marked down where the posts looked like they needed to be replaced while she kept her eyes peeled for the cow and her calf.

It wasn't even a mile down from the last wire she stretched and stapled back up that she found the cow with the calf that looked like it was already a day old and dried off. It didn't have much strength since it was having trouble getting the milk to come down in the udder.

Missy slowly approached the cow with the new calf and spoke quietly to it so it wouldn't charge her. Holding out her hand sideways, she gently approached the animal and rubbed her ears and muzzle as she spoke in a soothing, nonsense language. "There now, momma, you've done a good job with your little one there. I'm gonna let you smell this can of milk for your baby here, and I'll pop it open so you can smell the milk. I'm gonna let him drink, ok? There now, momma, you're doing a good job with your little one."

Missy kept rubbing and patting the cow as she gently worked her way down her sides and kept rubbing on her until she got to where the little bull calf was standing on wobbly pins. "Let's look at you now, little man." Missy kept talking in that low, slow voice so neither the cow nor the calf would startle.

"All right now, little one, let's see if we can get some milk in you and then get you back home." Missy slowly lifted his head and poured the milk down his throat as she kept talking and worked the milk down his throat. "There now, I bet you'll make the ride home with me across that saddle just fine now."

Missy lifted the calf and placed him gently in front of the saddle horn. While keeping one hand on the calf, she swung herself back into the saddle and said to the cow, "Alright then, momma, come along now." Proceeding at a slow pace, she started out, and the cow trailed right along beside her as they headed back to the ranch.

She wasn't surprised too much when she rode into the yard about 45 minutes later to see Jeth and Babs on the roof, placing screens on where the storm windows had once been. She wasn't surprised to see Marlow in the yard with a bucket of water washing off the storm windows and scrapping the old paint away to get ready for a new coat, either. She was surprised to see Nylee, all 100 pounds soaking wet, pitching hay from the barn loft, though.

She rode into the barn with the calf still on her saddle, and Nylee squealed with delight when she saw the calf. "Careful,

Nylee" Missy spoke in the same low tones. "Keep your voice about this level so the momma and her baby don't get spooked by your squealing."

"Oh, oh, oh!" Nylee said in breathless wonder, looking at the tiny creature. "Can I hold her or something, Aunt Missy?"

"Well, I think that'll be alright. Let me get down from the saddle, and you lift him off her while I put momma in the stall. Then, slowly set him down beside her. Just keep speaking it a low, soothing voice. It doesn't matter what you say. Just keep talking low and slow, alright?"

"Ok, I can do that." Mylee almost whispered but kept her voice at the same cadence as mine as I lead the cow into the stall beside my horse with a bucket of feed.

Nylee reached up and gently cradled the calf in her arms lifted it off the front of the saddle and spoke to the little bull as if it was a pet. "Here now, baby, I've got you. I'm going to put you right beside your momma now. Everything will be ok, you'll see."

Backing my horse out of the corner stall to give the momma and her little one some more room, I said, "Ok, Nylee, you'll have to let the cow smell you and the baby to make sure you haven't hurt him. Don't be afraid of her. Just rub her ears and talk in that same voice tone and tell her what a good momma she is and what a cute baby she just had. Then you need to back away slowly, and I'll close the gate."

Misty felt secretly pleased that this city niece listened and did exactly what she was told to do. It's amazing how the bond between women, both young and old, will blossom when given a chance.

"Want to help me unsaddle the horse and brush her?" Still not wanting to break this time with her niece just yet, she savored, letting the good will that was just blooming continue.

"I'd like that, Aunt Missy." Nylee replied, "I'd like that a lot."

"First things first, just call me Missy, ok? This Aunt stuff is getting to be a real drag, know what I mean?" I said and looked her square in the face as she loosened the cinches.

Nylee started to giggle, and even when the cow blew her nostrils at us for that startling laughter, she couldn't quit. "You're a riot, Auntie M, a real riot! Missy, it is then, seriously though, you use words like 'drag'?" And she burst out giggling again.

Lifting the saddle off the mare and placing it on the rail on the other side of the cow to prevent her from chewing on anything, Misty watched with pride as Nylee lifted the saddle blanket off and shook it out like she had been riding before and reached for the curry comb to brush out the horse. She started on the neck and rubbed the horse's ears and started talking gently to her. "What's her name Missy?" Nylee asked.

"She doesn't have a name Nylee." Answering honestly as I filled her water container in the stall, shut the valve off and moved to fill her feed container. "Dad, your grandpa and grandma would never let us name any animals since they are for work and not pets."

"That's the most ridiculous thing I've ever heard and I'm

not having it. As a matter of fact, I'm naming her right now, and probably by the end of the day the calf and the cow will have names too. If Grandpa doesn't like it, well then...I'll just tell him to jump it!" Nylee said as she continued to brush out the horse.

"So, what are you going to name the calf?" I couldn't help my curiosity.

"She'll be named Myrtle," Nylee said. "Are you making breakfast? Please tell me you are since Mom can't cook worth of beans and I for one, am starving!"

"Well, since you said it that way. I guess I am." I replied. "I'll head up now to wash and get started. Don't be too long down here. You don't want your surprise breakfast getting cold, do you?"

I turned on my heel and headed back out into the warming day to head to the house and get breakfast ready for the slickers. I'd let them know about my plans to go for a visit for about two weeks at lunch time when Marian would be there to soften any concern they might have.

I headed into the kitchen and noticed the eggs in the container on the counter, the fresh pot of coffee and Dad asleep in his recliner in the living room with a cup of coffee, a glass of water, his pills, his walker beside him and the TV on as he was gently snoring in his chair. Apparently, one of them had made another pot of coffee and helped Dad downstairs. I was grateful for that small service and quietly blessed them for their help.

After washing up in the kitchen, I got the sausage out and

made patties and set them on the back burner in the iron skillet while I whipped the eggs with some milk with grated cheese into it and set the bread out on a cookie sheet to toast in the oven since so many were eating all at once. It would be different cooking for this many mouths and something Missy was used to in the past. The skills just seemed to resurface when needed the most.

After breakfast was done Jeth and I settled Dad into his chair while Babs, Marlow and Nylee did the kitchen clean up. Dad pulled out his wallet and Jeth looked at Missy over the top of his head and raised an eyebrow as if to say, 'Does he think he needs to pay us?'

What we didn't know was that Dad had an old newspaper article, yellowed with age and covered with clear tape that was getting brittle. It was a copy of an article written in March 1902 from the Bis-Man Tribune.

In Dad's own way, he handed it to Missy first and said, "Here now, you read this out loud and then you tell Jeth 'bout that penny and Ole Thorson and what else is buried in the West."

Missy proceeded to read aloud to her brother and didn't even notice when dad fell asleep listening to her read, nor did she notice when Babs, Marlow and Nylee came into the living room and sat quietly and listened to what had come out of Dad's wallet:

Buried Gold

Correspondent at Standing Rock revives a tale about thousands of dollars in buried treasure.

March 20, 1902. -Somewhere in the sand flats of the Missouri River, twenty miles north of Fort Rice, is the rotten hulk of a rough scow and half a million dollars' worth of gold nuggets. A core of miners gave up their lives to protect this treasure, and only one man out of the party escaped death, and he because, like Capt. John Smith, an Indian girl interceded for and rescued him.

Montana in the 1860s was a place where life was held cheaply when whites were pitted against whites, but when the Sioux met the paleface, one or the other was sure to die. So, in 1865, when a party of placer miners at Virginia City decided that they had had enough of fortune-hunting, twenty-one banded together for the return trip. A scow was built, and in water-tight compartments on the bottom each man's gold was stored in buckskin bags marked with the name of the owner. A rough floor was laid over this, and above was packed with rifles, ammunition and provisions needed for the trip.

As they proceeded down the Missouri and entered the land of the Sioux, the danger of travel increased. So, they gave up trying to go by day, and sneaked downstream at night, and then as quietly as possible. When within two days' journey of Fort Rice, seeing no signs of Indians, the travelers laid aside caution and pressed forward by day.

Suddenly, from the shore one morning came the crack of a rifle and the man at the steering oar sprang to his feet, gasped and then fell into the rolling waters. The others seized their rifles and prepared for defense. Without a steersman, the boat swung around, and the next instant the prow crashed on a rock and the whites were held an open target for the concealed Indians on the shore.

All morning, the unequal fight was continued and one after another the miners were killed, white at noon with ammunition exhausted, a little party of four was all that remained. When the Sioux discovered this, they dashed to the boat with a knife and tomahawk to finish their work. The survivors were butchered, save one, Pierre LaValle, a Frenchman, whose Sioux bride crouched by his side. He was made a prisoner and adopted into the tribe. Later he made his escape and reached Fort Rice, the only man of twenty-one who knew where the treasure lay. For the Indians, in looting the scow, had not gone below the false bottom.

A few months later, he confided the secret of the sunken scow to an old Quaker, Richard Pope and *to his son. The three visited the scene of the tragedy and dug away the gravel and sand that had formed about the scow, but before they could get to the gold, the Indians attacked them again and LaValle was killed.*

Two years later, Pope told the story to J. D. Emerson, now an agent for the Northwestern Fur Company, stationed at Basin on the North Pacific. His son had died in the meantime, so the two determined to secure the treasure. They went to Fort Rice and started up the river in a boat. Before they had gone ten miles their craft sank. Pope was nearly drowned and died shortly after from the effects of exposure, but not, however, before he had given Emerson an accurate description of the spot where the scow was lost.

In the years that have passed since then, the Missouri has changed its bed, and where the scow sank is now a broad sand flat, covered with a sparse growth of trees. Many persons have sought the treasure and have dug trenches on various parts of the flat, but only one person, J. D. Emerson, knows where the spot is and someday, he says, he will return to recover the gold.

Bisman Tribune, March 22, 1902.

You could have heard a pin drop when Missy was done reading this and she figured now was the time to let the family know about the issues facing the ranch with funds, cattle prices being down, and Dad's medical bills. She told them about Ole' Thorson, the penny, George Grinnell and his roadhouse while trying to clean up the language for Marlow and Nylee a little.

Then she announced, "Since I'm missing Chuck, I figure I'll go spend time with him on the job site for a couple of weeks. The location is close to the Tobacco garden area and a dive location is marked on the map in the area where Lake Sacagawea and the river meet. I can dive and poke around there and spend some time seeing what the locals have to say about Grinnell's treasure.

It looks like this isn't the only place in Dakota where buried treasure can be found and it certainly can't hurt this family to hand onto the ranch, even though I know Chuck is against that and just thinks we should sell this place off if we have to, I don't know what the rest of you think, but I know both Ruth and her husband aren't interested; they have good careers in Grand Forks and are busy with their twins, and Sam is worried about completing medical school and he and his fiancé really aren't interested in the ranch as a career either." Missy turned away from the window when she said this and realized her dad had listened to everything she said and as usual Mort was pretending to be asleep.

"So, what do you all think?" and pointedly looked at Jeth when this was said.

Jeth cleared his throat and replied, "Personally, I think

some time away from here would be good for you. It would give us time to spend with Dad and help him out and see how we feel about living out here. I, for one, hate to think about selling this place off into the hands of strangers or a conglomerate from outside the country; kids and Babs, what do you think?"

Babs had a confused look on her face and remained silent. Marlow spoke first, "I think it might work. Honestly, Dad, this lifestyle isn't what we are used to at all. I guess I just wasn't aware of what was going on out here and was more concerned about losing our own house."

Nylee was quietly nodding, "Seeing the rough start we had at the airport and all, and everything that has happened with almost losing our house I guess I can see the struggles we are in for. It would be nice to get that treasure, but what if we don't? Can we keep the ranch going?"

Intelligent responses for sure from my brother and his family secretly pleased me that Babs said nothing. I was still waiting to see what would happen from her side.

Babs was chewing on her lip, a sign that she was nervous. She let out a deep sigh and looked up at us all, "Well, I suppose you want me to say I'd be delighted to stay here on the ranch, but honestly, honestly," ...as a tear rolled down one cheek. She continued, "I did have a good life in town, you know. I just don't know what else to say."

Missy replied, "You'll have to think about this since it will change everything for all of us. I'm going out to the shed and get my diving gear and pack up to go after lunch. I have a few things to cover with Marian when she comes out to check on Dad." Saying no more, Missy turned and left the room to head outside.

Jeth stood and said, "Think I'll help her check her gear out. Maybe I'll be able to go and visit and help with the dive one of those week-ends.

Chapter Sixteen
Corn Moon

Three years after Josephine left for the institute in Virginia in 1878, she was getting ready to return. Spring time was busy with farmers planting and tilling the soil. Trappers were still trapping out west and in the east, Josephine was getting ready to return home. In the dormitory where she had spent the last few years growing in knowledge and wisdom, she was silently packing her trunk and the valise she would carry on the train. She would not be returning in a cattle car as she did when she had arrived here. She would be placed with a full-service ticket, courtesy of the church and her scholarship, in a rear car. She and some of the other students returning to their tribes would be traveling with church members for most of the return trip. They would have a priest and a sister with them as an escort for the majority of the return trip.

When she went to the cupboard where her assigned drawer was, she heard light footsteps coming into the dormitory room. Turning with a smile on her face she said, "Hello, can I help you?" before she even knew who was standing there.

It was one of her favorite Sisters, Sister Theresa; she was holding a small package in her right hand. With tears glinting in her eyes, she said, "Oh, Josephine, you will be missed here my dear girl. You have been such a good role model for our other students, you need to promise me that you will write to me and let me know you are alright." Wiping her tears away with her free left hand the middle-aged nun quietly stepped close to Josephine and embraced her with a hug. "I have a little gift for you so I know you will write to me as soon as you can. I will be allowed to ride in the wagon to the train station to say a proper good-bye to you in place of Mother Superior." She laid the package on the bed and smiled sweetly at Josephine, blessed her with the sign of the cross and turned to leave Josephine to return to her packing.

Josephine allowed a few tears to trickle down her cheek as she thought of this favorite teacher of hers. Wiping her cheeks, she sat on the bed and then opened the package that Sister Theresa had left on her bed. "Oh my," escaped from Josephine's lips as she gently opened the packed that contained some thin paper for letter writing, envelopes, a fine quill pen, an ink well and a blotter. Josephine gently smiled and rewrapped these items and placed them in a corner of the bottom of her small camel-backed trunk.

Standing up she walked back over to her drawer and removed her two remaining petticoats, two pantaloons, two skirts, and two shirtwaists. She folded these as she had been shown how to do and in the center of each pantaloon, placed a pair of long stockings before folding them for packing. She was so intent on her task that she missed the other two younger Sisters who quietly came into the dormitory and saw Josephine intent on her folding task. Just as quietly as they entered, they left after placing two small packages on the bed.

When Josephine turned with the folded skirts and petticoats in her arms, she saw two more packages tied with twine on the bed. Her name was neatly written on small tags tied to the simple bows. After placing the skirts and petticoats in the trunk bottom, she sat on the bed once more to open these gifts. The first gift from Sister Margaret was a small book of poetry and the inscription read, 'To Josephine, may these poems give you peace as you travel. We will all miss you. God's Love, Sister Margaret'

The other gift was soft and flat and Josephine knew it was something even more beautiful since it was from Sister Agatha. When she opened this one the tears flowed freely down her checks. This gift was embroidered handkerchiefs that Sister Agatha had done herself with silk thread. The yellow roses and the blue crosses intertwined on the corners of each of the three handkerchiefs were beautiful and would always remind Josephine of how special roses were to these amazing Sisters of faith.

Josephine stood slowly from her bed in the dormitory and glanced out the window at the trees now beginning to spring bright green leaves. With a deep sigh she turned once again and completed packing her trunk and items in the small valise she would carry onto the train. She left room on one side of the valise as Sister Theresa had told her to do. That way, she would have room for the pieces of fruit, cheese, and piece of bread they would send with her for food along her journey.

The noon bell rang for lunch and she could hear the younger and older students coming into the building from the garden. She heard giggles that sounded like her younger sister Mary. She missed Mary more than even her parents and had heard about her from the Priest and Reverend's letters a few times over the years she had been here. It would be wonderful to see her and hug her again.

Josephine left her trunk and valise by the foot of her bed and went to wash and change her apron again for the noon meal. Descending the stairs, she turned the corner into the dining hall and saw most of the students and Sisters were already standing, waiting for Mother Superior or Sister Theresa to lead them in prayer. Josephine quietly stood beside her chair, bowed her head and waited with her hands folded in front of her.

After her three years at the Hampton Institute, it was time for Josephine to return to the Tobacco Garden area in Dakota Territory. After her last lunch before she boarded the train, she was asked to give a speech to her classmates. According to school records, this is what happened that day:

When actually facing the large audience, she was overcome with stage fright and, covering her face with her hands, moaned, "I'm so 'shamed!" A laugh from some fellow students stirred her and uncovering her face she exclaimed, "You laugh! You don't know what's in my heart!" and went on to express herself fluently about her hopes for her people.

After her speech and applause from her fellow students, teachers and Sisters, many hugs and well wishes for safe travels were shared with her and two of the other women who were returning to their tribal lands. These women were fortunate since it had been arranged for both a Priest, who was being sent west, and a younger Sister to travel back with all three of them to ensure safe passage.

They dray man who was to carry the trunks to the wagon thumped up the stairs as he followed the sister to the dormitory. He had been here before and didn't like it at all. It was quiet and clean and didn't smell like his house of dirty diapers, animals and food cooking. It made him feel strange to hear nothing but quiet, no laughter, no animals, no sounds but the ticking of the large hall clock that stood off to the side of the main entrance door. He thought to himself that 'haunts' lived here in this school. He picked up two trunks under each of his large arms and as he carried them down the steps, he was sweating and dripping on the floors. The Sister who followed him and noticed and would speak to one of the students as soon as all was loaded so the floors were cleaned as soon as the door would shut on him.

Up and down the stairs he went two more times as he sweated his way with carrying the items. After placing the three small trunks for the students and the larger trunks for the Priest and the sister in the dray wagon, he tipped his hat to the sister and waited for her blessing and prayer before getting up in the seat and heading to the train station.

The next wagon would carry the five travelers with their valises to the train station for the afternoon train that was headed west overnight and would travel to Chicago. The students, Sisters and Priests lined the winding front road that curved and met the main road at the base of the small hill.

They would wave and smile and clap loudly for the students who were blessed and would soon return home as changed people who would share their knowledge with their tribes.

All the valises for all five travelers carried two apples, a hunk of cheese wrapped in cloth, a small loaf of bread, a little tin can of tea, and a small metal container filled with water. This was all neatly tucked in beside their clothes, a wash rag and a precious small bar of soap.

For the final time, Josephine was assisted into the wagon with the other two women, Sister Ann and Father O'Reilly. This group would spend more than a month's time together as they traveled west. That time would be spent in prayer, meals, and laughter over silly antics they would see on the train. They were all excited for this next journey and going home again.

Slowly, the driver wound his way down the drive and allowed the younger students with flowers in their hands to approach the wagon and give the goodbye flowers to Father O'Reilly, Sister Ann and the three young women who were leaving the Institute. Tears flowed from the three women who were leaving this place of learning and smiles were large on the face of the Priest and the sister who were starting adventures in new convert areas.

Back in Dakota Territory, George was getting some advice from a trapper he knew, Fredric, who had sent three of his daughters to school back East as well. They were not in the same school as Josephine since he had paid the church funds for them to attend the school. All three of his girls had decided they would not return home. Fredric had just gotten a letter telling him that they would all be taking the vows of the church and become Sisters.

Fredric was telling George about what had happened 11 years earlier on July 7, 1863, where Tobacco Garden was located. The tribes had discovered that the agent was robbing them of their annuities and hey heard he had left and was on the R. Cambell steam boat. At the point where the river made a turn that forced the steamboat to slow down, the Indians hailed them to stop.

Outnumbered and outmaneuvered, the ambush was quickly over. Frederic discovered from his brother-in-law that the whites had no weapons worth taking. They only had worthless yellow dust on them. Miners from upriver had joined at the dock in the territory by the fleeing agent.

Upon hearing this, Frederic encouraged his brother-in-law to return to the Garden area and retrieve all of the yellow powder and nuggets he could find. He promised to trade them for guns and powder for the men. When they returned to Fort Buford, they not only had belts with hidden pouches of gold in them but also a coffee pot filled with gold dust and nuggets that the miners had thought would remain hidden in plain sight.

George liked Frederic since he also had an arranged marriage and because he had sent his three daughters to a church-sponsored school, the priest had left him alone. "Frederic, I need some advice from you. How in hell am I supposed to get the priest off my back 'bout Josephine?" George was already slurring his words since he had been drinking since he had ridden into the Fort that morning.

So, Frederic simply said, "You need some of that their gold coming down the river." George glared at him and nodded and pointed at his ear to signify he was listening closely.

"Here's how I got mine and how I sent my girls to that their fancy school out East. 'Member that raid on the steamboat that had the agent on it been a while back now?" George nodded in response and kept sipping his rot-gut whiskey.

"Well, you know my 'talker' has a brother in the tribe, right? Name of Red Shirt, he was in that their raid. When he comes back he and the others where mad as wet hens, I tell you! They come to me just about wailing about no guns, no powder, and only yeller dust! They ask me what is wrong with white eyes, yeller dust can't get meat to keep belly full. So, I just hinted that if they bring me back some of that yeller dust and yeller rocks, I'd see what I could do 'bout getting them some powder and guns." Frederic stopped at that point and swallowed his drink in one pull and, lifting his glass singled the barkeep to refill it.

Frederic wasn't sure at that point if the well-known George was still sober enough to understand what he was saying but he kept talking anyway. "Well, George, let me tell you what they brought back that day. I had five belts loaded down with dust in the lining they thought was hidden away. Then that their coffee pot was the sweetest part of the whole deal, damned if it wasn't filled with flakes and nuggets! Yer hears me, George?" since George's head kept nodding slowly down, Frederic gave him a nudge, "Hear me, George?"

George sat up as straight as his drunken self would let him.

"Yup, Frederic, heard every damned word yer just said. Gold in belts and coffee pots sure sounds sweet to me. Now if I could just figure out how to get some of that when it comes floating down river, I'd be set. That fool priest keeps telling me not to lodge pole her no more, that we need to get a church marriage. My ass if that'll happen! That priest is making my life the worst possible, just when I was ready to go at it with her again, that damned old fool would show up and sit and pray with Josephine on the porch and stay for supper. It got so bad before she left, I'd have to go the Blind Pig and have at one of the girls just to get rid of frustration!" George turned and looked at the older Frederic and said, "Did he stop you from having at yer pillow talker anyway you wanted it when the girls left?"

Frederic kept sipping his drink and just nodded yes to that question. "Course, now that my girls are becoming Sisters out East in their convent school he's left me alone pretty much." Then he smiled and licked his lips and told George just what his plans were for that night with his pillow talker. They included a bottle, a chair, and a rope and laid his pillow talker across the chair, laid down on the kitchen floor and tied her up once he got her drunk. He then lowered his voice so only George would hear the last part, "I'm gonna make sure that she won't walk tomorrow when I'm done stuffing her holes tonight if you get my meaning." He lifted his hand "Damn George, now I'm hard just thinking 'bout the fun this boy and I are gonna have in a short time. Think I'm getting that bottle now, so my fun will start this afternoon and if the old gal can hang on for a few hours, it might last until bed time. Won't matter though. She will be juiced up enough she won't feel anything I do until tomorrow!" Still cupping his crotch with his erection plainly visible, he grabbed the bottle and tucked it under his arm as he itched his erection once more and covered it with his coat. As he stepped away, he slapped George on the shoulder and headed out the door for his evening fun.

George was well on his way from turning into a sad drunk into a mean one and the talk about Frederic and his pillow talker really got him into a mood. He laid a gold piece that he had cheated a miner out of in a game of cards on the bar and said to the barkeep, "I'll have a bottle, a room and a gal that likes it rough."

George got strangely satisfied that night by using the bottle, a chair, a rope and a paid participant in his game. She liked it rough as well and even turned the tables on George that night by tying him up in the bed when he was done having her backside on the overturned chair. He was mad as hell when he was forced to watch her finish off the bottle of rotgut before she untied him and he lit into her with his riding quirt on her rounded bottom and had her squealing before he came into her twice more that night and filled all three holes well with his ejaculations.

Josephine did not move back in with George or her parents upon her return because she was made to promise the sisters and the Priest that they would have a church marriage and be considered married under God. She kept her promise to them all.

In 1881 she reported on the progress in a letter written to a favorite Hampton teacher.

I am getting along very pleasant indeed. Dear friend I want to keep to be a good girl and to help those Indian getting along very indeed, makes me feel so bad. I want keep try help all I can. Those white people, who live with Indian, never help Indian; never give any work, nothing to do Indian. I teach Indian children now. I study my books too. I stay Reverend and his wife, I never go home my father's house.

When I see Indian house, makes me feel so bad Oh! Dear me what shall I do with those Indian? I am going to try hard to help to them. I hope God will help me. If I live my father house I will very hard time because people do not know anything about God word, don't care about him. I love him myself. I hope he will care of me. I want keep try help them, I want show how good live and know Bible way. They do not know great word.

In 1881, Grinnell's success as a 'wood hawk', a saloon owner, a rancher, and a gambler had attracted a number of neighbors to the Tobacco Garden area. He applied for a post office position and on May 11, 1881, before Josephine returned, he became the first postmaster outside the military post.

Grinnell's losses the next year were close to bringing him to financial ruin and in an attempt to make up for the bad crops he formed a partnership with Bob Matthews to supply buffalo hunters in the Yellowstone Valley, Sensing the decline of the great herds Grinnell sold out to Matthews and got out in time. Speculation says that Matthews may have lost about $10,000 on the deal back then.

The roadhouse, 'The Blind Pig' was still doing a great business even though the rumors were flying about the suspected victims that turned up missing shortly after or during their stay at 'The Blind Pig'. The news traveled the length of 'Holes in Water' downriver and upstream into Montana Territory that anyone who had gold in their possession would be a bad place to stop.

Chapter Seventeen
Rest and Relaxation

Missy headed out to the storage shed located behind the garage to get her diving gear, followed by her bother Jeth, who wanted to talk with her alone.

"How long have you known about the treasure?" the first question out of his mouth was about that and not about how close their dad was to death.

Missy stopped and turned to look at him, "Are you some kind of stupid? I can't believe you're more worried about that than spending time with Dad and just listening during his final days! God, sometimes you and your family really piss me off, you know that?" She continued to stand her ground and glare up the few inches in height her younger brother had on her.

"I'm waiting for you to say something, dumb ass!" She finally said as Jeth stood there and had the momentary pause to look embarrassed.

"Geez Sis, I know, I know, I just was amazed at the story. I haven't forgotten how sick Dad is you know. I was the one who helped him downstairs this morning when I noticed he was having trouble getting out of bed while I was taking the storm windows off in the folks' bedroom." He still looked flustered and embarrassed by what he had first said.

"Forgiven this time little brother," Missy responded and lightly slapped his shoulder, "just try not to let yourself forget around me again."

As she turned and took out the keys to open the padlock on the shed, she added, "Hopefully Babs doesn't tell the story about Dad this morning differently than you when Marian gets here. I'll give her a snoot full if she does."

Jeth just nodded and waited beside her patiently as she unlocked the shed that contained the old fishing boat and the tubs of diving gear from each family member. When they were younger, both parents had insisted that they not only take swimming lessons at the pool located across the state line in Williston but also take scuba diving classes. Dad and Mom both had taken the family one winter down south to Florida. While there, they rented a house and fished off rental boats and piers and snorkeled and went scuba diving together. It was a wonderful break from ranching and the cold that winter and still made both Missy and Jeth smile at those memories.

At the same time, they both looked at the boat and said in unison, "Remember that trip to Florida?" and looked at each other and started to laugh.

"That was a great winter vacation," Jeth said.

Missy added, "A perfect family memory for sure, with cattle prices being high and getting to take those two weeks off from school and chores. Plus, the swimming and fishing were fantastic!" Then she added, "Jeth, have you been diving since the last time we went to the lake when Babs was carrying the twins?"

"Nope," he said and shook his head sadly. "You know, I really miss those times on the water. I really should have paid more attention to this when the kids were growing up."

"Always time now to get them signed up for classes and outfit them with some gear you know," Missy added. "Let's check out the goggles, hoses, regulators and such. I imagine everything is in good shape since I remember how Dad insisted everything be packed away correctly in case we ever needed or wanted to use it. Do you think he ever thought about diving in the Tobacco Garden area himself?"

"I don't know Sis," Jeth added. "I'll tell you this though, I just might be coming out to where you and Chuck have the 5th wheel parked and spending some time diving with you myself."

"I'd like that little brother; I'd like that a lot!" Missy added as they headed over to the side of the boat where the equipment was stored in plastic tubs with each of their names on their personal tubs and that had been covered with a tarp.

Missy knew her equipment was in good shape since she and Chuck had used their diving equipment just that past summer when they had spent time out here helping her dad. They had gone to the big lake to the east to spend time fishing and diving together. They had met their kids and grandkids out there and had spent almost a week and a half together.

Even Mort had come out to spend time with them for a while and driven Marian out with him for a day.

That was a sweet memory that Missy had before Mort had fallen off the ladder and been diagnosed with cancer. It was also a sad memory since she then remembered that Jeth had been having trouble at work and couldn't take the time off with Babs and the kids to join them even though they had been invited.

She quietly wondered if that was when Babs had really started having a problem gambling, and the kids started to really disconnect from both parents. She remained silent as she dug through her tub and then Chuck's tub to check items that might have started to deteriorate and needed to be replaced. If so, she'd call up the dive club in Williston and have them overnight her supplies there, then she could pick them up on the way to the campground.

Missy said to Jeth, "Want me to help you go through your stuff?"

He looked stunned when he picked up his items and said, "It looks like a great deal of this stuff needs to be replaced. I don't think I'll even fit into anything except my hood here. It looks like Marlow can wear it though."

"Tell you what," I volunteered, "let's take your measurements and Babs now and order new suits for both you and Babs. Marlow and Nylee will fit into your suits and we can get each of them a new hood. The four of you are really going to need new mouthpieces, flippers and goggles though."

Missy pulled out a small spiral notebook with a pen from

her back pocket and started writing down what she needed for herself and Chuck, turned the page and proceeded to write down Jeth and Babs at the top. Jeth held up his hand, "Wait a minute here, Missy. You know we don't have the funds for this right now even though I wished to God we did!"

Missy shrugged and replied, "I think as a family since we are selling off half the herd, the funds for some rest and relaxation time are just in order to keep you all sane at this time. I'm ordering these things now. Back to the house Buck-O and let me get the tape measure out and start with the twins. We've gotten a lot done this morning already and I'd like to have this stuff done and sent in on the computer before Marian shows up to make lunch. Move it little brother and take Chuck's tub of stuff out to the back of my burb, will you?"

"Since you put it that way, I'm in total agreement." Jeth nodded as he hefted Chuck's diving gear tub with both hands and headed out to the suburban to place it in the back.

Missy headed to the house and found Babs, Marlow and Nylee talking to Grandpa in the front room. Mort looked tired but happy as he enthralled his audience with tales from the 'old country' as he called the area where he had grown up.

Standing and watching the rapt faces focused on the story, I waited until dad reached for a cup and took a sip of coffee that smelled fresh to my nose. Babs looked up and saw me standing in the doorway smiling. She stood and walked towards me.

"Did you get your things loaded?" she asked quietly.

"Well, that's something we need to do here right now. All

four of you need to be outfitted in dive gear since we are going to go fishing and diving in the big lake probably next weekend. The kids can swim, right?" Missy asked.

Nylee heard this and started her high-pitched squeal again! "You bet Auntie M...I mean Missy! Both Marlow and I have lifeguard certificates and almost have our dive certification. We, um, had to stop last summer since money was tight."

Babs had the grace to blush at that point and looked down at her socks.

"I don't know," Marlow replied dryly then as he stood and stretched his frame up. "Seems like a long time since I've been in a pool or a lake anywhere."

"I'll get the tape measure and we'll get to work." I walked over and kissed my dad on the forehead. "Ok Dad?"

Mort nodded and said, "I think I'll just take my morning nap right here before lunch. Go on now and get that tape measure out. Swimming would do all of you good. Maybe you can check the tires on that old boat as well and try some fishing while you're at it." He reached for the light blanket that lay across the arm of the chair and Marlow beat him to it.

"Here, Gramps," he said, "let me fluff those covers out over you." And gently he spread the cover out over Dad's legs and tucked them around his shoulders.

I just smiled and led the merry band into the kitchen to take measurements for the pieces we needed to replace and new ones that needed to be provided.

Babs waited to go last before she would let me measure her and both Marlow and Nylee had left the kitchen before their mother would let me touch her with the tape. "OK," she said to me, "get the jokes over now about how much I've grown and just measure the chest will you!"

Without saying a word, I finished the measurements and just as I headed to the office to order the supplies Marian pulled up in front. I could see her talking to Jeth and the kids and figured they were filling her in on my upcoming trip to Tobacco Garden to spend time with Chuck and their upcoming fishing and diving trip to join us. Starting up the computer, I typed in the order quickly with a request to have it express shipped for all the items needed.

When Marian came into the house, she poked her head into the office and, nodded hello to Missy and said, "As soon as you're done there, come into the kitchen to talk to me. I need to hear the idea from you to confirm what I've been told six ways to Sunday out there." She jerked her head and pointed at the yard. "By the way, where is Babs? Is she awake yet?"

Babs was standing almost right behind her and heard the question Marian asked me and simply cleared her throat, "Right here, Marian, and yes, I've been up and helped. This afternoon, the plan is to scrape the paint off the storm windows that are all down now and get started on repainting them all, inside and out. Does that sound right to you?"

Marian jumped when Babs started talking since she hadn't expected to see her work that hard. She turned and glared at Babs and said, "Next time, speak up before you sneak up, will you!" Marian walked past her and headed towards the kitchen.

Babs just laughed as she headed out toward the now-opened storage shed to help get the scrappers, paint, brushes, and tarps out so after lunch they could start on the shady side of the house with scraping and painting the storm windows.

Missy just sent the order in with the credit card information and crossed her fingers to make sure it got into the system. Sometimes the wireless internet didn't work well out here but since the day wasn't cloudy and no storms loomed in the forecast, it looked like they were in the clear. The computer gave a gentle ping as a signal and a confirmation number showed up in her email. She quickly printed it out, folded it and marked it in the paid slip file lying on the corner of the desk with the other paid orders sent out that month.

Stretching the kinks out of her back, she smelled another fresh pot of coffee and headed to the kitchen to confer with Marian about her upcoming trip and the plans she and Chuck had made that morning.

The next morning, the sun rose a few moments earlier as June started to prepare for the warmth of summer. The same sorry songs that had been floating down to the kitchen were heard again that morning as Missy sat sipping her coffee. Missy smiled as she listened and couldn't resist shouting upstairs, "Hey, you city slickers! Daylights burning, chores and coffee are waiting for you." Met with groans and bed springs creaking as feet hit the floor and raced for the upstairs bathroom, Missy's laughter filtered up and blended with those sounds.

"Thought I'd beat you up this morning for sure Sis." Jeth nodded as he came into the kitchen and grabbed a cup off the hook under the cabinet and reached for the pot.

"I'm about ready to head out, Jeth," she answered and then kept blowing across the top of her cup as she waited for it to cool so she could slurp it down. "I figure I'll get to the construction site and surprise Chuck with lunch."

Jeth turned and as he sipped from his cup, he wiggled his eyebrows and then said, "Wow, a nooner at your age? I'm impressed that you two old fogies still have what it takes!"

Missy launched the flowered dishtowel at his head, the same one that had been left hanging on the back of a chair late last night after someone had come down and sneaked a bowl of ice cream before bed. Jeth caught it in his left hand as he continued to sip his coffee.

"Alright, smart ass, and tell whoever had the ice cream last night to rinse out the bowl, not to leave a wet towel hanging on a wooden chair and to remember to write ice cream on the town slip or to get some Thursday when the Schwan's truck stops by. Have you got all that?"

Jeth's eyes were smiling with delight as he just nodded and said, "Boy, it feels good to bet the best of you sometimes! Drive safe Sis and tell your 'man' all of the knot heads said hello."

Gulping down the remainder of her coffee, Missy stood and went to the sink and rinsed out her cup, placed it in the drain board, turned and hugged her brother. "I'll be back in two weeks unless I'm needed before then. I'll call daily around noon before Dad naps and talk to Marian and all of you. Don't be afraid to get advice from Marian if you need it." Out the door she went confident in her time away that her dad and the family place were all left in good hands.

As she headed down the gravel road and before she merged onto the highway she thought about the other slip of paper Dad had given her from his wallet. It wasn't a copy of the newspaper article from 1902. It was an internet copy of a report of sales from the 1940's. Sometime between 1940 – 1943 a C. Albert Grinnell had sold a rare $50.00 watermelon mark bill from the Civil War era. He received a large sum of money for it at that time, $1489.83 and at today's market price, that converted to around $150,000 to $200,000 in value. How Albert had come by that piece of currency is really no surprise since George had been a spy for General Sherman in the Civil War and it was reported that he had been rewarded for his efforts very well.

Missy merged onto the two-lane a few miles later and gradually onto the interstate with her Betty Burb before heading North. While she drove, she sipped iced sun tea and sang along with Mary Chapin Carpenter: 'I Am a Town' and thought about Tobacco Garden and the rich history of that prairie queen.

Matsie Non

"I Am a Town"

©Mary Chapin Carpenter

"I'm a town in Carolina; I'm a detour on a ride
For a phone call and a soda, I'm a blur from the driver's side
I'm the last gas for an hour if you're going twenty-five
I am Texaco and tobacco; I am dust you leave behind
I am peaches in September, and corn from a roadside stall
I'm the language of the native; I'm a cadence and a drawl
I'm the pines behind the graveyard, and the cool beneath their shade,
Where the boys have left their beer cans
I am weeds between the graves.
My porches sag and lean with old black men and children
Their sleep is filled with dreams
I never can fulfill them
I am a town
I am a church beside the highway where the ditches never drain
I'm a Baptist like my daddy, and Jesus knows my name
I am memory and stillness; I am lonely in old age;
I am not your destination
I am clinging to my ways
I am a town,
I'm a town in Carolina
I am billboards in the fields
I'm an old truck up on cinder blocks, missing all my wheels
I am Pabst Blue Ribbon American,
And 'Southern Serves the South'
I am tucked behind the Jaycee sign, on the rural route
I am a town
I am a town
I am a town
Southbound.

Missy played and sang that song at least three times heading north towards the construction site. As she sang she thought about how similar the song was to many small towns, not only in the south but all across the U.S.

The last phrase really struck a chord within her as she thought of the water rushing over the buildings at Tobacco Garden and how pieces of history were 'southbound' with river systems everywhere.

A town's life from anywhere USA is best told with stories of those who lived in her arms. Western prairie towns were no different and they were vulnerable, like others, to multiple sins that lead to their demise.

One dry year could render a town, and part of a country of over 30,000 acres, a death sentence. One year of deep cold and snow, or a year of ravenous insects could all yield the same toll. Whiskey, a rich wild life, loose men and women could produce a similar death sentence if the area saw an increase in migration of deeply religious groups.

Certainly, it was the water though that told of the life or death of those prairie queens and the families that lived in their embrace. Without water, trade was harder and gardens and families could not survive at all.

As Missy finished the last hour of her drive, she thought about how the water that had started this story and how the water had ended the story beneath her skirts as the waves had buried Tobacco Garden. Missy itched to dive again and discover what remained of the building, if anything.

Chapter Eighteen
Berry Moon

At the end of May, Grinnell found out that Josephine was back at the fort and just like previous days he went to the Blind Pig to have a drink and celebrate her return. Two days later, when he sobered up, he headed into town on his horse.

His first stop was the bathhouse where he could clean up and get a shave and a haircut. Two hours later a clean respectable looking middle-aged man with dark hair, a mustache, a clean pressed white shirt, clean trousers and new boots stepped out into the street.

Clamping his hat on his head, he set off at a steady pace for Reverend Wilken's house. He had an idea of what he was in for, but decided to keep his promise and try to court Josephine and then wed her properly so Father Piedmont and Reverend Wilkens would leave him alone. His challenge was to convince them that he was really sincere.

He stepped up to the door and knocked, taking his hat off he stepped back and waited for the door to open. Mrs. Wilkens opened the door and the smells of meat simmering and fresh baked bread came and went as will-o-wisp scents that made George's stomach growl.

"Afternoon, Mrs. Wilkens," George said and smiled politely, "do you remember meeting me last Christmas at the Fort party?"

Nodding her head politely and with a thread of ice in her voice responded, "Of course, Mr. Grinnell, I do remember having a lovely waltz around the room with you. We have been expecting a visit from you. Please come in and go to the parlor. The Reverend is waiting for you."

George nodded his head and smiling stepped into the cool interior of the sod house. One thing that was positive about sod was that it was cool in the long dry summers and kept warm easily in the equally long cold winters. Once the walls were white-washed and the dirt floor was covered, most women were pleased. 'Neat as a pin' was a phrase that entered Georges' mind as he stepped left into the small parlor.

Reverend Wilkens didn't stand and greet him and that was George's first clue he was walking a narrow line. Reverend Wilkens pointed to the other chair without saying a word to George. He lifted his head, smiled brightly at his wife and said, "Thank-you Martha, will you let us know when lunch is ready, please?"

Martha smiled in return and said, "Of course dear, about a half an hour I think." With a swish of her dark brown skirt, she stepped around the simple wood partition. George stopped himself from sneering and making a comment about 'uppity womin' and willed his face into a quiet look and turned to sit in the chair.

Reverend Wilkens removed his spectacles and set them on the simple plank that served as his desk until a better one was provided for him. "Well George, it's nice to have you stop by for lunch. How have you been?"

George shuffled his feet, placed his hat on his knee and leaning forward said, "Reverend, I really appreciate the home cooked meal and having this visit. We both know I'm here to take Josephine home with me. She is rightfully mine you know. It was a fair trade for land when I got her." He spoke with no more emotion than if he was talking about a horse trade.

Reverend Wilkens picked up his spectacles and replaced them on his face. "Let me remind you what scripture says about good women George." He opened his worn leather Bible and proceeded to read aloud to George; "This is a verse from Proverbs Chapter 3, verse 15; 'she is more precious than rubies: and all the things thou canst desire are not to be compared unto her.' And again, the good book reminds us in Proverbs Chapter 31, verse 10: 'Who can find a virtuous woman? For her price is far above rubies.'

George cleared his throat as if to speak, but Reverend Wilkens continued. "I'd also like to remind you of what the good book says about marriage George. You know the book of Genesis we read that God first created Adam to exercise dominion and then created Eve as the man's suitable helper. This is in Genesis Chapter 2, verse 18 and 20. It also says in Genesis Chapter 2, verse 24; 'Therefore a man shall leave his father and his mother and hold fast to his wife, and they shall become one flesh.' The Reverend lowered the bible and said to George, "This reminder tells us that God does indeed want us to be fruitful and multiply with our chosen mate. Now George I see that I've given you much to think about. I do see that lunch is ready since Martha just nodded to me. Shall we go eat now?"

George was pole-axed when he stepped around the simple wooden partition for he expected to see Josephine, either seated at the table or waiting to serve him. "Umm, excuse me Reverend. Where has Josephine gone?"

"Have a seat George, Martha has already started with things on the table. After grace I'll tell you where she is today." Reverend Wilkens quietly waited until Martha sat and they both folded hands and bowed their heads as they waited for George to follow suit.

George quietly fumed inside as he bowed his head and folded his hands while his stomach and head growled with different kinds of hunger.

George found out later that afternoon in the saloon that Mrs. Wilkens had slipped Josephine out the back door of the shot gun sod house they lived in and quickly walked her over to the Priest about ten minutes after George arrived at the bath house.

Apparently, the Reverend and his wife weren't above telling lies since they assured him that she had gone to see her folks. The same parents that had traded her off to him for that miserable little piece of land they now lived on.

The 'rabbit-in-hole' game of hiding Josephine and sneaking her out from one place to another continued for the better part of a week until George finally had enough. He went to see Father Piedmont and was surprised at how pleasant the man was to him after all that had happened, "Father, I'm not gonna pull any nonsense with you here. I'm serious about getting Josephine back and I guess I need to court her proper now. If you'd be willing to be our escort, I'd like to take her to the Fort and get her a few fancy things. What do you say to this Friday?"

Piedmont had been waiting for this opportunity and said firmly, "George, since your intentions are honorable now that is a great beginning." He reached for a hand shake that wasn't returned and dropped his hand and ignored the rebuff and said, "We'll see you Friday then?"

"Father I'll be here Friday at 1:00 after lunch to pick both of you up." Clapping his hat back on his head he stood and went out the door. Once outside he mounted up and headed back to the ranch to get the house in shape for company.

The next two weeks were a whirlwind of activity between keeping up with the fields of hay and oats at the ranch, the Post Office, and running the Blind Pig George was kept busy going back and forth every other day into town. When he got there, he would either take Piedmont, Wilkens, or Mrs. Wilkens with him and treated Josephine with great care and respect. He didn't drink when he was around her and was polite and considerate as he bought her dresses and some ribbons for her hair.

After a few weeks of courting George asked Reverend Wilkens and Mrs. Wilkens to come to Poplar, MT on the train with Josephine and him so he could marry her properly. On

June 1, 1882 they were wed, they became Mr. and Mrs. George Grinnell and the memories of a talking pillow started to fade.

When the ceremony was over George gently kissed Josephine on the cheek in front of his witnesses. After the honey moon night in the hotel, they took the train into Canada to travel for a month. Nothing was too good for the Grinnell's and George was generous in spending funds on dresses, a gold watch for his bride, and some nice pieces of furniture with marble tops that they had shipped to the ranch before going back home.

In the fall of 1882 Josephine wrote a letter back to her favorite teacher at the Hampton Institute and said; 'All is good here now. I have nice dresses, nice things, and even a gold watch. I go to Fort when I want and get nice things. All is good.'

The marriage started on a happy note and Josephine was truly content. Josephine was kept busy at this time of delight and happiness as well. Cooking and cleaning for the hands kept her occupied and kept George satisfied as well. George kept as many as 16 men working for him and kept them all busy. He paid his men in silver coin and not one dared ask him where that money came from.

George kept the ranch hands going from field to field with some very labor intense work. One day a man who had gotten lost when his boat tipped over along the river came into the yard asking for water, food, directions and help. George offered him all of those things, but George being George made this hatless, thirsty stranger work for his water. "Just cut up that cord of wood over next to the house and then I'll let you get water, food, and some directions stranger," George said to him.

"Sir, I've been lost for almost a week with nothing to eat, and very little clean water to drink. Can't you let me have something first?" the sun burned man asked.

"Nope, you heard what I said. You want to eat and drink around here you've got to work for it. No handouts to no one." George responded and from his seat on his horse pointed again to the stack of wood and axe waiting beside the house. "I'd advise you to get cutting right away, supper be in about." George pulled his watch up from inside his shirt on the leather horse hair chain to check the time, "about three hours. Best get a move on if you want to eat and drink at my table."

The sun-burned man weaved his way to the shade of the house and sat on the stump to catch his breath. He picked up the axe in a few moments and started to chop firewood for the ranch. George sat on his horse for about an hour and just watched. When he saw the man was intent on getting the job done, he left him and headed out to get the next group moving.

He headed to the hayfield first where one group of three was cutting hay. He pulled up alongside the hay wagon and got down to see if their bucket was full of water. The men had half a bucket of water left and he knew they each had their own canteens. He wasn't worried too much about them since he knew they would be ready to haul two of the three wagons into the fort the next day to fill his government contract for hay.

He went to the wheat field next and then to check on the oats. They were starting to turn color and soon they would be ready to take the sickle to and harvest. Some of his men would be moving those crops into the fort according to his contract with the government as well. George felt very comfortable with all that he was accomplishing but he wanted more.

He kept the other hands busy with the cattle moving them to the fort when he sold beef to the government or to the shopkeeper to sell to the locals. Most of the money he paid his hands came back to him at the local road house he kept going. And that roadhouse satisfied some of the longing in him for more as he was reminded of his wild youth.

The Blind Pig was busy night and day between the whiskey that came up river and the girls he kept going upstairs. George had a favorite soiled dove he would go spend evenings with when his wife wasn't up to rough sex. When she got pregnant that first year, he was so disgusted with her he spent most nights drinking, gambling and whoring at The Blind Pig.

He kept gambling and fleecing the miners headed home from the gold fields, some of them never made it past The Blind Pig and were never heard from again. Some of the miners with funds in their pockets looking to make a fortune were fleeced in a drunken game of cards and returned home. No one knew where he hid the gold he fleeced from them. Since he always paid his men with silver coins the men who weren't afraid to speculate would talk in low tones about where he hid his poke.

He became Post Master of Tobacco Garden and built a little shed where locals from Beaver Creek across 'Holes in

Water' would come and pick up their mail when the water wasn't running hard.

George was a busy man ad to allow himself time to relax he would often go into The Blind Pig before he headed back to the ranch house. Depending on how his day went he would drink more if he was having a bad day and end up in a room upstairs to have some rough sex with one of the soiled doves who worked for him.

Josephine was pregnant with their first child when the beatings and abuse started again. That first summer as she grew with her pregnancy George was so angered at seeing this he made her walk barefoot in front of him on horseback as he told her he was thinking about returning her to her parents, since she was so round he couldn't mount her she was no use to him. She walked for two miles this way until George got thirsty and wheeled his horse away from her and headed back to the road house.

Josephine continued to walk and headed to her sister Mary's house that was only a few more miles away. She knew Mary would make sure her feet were bathed and she would be safe until the baby was born.

George and Josephine's baby boy was born and they named him John, his Aunt Mary helped deliver him at her place.

Chapter Nineteen
Rest, Ride, Relax

Pulling in beside the camper she grabbed the cooler that had lunch already made and got a partial work out as she lugged it into the camper. Chuck was in for a hot meal surprise and a hot piece of his wife if he wanted that too.

Missy brought the rest of her clothes in and after checking the water tank was full she turned on the generator. She did the few dishes left in the sink, got the hamburger goulash ready to warm in the microwave. She tossed the salad and left it covered in the refrigerator, set the table with plates, cutlery, condiments and the bag of fresh rolls she had stopped and bought at the store.

All was ready for a surprise lunch except for her. After a quick relaxing shower, she slipped into her short sleep shirt that was Chuck's favorite. As an extra incentive she wore nothing underneath, she just hoped no one else showed up for lunch today with Chuck.

She didn't wait long and warmed the goulash so the smell of that greeted Chuck when he opened the camper door. Missy was seated at the table and Chuck took one look at her seated in the chair with her legs spread wide in his favorite see through sleep shirt and he hardened like a young bull in rut.

Chuck turned and double locked the camper door, dropped his pants and kicked them off and quickly walked over to his wife. "God I've missed you babe!" He bent down as he said this to deep kiss her and as their tongues locked he reached inside her shirt and pulled and tweaked her nipples until they hardened.

"Oh babe, I've got to have you now" Chuck moaned as he reached down and spread Missy's legs wide and inserted two fingers into her and rubbed her moist come out and around her opening. Chuck got down on his knees and lifted her shirt and sucked on one nipple at a time as he pulled his two fingers out and rubbed her come onto the other nipple before licking and sucking it off. He rose and quickly slid himself into her in one long stroke and said as he licked and sucked first one nipple than the other, "I can't last long here it's been too long babe." As he proceeded to spill his load Missy wasn't far behind him.

They ate lunch in the nude after Chuck got on his radio and told his foreman he was off air until tomorrow morning since his wife was here. Missy and Chuck spent that afternoon in bed that day resting, playing and involving each other in all kinds of games they liked to play that always ended with both sides being satisfied.

After the third satisfaction romp that involved a chair and towels tying her up, Missy laid in Chuck's arms and told him about the surprise information of C.A. Grinnell and the $50.00

watermelon mark bill he had sold in the 1940's.

Chuck speculated as he stroked Missy's hair and reddened rear; "Mmm, babe I wonder what else their Momma hid from them? Or George hid from her? I think you're right about diving and checking it out." He continued to massage her neck and shoulders as his other hand gently moved around her cheeks.

"Now you've got me thinking more of this 'love story' of ours you know." He bent his head and once again to proceeded to lick and suck her rigid nipples. "I think I need a snack before supper babe. Are you up for having a sausage first?" He tongued kissed her deeply before she could reply and stuck two fingers deep inside of her. "Can I interest you in eating my sausage?"

Before she could say anything Chuck spun her around on the bed as he continued to slowly stroke her in and out with his fingers. As she came he quickly plunged his rod into her mouth up to his balls and stroked in and out as he held her head in place.

Every time he would stroke deep Missy would gag a little and Chuck would pull her hair and stick three fingers in as deep as he could. "God I hope you can swallow this babe." Saying this he unloaded directly into her mouth as he held her head in place with one hand and continued to stroke in and out with his fingers as he forced her to swallow it all. When he finished coming all of it she still had some that dribbled out of her mouth on the corner and Chuck leaned down and licked it off and said, "Oh I think we need more practice swallowing right babe?" Missy was well satisfied and could only smile at this form of pillow talk.

Chuck went and got some warm washcloths and as he washed Missy up he gave her one to wash him up as well. "Sorry I was rough on the spanking earlier babe, I just got carried away after not being able to take you from behind in a month or so. I'll be gentler tonight I promise. Now what's for supper, I really need to eat to keep up my strength for tonight and tomorrow's lunch."

Missy only hoped Chuck's sexual appetite for her would slow down over the next few days because after four romps in four hours she was getting sore. It certainly would be an oil night tonight and tomorrow and they still needed to talk about when they could dive.

That evening after a slow supper of sitting on his lap and feeding each other the oil came into play. Starting in the kitchen then moving to the table, it continued onto the steps with more poking and stroking and finally made it to the edge of the bed. Chuck bent Missy over after laying a pillow down to place her rear at a higher angle. He warmed the oil in his hands and rubbed it over her cheeks and then rubbed more oil into her rear and let it drop down onto her clitoris. Chuck once again mounted Missy from the rear and started slapping her ass cheeks as he pounded into her fast and hard from behind with a yell of "God, I love to fuck you babe!" he came for the fifth and final time that day.

The next morning as the sun rose before six Missy lay in bed contented, but sore. Chuck was soft, but had a satisfied grin on his face as he bent to kiss her and said, "Stay in bed babe and sleep and rest. I'll be back for lunch in a few hours so we can catch up some more." He bent down and tongue kissed her and lowering his head and sucked one nipple then gently bit it and did the same to the other one.

Chuck left before sunrise and before Missy fell asleep, she reflected about what kind of life a woman who was trapped in an abusive marriage felt like. What had happened with Josephine over the years after the death of George? Maybe there was information in her Grandparents old books about the history of the county that she could dig into. She had brought the two volumes with her just in case she needed to find out a little more information.

Missy slept for two more hours feeling satisfied and sore, she had a wonderfully long shower and after scrubbing deeply and soaking in the little tub area she placed her second enticement outfit on underneath her clothes. She paused before putting it on since Chuck was so horny she wasn't even sure if she needed it at all.

Did all women have husbands that needed to be satisfied like this? After dressing and having her cup of coffee and toast to start her day, she moved outside into the screened off picnic table area and pulled the two volumes out of the backseat and started to dig for more information about Josephine.

She found out that Mort's information rang true, even to the fact that history was altered to make it appear that Josephine simply fell in love with George after she returned from Hampton Institute in Virginia, and that no mention was made of her being traded in a land swap by her father. Protection for the family was what Dad had said to her.

"No one wants to admit how women were really considered property back then. No one wants to admit that parents traded children for sometimes a lot less than a patch of land, ponies and whiskey., but that's how the world was then. Failing to shine a light of truth on the past and change it can make us all weaker for not knowing how it really was." Mort had said when he handed the other paper clipping about the watermelon mark bill from Civil War days. "Even today being a war veteran isn't a bad or a good thing, it is something you decide to do and for some individuals it changes them in bad ways."

Missy had lunch ready when Chuck came back for lunch and told him she was riding out to the site with him so she could see his work for herself. She figured being out there in his element would help her tame his libido down a bit.

Chuck looked disappointed when she said that and then as he scooped up the last of the baked beans with his bread, cleared his throat and said, "Um, well see I already told the crew I'd be spending the afternoon here with you and not to disturb us. Maybe tomorrow morning will work best. If that's ok with you babe?"

Missy could see the handwriting on the wall and the erection under the table from where she stood by the kitchen island. She proceeded to unbutton her jeans and let them drop where Chuck couldn't see what she was doing and slip into her kitten heels.

"Well Chuck, considering how you did say you wanted dessert today. I guess staying inside the trailer with you is a good idea now. Tomorrow will be good too." As that statement Chuck smiled and started to unbutton his shirt.

"Now you're talking babe! What's for dessert? Are you on my private menu?" Chuck happily asked.

As he was taking his clothes off, while Missy finished with her leaving on her second enticement outfit; a black bra with cut out nipples, crotch-less panties with garters and black stockings with kitten heels. Before she grabbed the whipped cream in a can and a bowl of cherries to go with it in the frig she opened the door so Chuck couldn't see the outfit.

The game was an old one Chuck had taught her when they were first married and she had learned how to give him dessert this way in Vegas. True it had taken her two days to keep repeating this until Chuck was satisfied, but some part of her loved having him repeat this for her to play with him.

She grabbed the red lipstick and put it on and then the cherry body paint from the frig and painted her nipples red as well as the lips of her vagina since cherries were Chuck's favorite fruit.

Even though Chuck was sitting in the nude waiting for his 'dessert,' he was on the phone with his foreman. He turned when he heard the frig door shut and almost dropped the phone when he saw her.

"Um yeah Bill, I guess I won't be right back. Something has sprung up here and I need to fix it. I'll call you back when I'm done. If not, just wrap it up at 5:00 and I'll see you tomorrow morning."

Missy sauntered over to the table rolling hips and pouting with her lips, she set the whipped cream can and bowl of cherries on the table in front of Chuck. She spread her legs wide and curtsied in front of Chuck.

Chuck grinned and his eyes danced with a come-hither look, "God babe, you remember it?" He said as Missy replied.

"Oui, mousier, I remember how you love the whipped cream with cherries." Again, with a throaty purr, Missy gently sprayed whipped cream around each nipple and leaned forward and said, "Perhaps mousier would like a taste before ordering?" (The game was perfect at this point, except the door was still unlocked)

With a quick hard slap across her rear and after licking his lips Chuck said, "You get your ass over there and lock that door now Kitty!"

Missy sauntered slowly over after picking up the can of cream and bowl of cherries from the table, making sure she kept her legs spread wide so Chuck could see it all. She bent over to lock the door and wiggled her ass so that all the painted vagina lips to her anus was exposed.

"Oh mousier, how will I lock this door with dessert in my hands?" she gave a throaty whisper.

Chuck had a raging erection and she heard him slowly walk over to the door. Chuck breathed heavily on her neck, kissed her and said, "Now Kitty someday you'll earn this correctly. Just stay bent over and let me find that hole to lock." He licked his two fingers and immediately stuck them in her center as he rubbed her clitoris with his thumb.

She didn't want a spanking if she dropped dessert so she allowed herself to come on the spot and when she caught her breath said. "Oh, monsieur perhaps you would like to try my cream first."

Chuck stuck his fingers in his mouth and licked them off and said, "Oh cherries would be really good with this." Then he locked the door.

Chuck turned his 'Kitty' around and bent down and sucked hard first on one nipple than the other one. "Oh yes, Kitty, cherries and cream are delicious. I think I'll have more."

Putting his 'Kitty' in front of him he stuck his erection partially into her anus and as he pushed walked her towards the table said, "You spill anything you know you get spanked right?"

Missy continued the game and pretended to spill some cherries out of the bowl and five of them landed on the carpet beside them. "Oh monsieur, I've lost some cherries, I'm so sorry what can I do?"

Chuck just grunted and continued to walk the two more steps to the table as he attempted to push more of his erection into her anus. At the table he took the bowl of cherries from 'Kitty' and set it on the table hard as well as the can of cream. Missy knew she was in for a spanking and didn't care since the game excited her as well.

"Bad Kitty, very bad girl, you are going to get spanked in a moment. But first I have something else to do." Chuck bent Kitty over the table and slid himself all the way in and proceeded to pump her anus as he moved her right leg over and then her left leg so he could really try to get his balls in as well.

It didn't take long before he unloaded in her and cleaned both of them off with the damp towel she had left for that purpose on the table. The game continued after a rest of about fifteen minutes with Kitty and Chuck feeding each other whipped cream and cherries. Then Chuck said it was time for Kitty's spanking and had her lay across his lap and he gave her five red handprints on each of her cheek bottoms and then proceeded to cover them in whipped cream and lick them off. Missy and Chuck were both satisfied and headed to the shower to wash each other up.

Before falling asleep on her second day Missy said, "Tomorrow morning I'm coming over to the job site and then checking out where the river and lake merge to see about any new diving regulations."

She was met with Chuck's snoring response.

The next morning, they were finally able to talk and discuss when to plan for a practice dive. Since it was Wednesday they figured taking off early on Saturday morning would be a good day to just have a practice run. The crew was ahead of schedule and Chuck had no problem with letting them off early Friday night. That way they would have enough time to go over the gear, make sure the boat was ready and the supplies got stowed for an early Saturday start.

Friday night came quickly and after supper, the tubs were pulled out and the equipment was given careful inspection. All personal dive gear was rinsed and inspected first and after pulling on suits, hoods, flippers and gloves and making sure they fit and were safe they finally turned to the face masks, mouth pieces and connections to the tanks.

Slowly and surely they double checked each piece to make sure that all the gear functioned properly to prepare for their short dive tomorrow. After loading the equipment in the back of the boat and hooking the trailer up to the truck they were both tired and ready to call it a night.

"I want to wish on the stars tonight honey," Missy said to Chuck as they sat outside in the screened in tent eating a fresh salad for supper.

"I bet you want a fire and some S'mores to, don't you?" Chuck replied

"Of course I do, and I brought along everything I need to have that treat. You don't think I'd plan on being out here for two weeks without some kind of treat, do you?" She challenged him.

"Just curious is all, I'd wondered if you still had that sweet tooth along with the rest of your sweet self." Chuck smiled and winked at her.

Missy realized something that night as they sat in their chairs beside the fire toasting marshmallows and getting sticky fingers that were easily licked clean. It made even hard times better when you had a mate who you could joke and tease with, who loved you for the person you were and who adored your children you had created together. Giving Josephine a gentle thought in the back of her mind she wondered if she had ever felt being loved or that her children had ever experienced that feeling from their father. She had a sick sense in her stomach that being loved was only given by Josephine herself.

Chapter Twenty

Ice Moon

That winter with the new baby in the house seemed to settle George down. George Jr. was a happy baby, content when he was full of warm milk and had a clean diaper on. He was a handsome boy and the hired men would often ask to hold him when they needed to come up to the ranch house. He would smile and babble back to the men and even to the few women who dropped by. Josephine was very proud of their son and would often see George smiling gently when he would overhear the comments of 'What a handsome boy.' 'He looks like his father; don't you think?'

The winter was deep and cold that year and visiting slowed down towards January when the cold seemed to seep into the line shacks, the ranch house, and the saloon. Little travel happened at that time since the steamers could not run up river and the cold could easily kill people and animals caught unprepared for the depth of the bone chilling winds.

That winter saw an increase in families, since the cold seemed to encourage people to cling together and create new life as they waited for spring to come again. Josephine became pregnant again during a cold snap that lasted for four days. Except for getting up to place coal and wood in the fires they kept going in both the cook stove and the fireplace most days were spent huddled around with all three in bed when they weren't eating from the constantly simmering pot of stew on the stove.

George Jr. was still nursing and was also eating cooked oatmeal in the morning and at night. He was growing bigger every day. His favorite game was to pull on his father's whiskers and when George would bellow "No", he would chortle in his baby laugh and pull on his whiskers.

This time was sweet for the three of them and George was excited again when he discovered Josephine throwing up in the chamber pot one morning. "We having another one?" he said as he heard the sound and discovered her in the kitchen corner.

Josephine wiped her mouth and simply nodded, still feeling miserable and sick to her stomach it was all she could do. She was able to drink tea and have a piece of bread in the morning until the queasiness passed. George just smiled and said, "It'll be all right. Just takes time, then you'll be busy with another one and George will have someone to play with.

George was pleasant that winter since he wasn't drinking. The saloon was slow, as well as sending and receiving mail at the post office. Most people weren't even traveling except for short distances to check on stock and make sure neighbors were fending well. George and some of the hands were still going into the fort at least once a month on a mail run. They would bundle up in the sleigh with hide blankets and baked potatoes on the floorboards around their feet for warmth. In case they got stuck the hands who were riding could help them get out of the drifts.

Josephine continued to grow with her second pregnancy and George Jr. grew right alongside the new sibling waiting to appear. George started walking before spring break-up on the river when the ice would crack and pop and the water would start to flow underneath the chunks of ice. Josephine would take George out with her and walk to the outhouse after bundling both of them up. The fresh air, though cold and stinging would put roses in her cheeks and give George red cheeks and lips. When her sister Mary and her husband Frank came to visit and spend time, they would travel in their sleigh the same way others did. They tried to time the visit about the same time George would be gone since neither Frank nor George cared for one another. The sisters could enjoy their visiting and Frank would play with George in the open space by the fire. The visits were always filled with happiness for the upcoming birth and the time spent with their nephew and each other.

Josephine was an excellent cook and would make fresh coffee and biscuits with some jam as soon as they would come in the door. After a hardy lunch of meat, root vegetables and bread she would start making cake or cookies. These would go home with them when they returned to their homestead as well. Traveling in the west was a hazard in the winter and no traveler left a house without food given to make sure they had enough to sustain them until they arrived. Josephine knew enough to have fresh bread and cake for George when he got back from the fort. She knew that he had favorite things to eat that she made and as long as he wasn't drinking, he was a reasonable man.

Josephine hoped for a daughter with this pregnancy, but would welcome a son. She continued to fill the bottom of her flour barrel with coins from George's pouch as a way to ensure her children would always have a way to get things they needed. If George suspected that every week his pouch was being searched Josephine was leery about what he might do. She made sure he was gone when she searched and always took only one coin or one bill from the pouch.

Her hidden stash of coins and bills was growing and she needed another safe place to hide them from prying eyes and little curious fingers. She had a good idea where to hide them, besides the bottom of the flour barrel, but she wanted to make sure both places would stay hidden and keep her growing pile of funds safe.

She went to her sewing basket where she kept strips of leather to repair things with. She had just finished making George another pair of moccasins for his growing feet to wear in the house since he wasn't old enough yet for boots and she had strips of leather left over. Since nothing was ever wasted, she sat down when George was napping and proceeded to whip stich the strips together, sewed up the sides and created a small leather bag of her own with ties that she could use to hide her growing pile of coins and bills.

Even growing with her second pregnancy she was able to bend over and dig in the bottom of the flour barrel and dig up her coins and bills. She placed the three coins and two bills she had into the leather pouch and tied it shut. Quietly going into the bedroom positioned off the side of the parlor she gently lifted the leg of the bed and stuffed the pouch into the hollow leg and replaced the cap right under George's side.

Before their second son was born Mary and Frank came for a visit to check on the growing needs of having another child in the house. George Jr. adored his Aunt Mary and followed her everywhere. When they went to leave in the sleigh no one noticed the toddler heading outside without his coat on and only thin moccasins on his feet. He was following his favorite Aunt Mary and Uncle Frank toddling along in the tracks left behind the sleigh.

When Josephine realized that George Jr. had wandered off, she became frantic and pleaded with the hired hands to find him. Grinnell, of course, had started drinking when Mary and Frank showed up and had been drinking all day.

He threatened the hands and said, "Any one goes after the squaw's kid and I'll kill you. Let him freeze if he's that stupid." One man stepped up who was not afraid of Grinnell and said, "Ma'am, I'll find him and bring him home."

Jeth took an extra blanket and bundled himself up and headed out after the boy. He followed his tracks easily and less than an hour later a cold and hungry little boy was returned to his weeping mother.

Jeth carried him into the ranch house and gently set him on his mother's lap and said, "I think he's got frost bite on some of his toes and fingers. You know how to save them: It might make him cry because it will sting but you'll save those toes and fingers."

Josephine waited and looked to Jeth to hear what to do about this. With tears streaming down her cheeks, she heard him say, "Soak them in kerosene it will sting, but bring the blood flow back. Then give him a bath in warm water afterwards and feed him good. Make sure he drinks some milk or something warm, tea is good if you've got it."

Jeth headed out the door, but not before he turned and glared at Grinnell saying, "Your son's back, and he will be alright. Next time I'll go again if I have to." He headed out back to the bunk house to let the others know that the boy was alright and what had happened.

Josephine realized just how important her little pile of money was that she was able to save. She almost lost her son and she wasn't about to lose this child she carried either. As she bent to cover George Jr.'s toes in a rag soaked in kerosene and his fingers, she had to hold him as he cried. The more she rubbed the kerosene on his skin the more he cried. Finally, the skin was turning red from the heat and she was able to stop. She gently washed his hands and feet in soapy water and dried them off.

When that was finished, she set him on the chair and gave him a spoon and a bowl of warm stew. Along with a warm glass of milk the little boy devoured it all and then laid his head on the table and promptly fell asleep.

Josephine carried him wearily into the bed and laid him beside her so they both could rest. With George still out in the saloon she knew they were safe for a while until he returned. She stroked her son's hair as she thought of what to do if George ever found the money she was saving to protect herself and her children.

If he ever did find her hiding place, she would tell him that is where he told her to place that money. Somehow, she knew she could convince him if she told him he had been drinking when he told her to do this. She hoped he would never find it. After George fell asleep, she returned to her chair and she proceeded to whip stitch three more pouches together with the scraps she had left. She would place those into the remaining posts of the bed with nothing in them until she could recover more from George's pouch.

When George came back from The Blind Pig, he stood beside the stove eating stew from the pot with warm biscuits and never said a word to Josephine. When he ate until he was full he belched loudly, wiped his face with a kitchen towel and headed right for the bedroom where he fell down in the middle of the bed with his boots on. Josephine and George made a pallet of blankets on the floor by the kitchen stove and fell asleep after they heard Grinnell start to snore.

Chapter Twenty-One
Diving Deep

Saturday morning the sun rose in the East with a clear light blue sky, no clouds and no hint of a breeze at all. The promise of a warm bright day glistened in the dew on the sage brush with diamond drops that gave off rainbow colors on the ground. The air smelled sweet with the promise of spring warmth and crops growing. Turning west brought the smell of cattle in the distance and new life being born in fields surrounding the large lake.

The boat was filled with their diving gear and the necessary spare parts; buoyancy compensators, regulator setup, spare weights, spare masks and fins, tank valve O-rings, air horn, marine whistle, life ring, charged cell phone, extra oxygen tanks, standard first aid kit, spare parts kit and the large net with ballast buoys to lift heavier items from the floor. Chuck was filling the fuel tanks on the boat, and Missy checked on the mooring ball and the two dive flags; red with a white diagonal stripe to notify other boaters a diver was down and the blue and white alpha flag to let other boaters know to steer clear of the boat where they were diving. When she knew those items were good for the dive, she went to the GPS on the dash, turned it on and entered the co-ordinates, N 48* 009.649, W103* 08.105. From that location they would be headed directly across the lake almost to the opposite shore where the location of the current Tobacco Garden is. Missy went back inside to finishing packing their lunch in the cooler. She felt the excitement she always felt before a dive skittering up her spine as she thought of the beauty beneath the water's surface.

She hummed a little tune as she made up five sandwiches and packed them into square containers inside the cooler and then carefully placed the grapes and strawberries in two more containers on top of the sandwiches. After filling the empty spaces with water and soda bottles, she dropped the bag of ice on the floor to break it apart and carefully dumped it on top of everything in the cooler. She didn't hear Chuck when he quietly came into the kitchen and nuzzled her on the neck without touching her with his fuel-stained hands.

"I've got to wash Babe." He gently nudged her away from the sink so he could wash the fuel from his hands. "Good thing I stopped kissing you now. I don't think I could handle any more of your passion and diving too right now."

Missy smiled gently and said, "Glad to know that hair trigger libido of yours is satisfied for a while. Personally, I don't think I could take another day like earlier this week! Good thing we have gotten older and a little tamer with our love time."

Chuck continued washing the fuel from his hands and agreeably nodded as he said, "It sure is. Except I do enjoy that wilder side of you when we have our moments."

Missy stood and watched him wash up as she thought about the deep sense of satisfaction being with someone who loved you brought. She thought about Josephine and wondered if she had ever thought that at all. She had just read more in the County Historical Volumes the night before about the fact that Josephine had remarried after George's death and the fact that the second marriage had not lasted long either. It left her wondering if the pillow talker aspect of her life had influenced far into her future. She was left with a twinge of fear that it impacted everything about her life, except for the love of her children, which remained steadfast and strong.

Chuck walked past her and gave her rear end a swat and said, "Let's go Babe, daylight diving is waiting! Lock the door when you come out, I'll be in the truck waiting for you." He headed out the door and left the screen door open for her to shut and lock up.

Driving the truck along the gumbo and gravel road left a cloud behind the boat as they headed to the boat ramp at Lund's Landing. The breeze blowing in the open windows smelled sweet like drying earth and sage and both of them were quiet as they listened to the radio and mentally prepared for their dive. Slow breathing was a must when diving so control of your depth and vision didn't become clouded. They both were in rhythm as they breathed in and out and listened to some easy listening music. Chuck reached over and caressed Missy's hand as they drove alone and simply said when one song stopped, "I dearly love you, Babe."

Missy only nodded and continued her deep, slow breaths as the next song started up. When they arrived at the ramp, Chuck backed the boat and truck down the ramp and expertly guided the boat trailer into Lake Sakakawea. Missy hopped out and unhooked the clamp and let the boat glide freely away from the trailer. Hopping off the trailer, she walked the boat over to the slip and tied it off as they prepared to load their diving equipment on board. They made sure the first thing loaded onto the boat was the cooler, then the diving floats with flags and then the equipment.

Missy had her swim suit on under her shorts and top and so did Chuck. It was just a matter of stripping off the outer layer and putting on the dive suits when they got to the coordinates they had researched. As soon as they arrived Chuck dropped anchor and Missy placed the mooring ball and rope with the weight down beside the ladder into the lake then placed the two flags out. She placed the flags in two spots, one at the stern and one at the bow of the boat. They kept their breathing nice and slow as they suited up and checked each other's equipment to make sure they had snug fits and their regulators were working correctly.

They were anchored towards the opposite shore about 100 feet out from the current Tobacco Garden where kinnikinnick would grow. This wild plant was used for hundreds of years by the tribes who traveled and followed the herds to this area for hunting. They would trade and smoke the leaves around campfires. The broad-leafed plant cannot be found in the area any more, and according to those who make the claim it has no medicinal or hallucinated components in it.

Missy went backward over the back platform first into the cloudy water and Chuck followed after a few moments. Missy was waiting in the slow-moving gray green water for him below the surface. With hand signals only, she let Chuck know the first dive of the day would be ten minutes down since it had been a while since either of them had dived. Chuck nodded and pointed below and held up his fingers for 15-20 feet and they descended beneath the surface together until they approached the bottom.

As they neared the bottom, they could see the outlines of what appeared to be both square shapes and octagon shapes of raised dirt. This matched the description of the ranch house and The Blind Pig Saloon; they decided they needed to get a little closer before ten minutes were up and they needed to start the ascent. Missy had thought to bring the tape with her and she was glad they did. They measured off the ranch house first and were about to head over to the octagon structure when both dive watches buzzed on Chuck and Missy's arms. Chuck motioned to start the ascent and Missy swam with him over to where the shadow of the boat floated above them. Slowly they ascended on the mooring ball line as they marked their time and watched some Northern Pike swim in the distance past them. Neither one of them wanted to get the shallow bends, so they took great care to protect themselves as they ascended and just enjoyed the sensation of floating and hanging onto the rope from the marker float.

When they were about five feet from the surface Missy cleared her mask. This only took her three easy steps by inhaling deeply through her mouth piece and getting a decent lung full of air, pressing the top of her mask firmly to her forehead and slowly opening the bottom seal as she blew hard through her nose and then tilting her head back slightly as she looked up and exhaled through her nose and then resealed her mask. She had about thirty feet of visibility underwater and could see form her point on the line the outlines of the buildings in the distance. They would return once more that day with the underwater camera to take pictures of the site to check on the computer when they returned to their trailer.

Chuck had broken the surface and was climbing onto the back of the boat when she finally surfaced and removed her mask. He gently reached down and helped her up onto the platform on the back of the boat. As she climbed up the ladder, she noticed Chuck was waving and smiling at the DNR boat that was trolling off their starboard bow. He helped Missy get her tank off and waited to take her headpiece from her. He said gently, "Don't look now, but we are about to get checked out by the big boys for diving here."

The DNR boat pulled alongside as soon as Missy stepped from the platform onto the deck of the boat.

"Hello folks." The young officer said, "We see you're diving today and we'd like to run a check on your equipment and licenses if you don't have a problem with that."

"No problem officer." Chuck smiled as he reached for the packet of licenses and equipment list, we always kept in a sealed plastic container below the dashboard. "You're welcome to board or I can just toss this to you. What's your preference?"

"I'd like to come aboard if that's fine with you." He said in return.

One younger officer was manning the steering wheel as the other one swung a line over and tied the DNR boat to ours. He quickly stepped across with little motion in a smooth, practiced move. Our flags were still out, so other fishing and water-skiing boats were giving us a wide berth as well. They would wave and smile happily that they were not the ones being checked out as they trolled around us. As soon as the officer boarded, he took the waterproof container from Chuck and proceeded to fill out a form with our information. He included our dive certification numbers and listed the last two times we had been diving along with our current location.

He was pleasant and polite as he went about the business of ensuring our boat was well-equipped for safety and that we knew what we were doing when diving. As his list got shorter Missy stood and said "I have some fresh fruit I'd love to share with you if you're allowed to accept it."

The young man smiled behind his dark sunglasses and said, "Ma'am, I'm sorry we aren't allowed to accept anything. Let me assure you we do have sandwiches, fruit and water aboard our vessel. I do appreciate your kindness, though."

Missy just nodded and smiled back but took out the box of grapes from the cooler anyway so that the DNR officer could see there was no alcohol in the cooler. Popping the lid off the container of grapes she took a small bunch of green grapes and started to eat them. Walking over to Chuck, she handed him the box and let him grab some as well since she had no idea how long this little check stop would take. They could at least enjoy part of their lunch as the field agent went about his business of checking the boat out.

Finally, he was finished but had some strange advice to give them before he stepped back onto their high-powered boat. "Make sure you keep listening to the weather channel in case the winds shift. You can never be sure around here what will blow in. You also need to be careful if you move any of the structures below. Some of the logs from the original Tobacco Garden are crumbling and in a sorry state. We've had other divers looking for treasure around here, so I need to remind you that if you find anything, you will have to fill out the paperwork to report it and pay taxes on it. Have a nice afternoon dive folks." With that said he touched the bill of his hat with his fingers, smiled and stepped back across to their boat, untied it and the other agent gave a little wave and off they went across the lake.

"That was strange," Chuck said as he turned to me. "Not the checking out the boat equipment, but about the treasure. I wonder who has been diving around here that they're worried about."

Missy only shrugged her shoulders and bent down to get the rest of the lunch out. "Let's not worry about it. We have no idea and probably will never know anyway. Let's just have a light lunch and rest and then go back down with the camera and see what we notice. Does that sound good to you, honey?" Chuck just smiled and nodded as he bit into his ham and cheese sandwich.

They moved the boat closer to the location so they could be almost directly above the original buildings but slightly north of them by about twenty feet. Chuck had the camera and had checked it the night before in the camper sink to make sure it was working properly. Check descended first on the mooring ball line with the camera strap looped around his shoulder and the camera tucked under his left arm. Missy followed him and worked her way down the line hand-over-hand until she approached the bottom and let go. She flipped her fins and caught up to Chuck just as he was taking pictures of a small school of walleye swimming towards them.

Missy smiled behind her mask and gently swam towards the school and watched as they scattered as she got closer to them. She hovered over the building outlines on the bottom and watched as Chuck took pictures from multiple angles. She swam a little further away from the buildings where she imagined either the well, outhouse or barn might have been. Seeing a deeper depression in the ground, she swam back to Chuck and tapped him on the shoulder to motion him over to where she had seen the deeper depression.

Missy was rewarded with a big smile, a thumbs up and Chuck's wiggling eyebrows as he dove a little deeper and started snapping pictures of the squared-off depression she had seen. It had seemed like a short time, but the 24 minutes they had allowed themselves on this time was up and both of their dive watches buzzed on their wrists. They leisurely swam back to the mooring ball line and started their ascent. It promised to be an exciting evening when they would look at the photos they had taken.

Chapter Twenty-Two
Planting Moon

Eleven miles northwest of Grinnell's, a former employee of George's had located, Frank Fleming. Frank argued with Grinnell many times and always had a chip on his shoulder against George. Frank was looking for a bride and finally married All-Goes-Out, now called Mary, who was Josephine's younger sister. Frank and Mary lived about 10 miles northwest of Tobacco Garden on a homestead claim. It wasn't as big a spread as George and Josephine's. It had a little porch on the front for saddles and muddy gear to be hung before going into the kitchen. It had a loft above the kitchen where their two children slept. The bedroom for Frank and Mary was nice in size since Frank was a big man and needed room. He had even built an area off to the side with a wash tub so Mary could bathe and wash clothes in the house. Even though he was a man who complained a great deal, he was thoughtful of his wife and children.

Frank was proving up his homestead slowly and was careful with his money. He would often tell Mary about some of George's illegal funds he got from stealing from river traffic, gambling, and even reportedly murdering unsuspecting miners. His favorite thing to do was to make sure that Josephine always knew she had a place to come to with her children, and he mentioned it whenever he could around George. George also knew that Frank didn't care for the way he treated Josephine and hated the fact that he never referred to his children as his own but called them 'that squaw's brats.'

Frank was a decent man to Mary but was difficult to like as a neighbor and an in-law. Frank would go at least once a week to the post office in Tobacco Garden, where George was still Post Master. Frank was a big man who liked to eat and have coffee and would often stop in the bar/restaurant that George owned as well. He would always eat a big breakfast of steak, eggs, fried potatoes, and biscuits. Then he'd drink at least half a pot of coffee himself. When it came time to settle the bill, he'd smile and say, "Oh, my brother-in-law George said he was paying this for me."

The Blind Pig also had a 'soiled doves' area on the top floor that Frank never visited. He knew how mean and ornery George was with Josephine and when he was done eating his free meal of steak, eggs, potatoes and biscuits, he'd sit and slowly sip his cup of coffee. When he would sip his coffee, he'd share nasty comments about George with whoever would listen to him. Every week, this little game was played out by Frank and soon enough, those nasty comments eventually made their way to George.

When he heard about them from his hired men and the free breakfast Frank was eating at his expense every week, his dislike of Frank slowly turned to anger. That anger simmered for a long time underneath the surface with George. He wasn't a man who forgot and was always looking to pin the blame on someone when things went wrong. Now he had another reason to lodge pole Josephine since her sister was married to Frank. He quietly kept silent about this until the middle of February.

February skies were a bright turquoise blue with winds sweeping across the prairie and the wind held a chill with a late promise of storm brewing. George cared little for the upcoming Valentine's Day and he personally thought it was a waste of time and money. Josephine was always looking for a way to make George feel more appreciated and loved by her. She decided to make a cake for him and the children for Valentine's Day to celebrate the holiday. Chocolate for baking was very expensive and she had part of a baking chocolate bar left in her Hosier Cupboard. She carefully cut off the pieces she would need to melt to create the delicious dessert and she made sure she had enough left for more cake for visitors as well.

Outside, the skies were turning a deep gray and snow started to fall thicker and faster through the day, bringing the promise of a blizzard. Josephine had the children quietly playing together in the kitchen when the door blew open and a snow-covered George thumped into the kitchen and shook the snow off on top of the floor and the three boys. The baby, Ellen, was asleep in the cradle close to the stove to keep her from getting chilled. Josephine turned and said, "George, please, the door. The children will get sick."

George responded by throwing his snow-covered hat on

top of the oldest boy and his coat on the other two and said, "Snow isn't gonna hurt 'em. They should be outside playing instead of staying in here with you anyway!" Then he turned to the boys and grabbed his hat and coat off of them while covering them in snow, "Git out of here and head upstairs now unless you want to feel the belt!" The boys looked frightened for themselves and their Mother but turned and ran from the big man they didn't understand.

George turned to Josephine, who stood at the stove with a wooden spoon in her hand, dripping chocolate batter on the wooden floor. George smiled and said, "MMM, making me a cake are you? I love chocolate and you know what I like best about it?"

Josephine only shook her head no, too afraid to speak. She didn't know if George was drunk or not since he wasn't close enough to her for her to smell his breath.

George reached to top of the shelf and got his riding quirt and a bottle of whiskey and pulled them both down. "Yup, I do like chocolate with my whiskey and a mount right here on the table." He pulled the cork out of the top of the bottle and gulped down half of it. Wiping his lips with the shirt sleeve, he proceeded to shuck his shirt over his head and stood bare-chested in the kitchen and walked closer to Josephine.

Josephine was quaking in fear, but stood still with the spoon still dripping down to the floor. George slowly walked up to her and grabbed the spoon. "Now squaw, I want you to lick this spoon." He picked up the spoon and licked some of the batter from the handle and then proceeded to grab her mouth and stick the spoon down into her mouth. He wasn't gentle either since he was getting her ready for what he planned next.

George laid the riding quirk on the table while he proceeded to stroke her throat with the chocolate batter=covered spoon and with his free hand, he unbuttoned his trousers and let his member spring out. He stuck his hand in the batter bowl and smeared chocolate over his penis, and kept stroking the spoon in and out of Josephine's mouth. Since she was nursing, he avoided her breasts, but focused on her bottom and mouth. He planned a riding-sucking game right there on the table as soon as he could.

He took the spoon out of her mouth and said, "Want it hard? Are you thirsty? Best answer right, or the quirk will go harder on you and those brats upstairs." George whispered this meanly in her ear as he pushed her to her knees. "First things first, though, I've got more than one load here, and you're gonna take it in the mouth first and drink all of me." Josephine had played this game before and really didn't know that sex didn't always resort to mean pleasure.

"Please, sir, may I have a drink? I'm powerful thirsty." She said in a whisper as she knelt on the floor by the table. Before George grabbed her hair and pumped into her mouth, she glanced to see that the outside door was locked, and so was the kitchen door. No one would disturb them not matter what happened here. She took a deep breath and tried to relax as George grabbed her head with both hands and pumped into her mouth until he exploded. She swallowed his come just as he expected her to.

George looked satisfied, but then he reached for the bottle

and finished it off and as he lowered it to the table, he said, "Now lick all the chocolate and come off me and off the floor right now." His face was red and his breathing was hard as he watched her clean off the come and chocolate from his penis. As she bent to clean up the floor, George took off his boots and pants and stood in the kitchen bare-naked by the stove. He threw more coal into the cook stove to warm the kitchen up since he planned on stripping Josephine naked so he could watch her breasts jiggle as he rode his mare hard from the rear.

Josephine thought she was finished with the game this time and stood and turned to see George standing naked in front of her, holding the riding quirt. "Think you're done there? Gonna have to ride you hard there. You missed some of my chocolate and come from the floor." George pointed at a spot that had been hidden under her dress and as she looked down, he slapped her hard in the face. "Better not hear nothing from you neither, you'll take it and like it!" George said as he slapped her again and bruised her cheek. "Take off that dress and all those damn petticoats right now."

Josephine unbuttoned and removed her shirtwaist and glanced at the sleeping baby who hadn't stirred. It was a good thing she had nursed her before George came into the kitchen. She wasn't full of milk but knew that George liked to see milk dripping from her onto the table. George grabbed her hair and pulled hard to loosen the bun, "Hurry up and get these clothes off." He stroked himself up and down to keep his member hard as he watched her slip out of her blouse, skirt, and pantaloons. George's penis increased in size as she stood naked before him, waiting for him to say what he wanted.

"Now squaw, know how I like to ride? Get ready because it's gonna be fun and hard." He pushed Josephine over the table and drug two chairs on either side to elevate her rear. George hadn't mounted her from the front since their daughter had been born, and he was filled with booze and need to have at her. He dipped his fingers in chocolate and rubbed them on her ass cheeks and then plunged his fingers inside her to get her wet. He moved her left leg up onto a chair rung and did the same with her right leg. He went to the peg by the door and grabbed two ropes. "Now we're really gonna ride." George tied her left hand to one table leg and her right hand to the other. He then bent down and tied her left leg to the chair rung and did the same thing with her right leg. He dipped his fingers into the chocolate and spread more on her ass and then took more and reached around and forced chocolate batter into her mouth. "You like it?" George was red-faced and breathing hard as he forced chocolate down her throat and around her lips. "Better answer right squaw or the quirt will be hard."

"Please sir, may I have a drink? I'm powerful thirsty." Josephine replied as was expected.

George bent down and licked her ass down the crack and then stood and slapped her hard with his quirk leaving welts across her ass. "Get ready. We're going riding now." He mounted her from behind, and as he pounded in and out of her, he would slap her ass with the quirk as he rode. When he bent down and saw the milk dripping from her nipples onto the table, he finally released the rest of his load with a roar. He took the ropes off her, grabbed a towel and washed himself off, slipped his pants and shirt on, carried his boots with him and left the kitchen without a backward glance or look at Josephine.

Josephine slowly stood and went to the wash basin and proceeded to wash herself first with cool water, and then she dumped the water in the slop bucket and filled the basin with warm water from the reservoir beside the stove. The baby started to stir wanting to be fed and changed so Josephine quickly completed washing and dressed, then turned to the cradle. Bending down, she murmured to Ellen, "There now little one, there now. Momma is here for you."

Lifting her onto the table she quickly wiped the little girl down and changed her diaper, sat in a chair and unbuttoned her shirt waist and let Ellen nurse her fill. When that chore was finished Josephine took the now curdled cate batter and poured it into a pan. What was left would make one small cake that George would eat by himself. She decided that the boys would have a fresh small cake as well and that George would never know the difference between the batters, but she would.

After placing George's cake in the oven, she turned to the cupboard for more ingredients to make a small batch and noticed a cloth sack that George had placed on the counter. She had started to pay more attention to the things that money could purchase for you, food and clothes for the children, education and maybe some fine things like their brass bed, and the marble-topped side table in the parlor area.

George always carried coins and some bills in that sack and today, she decided to look for herself.

She cautiously looked and quietly listened at the kitchen door, but no sound except for snoring came from their bedroom. She heard the boys playing upstairs in the bedroom loft and decided not to call them down until their cake was done. She gently untied the knot on the bag and quietly emptied it into her hand. Four $10 Gold Eagle coins slipped into her hand along with five bills that were crumbled up. She gently spread out the bills and took one. It was green on the back and the zeros looked like watermelons. It had a red seal on it with the face of a man with whiskers. She quietly sounded out the name 'GRANT' on the bill. She took that bill and one of the Gold Eagles and placed it in the bottom of the flour bin and, covered it up and returned the coins and other bills to the sack. After tying it the same way she returned to her task and made more chocolate batter for the children. She took George's little cake out of the oven and set it out to cool on the cupboard and slipped another little cake for the boys to eat into the oven.

Before finally sitting to rest, she went to the door and listened again. Snoring still came from the bedroom and giggling floated down the ladder from the loft. Ellen was sound asleep again in her cradle by the stove and Josephine knew she had to add more coal to the stove before going out to use the outhouse. She sat for a moment and thought about that gold coin and the bill she had taken for her secret hoard of funds. She had been checking that bag whenever she could for the last four years and would hide the money away in the bottom of the flour bin until she had a chance to place it in one of the leather scrap bags to hide it away from George. She would make sure she had the money she needed for her children to have enough clothes and food.

After sitting and finally catching her breath, she rose and went to the pegs beside the door and wrapped herself in her warm wool shawl since it still had not stopped snowing. She grabbed the slop pail in one hand the coal bucket in the other and went outside into the cold. The outhouse was around the back of the ranch house and the coal bin was closest, so she filled that first with chunks of coal and set it down for her return trip. After dumping the slop bucket out behind the outhouse, she set the bucket by the door and went inside the outhouse to finally have a few cold minutes to herself. She still was sore from George riding her hard, but she felt better now that she had added more funds for her children.

The snow kept falling as she made her way back to the house, and when she got inside found George in the kitchen eating his cake.

Chapter Twenty-Three
Back Home

After two weeks of investigating the county history books, diving and taking photos, cooking and spending passion-filled nights with her husband, Missy felt the need to return to the ranch and check on how the family was doing. It was true that she had spent at least an hour every two days speaking to them on the phone, but she also felt the need to return and see things for herself, even with the assurances from all them things were working out well. Chuck, of course, didn't want her to leave at all and made her promise she would be back to spend time again in no more than two weeks. She didn't want another two days of intense and passionate lovemaking like she had experienced after being away from him for a month.

With the promise made the next morning after making love, she headed back to the ranch on Monday. She felt both satisfied and content with her decision to return for a short time. She was excited about all the discoveries she had made about Josephine and George and what had happened to that family. Missy was also eager to share her research with her brother and his family. Chuck was content that she was sharing this before they attempted to dig anything up and promised that when they came out, he would round out another work camper for Jeth, Babs and the twins to stay in when they went diving.

Bumping along the gravel road she sang along with a country western station on the radio and made a decision to stop by Fort Buford on the way back. She wanted to see if any record of where George was buried was even left there. Those promises she made to herself she intended to keep. She headed north when the highway merged both north and south and then a few miles into Montana, she turned left onto a gravel road to head to the historical Fort Buford site. She was pleased to see the parking lot was about two-thirds full and smiled as she thought of the others here who were interested in history.

She headed to the trading post along the gravel path and when she stepped inside, she quietly listened as 'Charley the post-trade' was answering questions from a group surrounding him. Charley was round, with wire-rim glasses on his round face, balding and gray-bearded. He was dressed in costume and looked the part of a trader. His voice matched his twinkling smile and eyes as he answered all the questions the group would ask him. They were held enthralled until Charley himself broke the spell by lifting his plastic water bottle to his parched lips to take a drink. They all took a step back, shook his hand, thanked him and headed out the door to investigate the remains of the fort and the buildings left standing.

Missy stepped up to Charley and introduced herself, she had brought along a spiral notebook and pen to write down his answers to her questions. She placed her pen on the surface and, smiling at him, said, "Charley, I'm doing some research on who lived here in this fort and the area around here. Can you give me any information about this fort and what was happening around our country at this time?

Charley answered with a smile, "I'd be delighted to, just try and keep up with my information. I'll repeat and slow down when you need me to. Does that sound good?"

Missy's response was a returned smile, a nod and a soft "Go ahead, I'm ready."

So, Charley began, "Fort Buford became a bustling hub of activity and housed six companies of soldiers when it was a busy area. A census that was taken in 1885 showed that Buford County's population, that included the fort, was five hundred and twenty-four. Three hundred and six were officers and soldiers and two hundred and eighteen were civilians. Only seventy-eight of them were women.

A further breakdown classified by occupation revealed eleven farmers, two wood dealers, one hotel keeper, one lawyer, one druggist, five clerks, one bookkeeper, two laborers, four railroad workers, four cooks, one beggar, twenty-five teamsters, ten woodchoppers, two herders, twenty-seven musicians, one post trader, one interpreter, two blacksmiths, one saddler, one wheelwright and a bartender. No citizens of the eastern half of Williams County were included at this time and this only included those living in Flannery County." Charley stopped to take a sip of water as

Missy continued to write she added the following sentence.

George and Josephine lived in Williams County and were not included in this census but their roadhouse and the ranch continued to grow and become successful as George continued to fleece water traffic and any immigrants who were headed to the gold fields and bothered to stop there.

Charley continued with the information below. The starred timeline items were added by Missy from facts she had already researched.

"Further Historical Time Points to consider:

- *1840 - George Grinnell born in Baltimore, MA
- 1859-First major Silver strike in US, Comstock Lode discovered
- *1860-Josephine "Comes At Night" Malnouri born in Dakot1863a Territory, daughter of Charles Malnouri, b. 1828 in France, d. June, 1910; m. Beaver Woman, b. 1838 in Elbow Woods Dakota Territory (Gross Ventre). M. Indian custom, 1853 @ Elbow Woods
- *1861- George Grinnell enlists in First Regiment of MN volunteers in May
- *1862-George Grinnell, discharged in October, enlists in Tropp B, Battle of Gettysburg under General P. Sheridan, Battle of Gettysburg.
- 1863-Tobacco Garden raid on steamboat to recover promised goods, July 7, Sitting Bull (Buffalo)
- *1865-Civil War ends, steamboats make it to Fort Union, George Grinnell comes to Beaver Creek/Tobacco Garden area, age 25

- *1866-G. Grinnell worked a year as a wood hawk
- *1871-1872- G. Grinnell takes a 'sleeping dictionary pillow talker' in land trade, J. Malnouri
- *1871- Ole Ambrose Thorsen born June 23, 1871 in Dakota Territory
- 1876-Red Blanket and Whistling Bear participate in raid on boat of miners at Tobacco Garden
- 1876-Party of miners from Boise, ID had 32 people on board mackinaw boat, all killed in raid near Fort Union (Buford), miners carried one hundred thousand dollars in gold dust
- 1876-Fred Gerad gains funds from Tobacco Garden raid from brother-in-law, Whistling Bear. He and Red Blanket told to Joseph H. Taylor about what miners had on boat, no guns only 'worthless yellow dust'. Fred had Red Blanket and Whistling Bear go back and get the yellow dust for him with a promise of exchange for weapons. They found belts filled with gold dust and a coffee pot filled with gold dust and nuggets hidden in plain sight
- *1876-G. Grinnell has conversation with Fred about Red Shirt and Whistling Bear about raid and gained funds
- 1876-Battle of the Little Big Horn
- 1876-Steamboat carrying over $3 million dollars in gold bars stops to bury bars along the river to return to pick up bodies of soldiers from the Battle of the Little Big Horn
- *1877-Fred Gerad sends his 3 daughters to Indian School on East coast; all three girls become Catholic Nuns when there

- *1878-Priest intervenes with Grinnell and Josephine, she is sent to Hampton Institute in Virginia with funds from John Southworth scholarship from Hampton Institute, VA
- 1880- Billy the Kid is brought to justice
- *1881-Josehpine 'Malnouri' Grinnell returns to Tobacco Garden area
- 1883-Brooklyn Bridge is opened
- *1885-Hans Barstead, built log house in Tobacco Garden area, worked for G. Grinnell, friend of Ole Thorston and Nels Kamp
- 1885-Last buffalo in area shot near Cusik Springs in Dakota Territory
- 1886-Statue of Liberty is dedicated
- *1889-Hans Barstead picked buffalo bones for $14.00 per ton, picked a ton a day
- 1891-Carnegie Hall opens
- 1898-The Spanish-American War breaks out
- 1921-Last Morgan Silver Dollar is minted."

Charley stopped speaking and took another sip out of his water bottle. "I hope that helps you Missy. Many people need an understanding of how fast this country expanded and what was happening all around different areas. The timeline really helps them place things in perspective. I hope you enjoy your tour around the fort. Feel free to stop back if you have more questions and I'll try and answer them." He smiled and offered her his hand again.

Missy shook his hand, turning she walked out on the

porch and decided to take a quick walk around the graveyard and see if any markers identified were George Grinnell. She checked her watch and then looked at the sun since she had another two hours to drive to get back to the ranch. Not seeing any markers with his name on it she decided to take her brother's family here and see what they could find out next month. She headed to the parking lot and got into the truck. As she headed out both the radio and air conditioner were on high for her own comfort.

Pulling into the ranch yard always brought a feeling of homecoming and comfort to Missy. The wide porch with rockers that were covered with pillows seemed to beckon to come and sit and visit, the house was beginning to shine with the new coat of paint on the second story and around the screens. They would soon be replaced with newly painted storm windows in just a few months, but now the house looked ready for summer warmth and welcome visits. Missy slowly rubbed her neck and stretched her arms around her neck and shoulder as she slowly rubbed away the kinks from driving without a stop.

She knew the coffee might be cool, but she was ready for either hot or iced coffee when she would step into that kitchen of the old home place. As she carried her duffel bag up the steps and opened with door she was met with a delightful and unexpected smell of peanut butter cookies coming from the kitchen and the not so unexpected sound of her father snoring in his chair off to the right. She headed up the stairs to get her bag into her bedroom first and to wash up before they realized she was here.

As she washed she heard the screen door slam and heard Nylee's voice as she pounded up the stair, "Missy, you're back! Where are you?"

Missy opened the bathroom door with her foot as she continued to wash her face, neck, and arms off. "Hey, Squirt, you're loud enough to wake the dead in the next country! I'm in here washing up. Where is everyone?" Nylee stood at the door with a huge grin on her sunburned face and waited for Missy to finish before she launched into all the information she had to share.

"You know Gramps is sort of doing better since we got here. Isn't that just kind of weird and wonderful? And you know what else? That calf that I named Myrtle isn't a Myrtle at all, he's a Melvin, and Grampa said he thinks we should keep him as a bull as new stock. I'm even teaching him how to follow me with a halter to show in 4H at the fair. And diving lessons are really great, except that dork that rescued me and our luggage is taking them too. He's nice, but sorta weird; he just stood and stared at me in my two piece at the pool the first day of lessons. I guess he's alright though. We were in town getting groceries and he bought me a shake so I'm not gonna complain too much. But I guess I need to ask how you've been and how Uncle Chuck is, don't I?"

She finally had to pause to breath and Missy had finished wiping her face, neck and arms with a hand towel and stepped out into the hallway and grabbed her niece in a big hug. "Boy I forgot how chatty you are when you want to be. It's good to be back, Chuck is fine, I have research to share, and I'll be headed back in two weeks. Now tell me who in the world is making cookies! I'm famished!"

Arm-in-arm the two headed down the back stairs to the kitchen to snatch fresh cookies along with some iced tea that was waiting for them, courtesy of Babs.

Chapter Twenty-Four
Strawberry Moon

Lovely blue skies filled with wind swept clouds that looked like mare's tails greeted every morning sunrise that spring. Oat and wheat fields were planted and the fresh crop of calves that had been born were growing and promised a great cash flow later in the season. Wild berries were growing in the draws along the river and the sweet smell of earth drying greeted everyone when they would step outside. George and Josephine had four children living in the ranch house with them that spring; George, John, Charlie and the baby Ellen. The three boys bunked in the loft and the baby slept in the cradle on the floor in the main bedroom downstairs. Josephine was delighted in all of her children and was content that her last birth had given her the daughter she had hoped for.

That morning saw George headed out before the sunrise; Josephine was feeding the children in the kitchen and busy preparing fresh bread dough for lunch to have with bacon and beans. They had butchered a hog the month before and the bacon had been smoked in the smoke house and was still fresh. She gave no thought to where George had gone and imagined he would show up sooner or later that day.

The children were dressed in light jackets and the boys were sent out to play in the yard when Josephine rested with Ellen on her lap on the porch. The hired men came by and would tip their hats respectfully as they were busy with chores. Josephine decided that today would be a good day since on one appeared to be in a bad mood. Two years ago, on a morning almost like this one, two visitors had arrived from the Hampton Institute to check on her.

They reported back to the Administrators the following and in 1885, a report on the progress of Josephine's life was received at Hampton Institute.:

"Christian marriage. Visitors report a nice house, marble-topped furniture-two boys, civilized living."

Nothing in the report mentioned the Road House George operated, or the fact that he sat beside her in the kitchen with the two boys, George and John, on his lap and held them tightly around the legs in case they decided to misbehave.

Gray gumbo clouds flew up around the wheels later that afternoon when George pulled into the yard with a team of green broke horses pulling a wagon. He drove around the ranch house three times yipping at the top of his lungs. Josephine finally stepped out on the porch with the boys and remarked to Hans Barstad who had stopped his mount and moved out of the way. "Here comes my grandfather, drunk as usual."

Barstad told Josephine, "Maybe if you greet him with a

hug, it will soften him up and he'll be nicer." Josephine decided to follow his suggestion when George finally came back to the house from the barn. As soon as he stepped into the kitchen Josephine stepped up to him and gave him a hug and said, "Welcome home George."

George looked at her with a strange look on her face and replied, "Josephine, are you feeling ill?"

"No, Barstad told me to do it." Grinnell turned to Barstad who was watching into the kitchen from the open door. George glowered at him and slammed the door shut. Barstad hoped his idea would not turn into a beating for Josephine later on that day. Other news would interrupt George's anger for a while the next morning as news of a neighbor's death would start him celebrating with his men at The Blind Pig.

Frank Fleming, brother-in-law of Josephine and George, had been involved in another partnership after he and Mary were wed and this included a joint claim to a quarter section of land. Frank was a difficult man to get along with and when the partnership didn't work out with John Jones, a neighboring settler, they decided to split their interests over the land. This ended up in a quarrel and they were trying to settle the matter. The bad feelings between John and Frank ran deep from these two men who used to be partners.

May 6, 1888 was a Sunday and a beautiful spring day. The breeze from the West was blowing in smells of dry soil ready for planting crops. The sky was a stunning blue with a few wispy clouds called 'Mares Tails' that looked exactly like a horse's tail when blown by the wind. Frank woke up that morning in a fine mood until Mary told him she had heard

Grinnell's hands talking about him at the Post Office in Tobacco Garden. That Sunday morning Frank headed out for Jones' cabin with the intention of ending the argument with his fists. He didn't hurry at all but enjoyed the ride over J. Jone's cabin. When he got there he shouted to the house; "Hello the house I'm here." And then he announced from his saddle; "I've come over here to whip you."

Jones was a slight and slender man and not one to get involved in fights at all. He avoided arguments whenever he could and he wanted no part of a fist fight with the larger and stronger Fleming. Jones, like all settlers, had a loaded shotgun beside his cabin door, prepared for any wild animals or thieves. He announced to Frank from the doorway of his cabin. "You get off that horse, I'll kill you!"

Jones reached up and took down his double-barreled shotgun loaded with buckshot and pointed it at Frank. He cocked the trigger and prepared to defend himself and his homestead from a larger and stronger bully.

Frank thought it was a bluff and slid down from the saddle and dropped the reins and headed toward John. John fired twice and at that close range the charge caught Frank in the neck and shoulder. Killing him instantly with his back hitting the ground before his feet came down. The dust swirled around Frank's head and body and slowly turned a brownish red as the fatal wounds bled out onto the prairie.

Jones panicked and saddled his horse quickly and fled over to The Blind Pig for a drink. He was looking for someone to sell out to so he could hurriedly sell his horses, cattle and land to anyone in the road house. After one stiff drink he headed to the Post Office to find Grinnell. When he told George of the shooting George slapped him on the back and said "Good shooting! That's the best news I've heard all day! Let's go have a drink to celebrate."

The two men headed to the road house and toasted the death of their common enemy. George helped John figure out a way to get out of the country fast as they continued drinking into the afternoon. Who John finally sold out to was a mystery until later that spring.

Grinnell's hired men got word of the shooting and stopped working. They saddled up and rounded up some of Frank's neighbors. As they approached Jones' cabin they saw Frank lying in the doorway of the cabin where John had left him lying. Two of the men grabbed shovels and two more went into Jones' cabin to retrieve two blankets to wrap the body in.

That perfect prairie breeze soon turned cool as storm clouds gathered in the West and seemed to swirl with moaning sighs as the men dug into the sod and prepared to bury Frank on a little hill behind the cabin that now belonged to someone else. They used a piece of rope and tied two sticks together to form a small cross. The four men rolled the body covered in blankets into the hole and covered him in the soil. They tapped the cross at his head into the ground, got on their horses and rode over to let Mary know what had happened to her husband and where they buried him.

Josephine found out about Franks murder later on in the day when one of the hands approached the house to let her know what had happened. They told here where they had buried Frank and that they had ridden over to let Mary know.

Josephine began to keen and moan in the tribal way of mourning for the loss of her sister's husband. Sobbing she moaned, "Oh, poor Frank, and poor Mary!"

George had come in for supper and was already drunk when he heard Josephine wailing and grunted, "It was good enough for him!" His stern look reminded her that she was close to a lodge poling so she moved away with the children to outside the ranch house until George left. Josephine had made biscuits and stew that night so George ate alone in the kitchen and then left.

Grinnell kept on drinking that day and somehow managed to help Jones get away on a fast horse with money. Jones left in the dark of night with only the stars to guide him, no one bothered to search for him or stop him and he was never heard from again.

Josephine now had her younger sister to worry about since Mary had just become a widow. The next morning May 7, 1888 dawned clear and bright, a perfect day for some planting and rounding up the new calf crop. The day began like most of the other days since Josephine and George had children. The children were growing fast and the youngest, a toddler named Ellen, was the daughter Josephine felt blessed to have.

George, on the opposite side of the fence about his children felt frustrated with all of them. George would often accuse Josephine of sleeping with other men and called his own children, "that squaw's brats".

Josephine had already fed Ellen and was spooning oatmeal into bowls for their sons: George, John, and Charley when

George strolled into the kitchen area and casually laid his bullwhip on the table next to his oldest son.

The children shivered since all of them from an early age and felt the sting of the whip across their backside until their Mother intervened and George would turn his wrath on her. The only one he spared was the baby. But now that she was trying to walk the boys and Josephine feared for her as well.

The boys silently continued to eat their oatmeal without looking up and saying "Good Morning" to their Father. George picked up a cup and tried to pour himself coffee but his hand was shaking so badly from the day before he couldn't even pour anything into the cup. He slammed the pot back onto the range and the cup and headed out the door as he went for the hair of the dog back at the road house.

As the sun rose higher in the sky George continued to drink in the road house. A younger man, Ole Thorson, approached The Blind Pig from the North West and tied his roan at the post. As he slid down from the saddle he dusted off his shirt, hat and pants and strolled into the road house. He walked up and asked the bar keep for a beer and as he took a gulp he asked where he could find the owner George since he was looking for a job.

Ole was a hard-working Swede whose father owned a spread across Holes in Water. Ole had been born and raised on that ranch and dearly loved this country. He was the boy who had reported about Red Mike to his father and now he was ready to add to the family funds. George recognized him from both sides of the river and knew he would work hard for him so he hired him on the spot. As Ole and George saluted each other with a beer mug and a shot glass they toasted his new job. The clouds continued to gather in the West and the gentle prairie breeze once again began to moan as the clouds grew darker gray. What Ole didn't know then was that by that afternoon he would be without a boss.

Another local rancher, Hans Barstad, stopped by the post office to check on his mail about an hour later. He tried to talk to a thoroughly drunk George who was standing outside The Blind Pig, weaving back and forth. He was so drunk he could barely stand. Hans had George lean on him where he led George to the house with two of his hired men and got him into bed where they believed he would fall asleep. George had no intention of staying in bed when he was woken up by Josephine's keening sobs over Frank.

George got out of bed and stumbled into the kitchen and picked up his bullwhip from that morning still on the table where he left it. Josephine grabbed the children and left the house when she heard George getting out of bed. She knew George was very drunk and very angry at her for mourning Frank's death. George tried to catch her, but he was so drunk he could barely walk. A saddled horse that was rein drop trained was dozing near the porch and George awkwardly clambered aboard and set out in pursuit of his wife and children.

Not far from the house one of the hired men was plowing. The mother and her four children ran toward him seeking protection. As Grinnell caught up with them she dodged between the team of horses. With the drunken rider swearing and the hysterical and they hysterical family weeping and screaming there was such turmoil that the horses went out of control and reared. George's horse was nervous and started bucking so George rode a short distance away.

As soon as the hired hand, Robinson, settled the horses down he said, "Ma'am, I think you and those young'uns' would be better off locked up in the house until George there sobers up." He persuaded Josephine to lock herself in the house for safety until George sobered up. As she and the children fled for the house George again galloped after her as he swayed in the saddle.

George rode his wife down and the horse knocked Josephine to the ground as they baby went sprawling out of her hands. Repeatedly George slashed with his whip at Josephine as he leaned far off his horse he swung to strike her again. As she fought for her life Josephine threw up her hand to ward off the blows and caught hold of the leather and hair watch guard that George wore around his neck.

With strength born of desperation she pulled as hard as she could, the horse shied away from her and George tumbled out of the saddle on the opposite side as Josephine hung on. The sliding knot on the watch chain tightened around his throat and Josephine hung on as long as she felt his struggles. When movement stopped she relaxed her hold and George slumped to the ground, dead.

Robinson and another hired man, M. Egan reached Josephine's side. "Is he dead?" she spoke to Robinson.

Robinson looked at the livid red face with the tongue sticking out, blank eyes protruding from their sockets and felt for a pulse. Standing up he turned to Josephine and said, "Yes, he is."

No one spoke for a while and finally one man said, "Let's go get a drink." They left the body where it lay in the field and Josephine gathered up the crying baby and the three boys and headed for the house. The men returned after they had swilled down a few drinks and picked up the body and brought it in, stripped the boots and watch guard from George's body and propped it up on a chair in a corner. They toasted the late George W. Grinnell, dead at the age of 48.

That night the hired men, together with some drifters and outlaws in the area threw a party in the cottonwood slab roadhouse as a wake. It was a tradition in those days that a host drinks with his guests. In an effort to keep tradition alive, the men poured a drink on George's head every third round.

The next morning three men from Williston arrived to investigate the death, everyone spoke that George was well preserved when they arrived. Many of Grinnell's personal effect and some of his clothing had disappeared by that time. The three men loaded his body into a wagon, covered him with a cotton tarp and set out for Williston.

When Hans Barstad heard the news he wondered how anyone as drunk as Grinnell was could have possibly got on the horse in the first place. He really believed that he was in bed to stay when they put him there.

That night at Bob Matthews' place in Little Muddy after viewing where the body had been buried, the coroner ruled that first of all no inquest was needed in the death of Frank

Fleming since Jones had left the country. The neighbors he spoke to felt the homicide was justifiable as well. An inquest into George's fate would be held later on in Williston with Josephine being required to be there in order to be interviewed concerning his death.

Chapter Twenty-Five
Return Dive

Flying by the two weeks back at the home place went quickly with checking fences, painting, rounding up and branding the new calf crop, planting a vegetable garden, and finishing the windows and starting the barn upgrades. Missy was delighted and amazed that even Babs seemed more relaxed around the home place. Frowning less, laughing more, and even stopped chewing her fingernails; all were signs for Missy that she was fitting into this rhythm of life. She hoped it would continue as the days got shorter and cooler before deep winter set in.

The twins were both growing as well, Nylee and Marlow now wore golden tans. Lean built when he came to the ranch Marlow was developing broad shoulders and a rangy rider build that was certain to make the local girls give him a second and third look. Nylee was still a beauty who wore little makeup to enhance that healthy tan look. She had developed muscles, but they were leaned and whipcord strong. Missy watched her wrestle a calf to the ground as she helped with the branding, sprayed and back to his bawling mother.

When a younger brother like Jeth it was pure delight for

Missy to see how his face had gone from worry lines to smile lines. Lovingly teasing the others in the house happened daily courtesy of Jeth, he even included Mort in the gentle teasing to make their aging and ill father a part of the giggle fests. One part of Missy was sad to know that she would soon head back to the construction site, and the other part was delighted.

She had contacted the Hospice nurse to arrange for someone to spell Marian when Jeth, Babs, Nylee and Marlow would head over for their week-long adventure. Mort would not be left alone, much to his dismay. Missy had no way of knowing that he had already asked Marian to stay with him since he felt his house was hers. Marian had said yes and they figured the two of them would have the Hospice nurse come in when Marian wanted to shop or go home and feed her cats.

Neither Mort nor Marian planned on letting Missy know about this arrangement since they wanted no worries when the family went out camping and diving for a week. They also wanted no unexplained finds so Mort had called the Historical Society in Bismarck to arrange for an archeologist to show up on site in case something was recovered. He made sure the man was dive certified and would bring his own gear and camper to the site to assist in their exploration. The next day after supper when everyone went to the porch with coffee in hand to sit and talk about the events of the day and the plan for the next day Mort planned on giving the information to his kids. Missy would leave in three days so he wanted no stone left unturned when she left.

The conversation started simply with Marian seated in the

rocker next to Mort and after taking a noisy sip of coffee and releasing the little happy 'ahhh' sound from a satisfied sip he set his cup on the porch floor and simply picked up Marian's hand and gently held it in his gnarled and weathered larger hand. "Marian and I have been doing a little research about the dive over at Tobacco Garden area. We have some information to share about what we found and how we can help with the search for any items you find."

Mort turned to Marian as he released her hand so she could dig out the folded papers she had tucked into her front jeans pocket. She cleared her throat and started to read from the paper.

"According to the Archeological Resources Protection Act of 1979 it tells us about any treasure hunting done on public land and it says; 'archeological resources found on these lands belongs to the government. This law has been extended to just about anything over 100 years old." So, the way I figure it if you find treasure you are legally obligated to take it to the police. It goes into their custody and is handled like any other case of lost property. Except in 2017 the U.S. Gold Bureau posted this information; "Exactly how old an object must be to be considered treasure is unclear, but court rulings have defined it as both after a point that the original owner is unlikely to claim it or after at least a few decades (in 1991 an Iowa court ruled that 35 to 59 years should be sufficient). We also found that the Antiquities Act of 1906 basically says that the superior claim goes to the finder except for a 'treasure trove'. A treasure trove is stated as being gold, silver, gems, money or jewelry and it reverts to the finder immediately if the owner is not known. Now the government is always wanting a piece of any extra funds they can get their hands on so they also have a 'Reservoir Salvage Act of 1960 and that says 'a historically valuable shipwreck can be treated as an archaeological or historical site instead of a commercial property. The term they use as embedded means submerged in the states submerged lands that belong to the State under the embeddedness doctrine." Marian cleared her throat and lifted her cup of cooling coffee to her lips and waited patiently for Mort to continue with the rest of the important information.

"Marian and I decided after reading all this information that when you find something you can be sure the lawyers and the government will come with their hands out. We figured the smartest way to handle this was to involve the Historical Society and get ahold of a certified archeologist that could dive so we can get some protection under the law for our work. Maybe even get a rightful share of the finder's share. We have talked to Alfred Fairland about this and he has a camper, his own boat, is a certified diver and will be assisting you in recording any items you uncover. I'll always be your Dad and Grandpa and we; Marian and I love you dearly. We don't want any trouble happening when you dive and this way we can cover ourselves six ways to Sunday." Mort's gravelly voice paused and he bent down to have another sip from his cold coffee.

Jeth started out, "Dad, you two have really gone to a great deal of trouble with researching all of this. We're sorry to have you worry about us since you have your own worries." Mort just waved his hand as if to say 'enough', but Jeth continued. "You know we love you and I'm looking forward to the dive and a little time away with the kids for some fun. Maybe I should just stay behind with you instead."

Mort snorted into his cup and as quickly as his aching bones would allow he set the cup down. "Listen here young man, I'm still your dad and I'll have you know..." his tirade of letting his son know how he wanted the dive to go stopped as Nylee's giggles turned into a full-blown laugh.

"Oh Gramps, you are just perfect! Imagine calling Dad a 'young man' I love your humor and how you always try to take care of all of us and protect us." She got up from her chair and embraced her Grandfather from the back of the chair and wrapped loving arms around him. She then went to Marian and did the same for her; Marian and Mort wiped the tears away from the corners of their eyes at this unexpected and welcomed show of love.

Marian simply said, "Thank you dear for blessing me with your hug and that wonderful laugh of yours. We both certainly feel blessed to be caring for you as much as you care for us."

Mort lifted his hand and patted her shoulder and said, "We surely do."

Jeth, Babs and Marlow all stood and went and embraced the older couple as well and murmured words of kindness, love, and thanks for all they felt blessed by being there. Marian was the one who broke up the party by throwing her cold coffee over the porch railing onto the bushes and doing the same with Mort's cup she declared; "Time for this old hen to head home again and feed her cats. Time for you to head to bed and get out of the cooling air" she said to Mort as she patted his shoulder in farewell. "I'll see you all in the morning and we'll talk about the hospice nurse tomorrow, I feel like we've shared enough for today." She handed the empty cups to Babs, gave her a quick hug, dug her keys out of her pocket and stepped down the steps to her waiting pick-up. She honked as she turned before turning on the headlights so she wouldn't blind them on the porch.

As promised the next day at lunch Mort and Marian shared the plan about the Hospice nurse that was a younger friend of Marian's. They also let the family know that Mort was moving his bedroom down to the office area and that Marian would be staying here with him. No one questioned their plan because it was so well laid out and thought out for Mort's comfort and for including Marian in his care. It occurred to both Jeth and Missy as they headed out to the barn just how much love their father had given to them over the years. It wasn't deeply spoken of beyond a few words but was deeply felt by both.

As Missy helped pound nails into the garage addition on to the side of the barn she thought deeply about how much she would miss her father when the natural end occurred with this disease, she also thought about the townhouse that she and Chuck owned further west of here and their plan as they aged and their children and grandchildren grew. The breeze kicked up later in the afternoon lifting her sweaty curls off her neck as she continued to pound nails into the sheets of plywood siding on the garage. This would soon be covered in an insulated siding that wouldn't need paint. This addition to the pole barn would provide parking space for at least four vehicles in the winter months and allow an area for vehicles to be repaired when the weather was warmer.

The metal roofing on the garage area was brighter than the faded metal on the barn, but the colors matched and after a few years of prairie sun and wind would blend together nicely. Tomorrow before Missy left the Olsen family; George, his wife Hilde and their son Bart, were coming over to help finish up with the siding and installing the garage doors. They would have a pitchfork barbeque and other neighbors had been invited to come and eat even if they couldn't lend a hand. The way of western friendship and sharing what you had continued to this day. Missy would leave right after helping with the pitchfork barbeque and eating some 'bull'. She smiled when she thought about Bart who had become a friend to both Nylee and Marlow. He had proven to be a blessing since he introduced them to other farm and ranch kids who they would go to school with in the fall. Missy knew a crowd of friends who would show up bringing their own specialty dishes to share at the Pitchfork barbeque so she needed to get coolers loaded with both kid friendly drinks and adult beverages.

The new from the store pitchforks had to be scrubbed to get any trace of machine oil off them before they would barbeque hunks of meat over the coals on them. There was plenty to do and that included setting out the newly painted picnic tables, getting the umbrellas up for shade and making sure the grass clippings from the side yard had been picked up. Between Babs, Nylee, and Marian they managed to set everything up before the sun started to dip. The badminton net was set up in the side yard for those who wanted to beat the volleyball or badminton shuttles around; horseshoe pit was ready and had been raked. Coolers would be filled with ice and drinks tomorrow, but had already been labeled; KIDS and GROWNUPS. Babs stood on the porch and looked out toward the barn to see how the roof was going; she said quietly, "I don't think all these chairs and tables will be full tomorrow."

Missy just smiled and said as she walked past her, "Prepare to be surprised. We probably will need more; I just hope some folks bring lawn chairs too."

The next day dawned clear with a bright blue sky streaked with shades of orange and yellow and no chance of rain in the forecast for miles around. Missy had overslept and when she woke up she heard saws, hammers and drills already in motion. She wasted no time in throwing her clean clothes in a duffel bag then hastily dressing in her usual jeans and button-down denim shirt. As she took the back stairs down two at a time she smelled coffee and caramel rolls and the sweet smell of bread rising waiting for a turn in the oven.

"Grabbing a warm roll and sipping her coffee right by the sink she hadn't asked who made them since she recognized Babs's recipe by taste alone. Babs showed up moments later with containers of frozen cookies from the freezer in the basement. "Do the rolls taste alright Missy?" she asked and she set the containers that held over four dozen cookies in each on the counter. "I used the same recipe your Mother gave me years ago. It felt like she was right here with me when I was making them. I just hope the others like them."

Not wanting to talk with her mouth full of gooey goodness Missy just raised her cup, smiled and tried to say 'yum', it sounded more like 'mmm' to her ears, but the smile on her face when Babs turned and looked at her said it all. Babs just nodded and smiled back and reached for a roll after pouring a cup of coffee for herself. "Great idea before more show up. Do you know there are already six men and boys out there working?"

Missy waited before speaking until the last bite of warm caramel roll was safely tucked away inside her stomach; she took a sip of cooling coffee and finally said, "I'm not surprised at all really, the folks are well known around here. Most, if they can will be here to help and then eat with us. It was a great idea to make these rolls for them. I'm going to get the big pot and make fresh coffee and take it down in the wagon with a cooler filled with water. You want to separate the rolls and wrap them in parchment paper so they can eat them quicker when they need a little break? I'll take all of it down in the wagon and you can help me and say hello. Does that sound good to you?"

Babs said, "You think they know how stupid I've been? Will they be mean to me or like me? Should I take cookies down in case some don't like rolls? What do you think I should do? Do they need napkins then to wipe their hands off?" Finally, she stopped talking and paused to let Missy respond.

Missy said, "You'll be fine, no one in the family has said a word about you at all. They are happy you and Jeth and the kids are back here helping Dad. The cookies are a great idea; napkins can always be used. You really did a terrific job on these rolls and the men and boys working will love them I guarantee it." Missy gave her worried sister-in-law a quick hug and headed down to the basement for two cases of water to place in coolers labeled "WATER ONLY". She was up and down the steps a few more times as she took the large coffee urn up, filled it, lowered the basket with coffee grounds into the water, capped it and plugged it in to get ready for the trip down to the barn.

Babs helped her load the two coolers filled with ice and water bottles into the wagon and they pulled it down by the barn. They helped themselves to a plank of plywood and set that up on top of two saw horses. Babs had taken a container of cookies and popped the corner of the lid off and set the napkins beside it and placed a rock on top of them to keep them in place. They took the coolers out of the wagon and placed them in the shade under their plywood table top and headed back up to the house for the next load of wrapped caramel rolls, hot coffee, cups, and milk and sugar for those who wanted it. When they entered the kitchen Nylee was there with Mort and they were both eating caramel rolls and having coffee and giggling over some silly story Mort was telling her. Missy said, "Oh good! When you're done eating Nylee you can help put rolls for the men outside into parchment paper sacks and get the coffee cups out from the top shelf in the pantry.

"Oh, ok Missy, sorry Gramps and I didn't even hear you two come in. He was just telling me a story about how Grandma fell in a hole one time when they were coming home from a party and was full of mud. She was wet from her rear end to the top of her head with mud. Gramps and I were just laughing about how the term 'mad as a wet hen' fit her just perfectly that day. I'll help out as soon as I finish my roll and coffee." Nylee was slowly turning from a snarly teen into a beautiful young woman and the relationship with her grandfather was clearly helping her along as well.

The day picked up pace and went from an easy busy to a full-blown cyclone of activity in the house, outside by the barn, in the yard, and on the porch. Mort would frequently try to get away from his neighbors by saying "I think I need to take a break and get a nap." That would work for about thirty minutes until someone else would say; "Hey Mort, thought I'd take a break from hammering and come visit a spell." By mid-morning the coals were ready and Missy tied on her canvas apron and went to work on barbecuing meat ahead of schedule. Once the large chunks were cooked they were sliced and placed in a crockpot with sauce for sandwiches at lunch. The salads were already out sitting in pans filled with ice, along with fresh buns, chips, cookies, brownies, pies, watermelon and other fresh fruit. Directly at noon with the sun shining brightly down on them, Missy stepped out on the porch and rang the bell for them to stop work and come eat and then rest before putting the finishing touches on the garage.

She placed her hands on Mort's shoulders as she stood

behind him on one side and her brother stood on the other side. "Folks, I'd sure like to thank you for coming and helping with this little project today. We certainly couldn't have done this without your blessings as being our great neighbors. And now Reverend Huston, I see you standing there waiting. I'd like you to say grace for us here and give us a blessing before we eat." Her father removed his hat as did all the men. They stood as one family, the women quieted the children and they bowed their heads as one, folded their hands, and listened to the Reverend give his blessing to the food and to them.

Then the noise started as people began loading their plates and working their way down the line of amazing food. Mort sat in the shade and ate some of the beef he had provided along with a wonderful potato salad made by Hilde Olsen. He saluted her with a big forkful of it before he placed the large bite in his mouth. Missy had eaten a sandwich while standing and checking on the coolers to make sure they were being kept full.

She had given herself an hour to do this as she continued to help and also was loading her duffels into the back of her suburban to head back to Chuck for a week alone before her brother and his family would come to visit, fish, swim and dive with them. And of course, a week before A. Fairland, PHD showed up to inspect what they were doing. She made her rounds saying her goodbyes to good friends and neighbors and saved her dad and Marian for last.

Bending down to hug her dad, she promised she would 'drive carefully and arrive in one piece' and that yes, she had taken some buns, barbequed beef, and other items in her cooler to share with Chuck for supper that night. She hugged Marian tightly and whispered to her, "Don't let him get too bossy with you. Make him go in when he starts to get tired."

Marian responded with her usual smile and said saucily, "Yes Mother, I promise I'll be good. You make sure you are as well girl."

Missy headed back and honked and waved as she left making sure she kicked up no dust and gravel to pepper the food with. She had a feeling Chuck would be feeling slightly less horny than he was the last time since it had been less than a month like last time she had returned.

Chapter Twenty-Six
Thunder Moon

The men were assembled in a long narrow room, some seated on chairs and some standing along the outside walls. The windows were open at the top to let the breeze blow though, since most of the bodies standing shoulder to shoulder were unwashed like the clothes they wore. The sweaty smell would have been more like a barn if they hadn't bothered to scrap the mud and offal from their boots before coming into the inquest room. A few pictures hung on the walls, the small carpet had been rolled up and some chairs from the kitchen had been moved out into the parlor to make room for more men to be seated.

The coroner, George Carpenter, was in charge and pounded with a stick on the cloth covered wooden table at the front of the room, "I'll have it quiet in here now." They were holding the coroner's jury inquest at the home of John Heffernan in Williston. The parlor at the front of the house was long and narrow and could seat almost ten people if all the chairs in the house were used. Mrs. Heffernan stayed in the kitchen with Josephine until they called her into the parlor room to testify. She had kept two chairs in the kitchen so she could sit when needed and Josephine's youngest boy Charley had a place to sit at the table and eat the cookie she had given him with a fresh glass of milk. Josephine had brought her two youngest children with her and left the older two boys with her sister Mary.

The two women talked while Josephine nursed Ellen as she sat at the table. Keeping their voices at whisper level so they could hear when Mr. Carpenter came to get Josephine to testify. Mrs. Heffernan asked about the older boys and how they were doing; "Are both George and John going to be okay out at Mary's place?" she knew that Mary was a widow now and she thought about the power that Josephine and Mary would need raising their children almost alone. What Mrs. Heffernan was not aware of was the impact of the tribe the two women belonged to and how the elders would help raise their boys into men.

Josephine smiled and responded, "We will do well with the boys and my beautiful daughter Ellen. All will be fine with help from the church."

They heard George speak again, "This is the inquest about the death of a Civil War Veteran so I expect you all to show proper respect here." With that the slender man with the graying beard sat down in one of the few chairs in the room and cleared his throat as he started to read aloud about the condition of the body to the assembled group.

"The victim's name is George Grinnell; age when deceased was 48 years on May 7, 1888 between the hours of 1:00-2:00 p.m. He was strangled to death by a leather and hair watch chain he was often seen wearing around his neck. We will be taking testimony from his widow, Mrs. Josephine Grinnell, who was present at this time. She is currently waiting to come forward and has brought two of her four children with her, one an infant daughter by the name of Ellen. I'll go to the kitchen and escort her out here. You men in the jury can ask any questions after she tells her story about what happened. No interrupting her until she is done telling her side. I'll ask you if anyone needs to ask her questions. Are we clear about this gentleman?"

When all heads nodded form the Coroner's Inquest Jury as a yes, Mr. Carpenter stood and pushing a man by the shoulder as he said, "She'll need a chair to sit in." he moved the chair in front of the table facing the jury members who were seated along the outside wall. They would have a good look at her face that way and Mr. Carpenter shuddered as he thought about what he had seen just yesterday when he went to the ranch to escort her into town. Badly bruised and her face with scars told of a story of multiple beatings and Mr. Carpenter knew they would hear more.

He headed into the kitchen and saw Mrs. Heffernan holding baby Ellen and the little boy, who he thought was Charley, sitting at the table eating a cookie and having a glass of milk. Josephine was just washing her hands and when she turned towards him he quickly glanced at the floor. The sight of her battered face made him want to punch someone, the woman had been battered repeatedly and the light from the window showed the scars inflicted from the past.

He calmly said, "Mrs. Grinnell, we are ready to hear about what happened. I'll escort you in Ma'am." Taking her arm into the crook of his he pushed open the door into the parlor to lead her in. The murmuring didn't start until the men in the room saw her face in the light after she was seated. Once Mr. Carpenter took his seat he pounded the stick on the table and Josephine flinched at the noise. "I need to have it quiet in here now. Mrs. Grinnell is going to tell us what happened on May 7 between 1:00-2:00 in the afternoon out at their place."

Josephine told the Coroner's Jury her story about when George had started beating her. Three weeks into the marriage was when she first reported that he struck her with his whip. According to the county records she also told that he had whipped her often and three times attempted to cut her with a knife. Grinnell had broken her nose nine times and once blinded her for seven months from his poundings.

"He run over me the last time with the horse. That's what make my body sore," she told the jury. At one time I stood in a creek for two days, standing up to my neck in water to get away from him," she continued. "I left home lots of times and once walked barefooted for miles while he followed me with a rifle."

Finally, she told of the final tragic day where she killed her husband. The trouble had started two days before with the murder of her sister Mary's husband, Frank Flemin. She was mourning for her sister and her deceased brother-in- which was George's enemy. George had celebrated with his hired men the day before and started drinking early that morning again. At dinner time he threatened her again if she continued to mourn. She grabbed the baby up in her arms and ran toward the field where Joe Robinson was plowing as she screamed for help.

Grinnell followed her on horseback and pulled his revolver, she ran between the two horses that were plowing holding the crying baby and screaming hysterically herself. The normally calm plow horses were not used to such noise. They started to buck and rear up so Robinson told her to take the kids back to the house and lock themselves in until George sobered up. She went around the horses and headed toward the house. Grinnell had ridden away from the plowing and when he saw her making a run for the house he took out after her. George pulled out a revolver and slugged her in the head. At this point in the testimony Josephine touched the side of her black and blue face and said, "I fell to the ground and the baby fell beside me."

Her testimony continued; "George came at me with the horse and I reached my hand up to stop him from running me over. I grabbed onto the leather-hair watch chain and held it. This chain went around his neck through a gold slide and fastened to his watch. He was drunk and leaned over in the saddle to strike me with his riding quirt and he fell off the other side. I held onto the chain until I didn't feel anything. I took the children to the house and locked the door."

The room went quiet and still as the men on the coroner's inquest jury stared at their boots. Some would bravely look up at Josephine's face and then glance back down at their boots as if both disgusted and saddened to look at her bruised and battered face. She had been a beautiful young woman once and now was carved in a steely countenance that showed both dignity and quiet power.

Mr. Carpenter broke the quiet by clearing his throat and then asked; "Any questions gentleman?" One man seated closest to the door raised his hand, "Yes, Mr. Linsen?"

"I would like to know when Mrs. Grinnell realized that Mr.

Grinnell was dead, if it's ok to ask her that George."

Turning to Josephine while he nodded yes to Mr. Linsen, he simply repeated the question; "Mrs. Grinnell when did you learn that your husband Mr. Grinnell was dead?"

She testified, "I didn't think I killed him, I tried to get along with him, but I couldn't. The men brought George back home about 5 o'clock and told me he was dead."

Josephine was escorted back into the kitchen where Mrs. Heffernan was waiting and holding baby Ellen. She smiled and said, "Josephine is it ok if I hold this angel a little bit longer? She is almost asleep in my arms. We can lay her down on the blankets closer to the side of the stove when she falls asleep." Josephine was so weary she simply nodded yes and laid her head down on the table and shut her eyes.

The man who was plowing, Mr. Joe Robinson, was called next to testify. After they swore him in and he was seated the men assembled in the room relaxed. They waited patiently as George asked him to tell what he had seen that day. Joe like to talk and spent time explaining how he had hitched up the two horses to the plow after George Grinnell had come out to the bunkhouse drinking from a bottle and called his name and said, "Git yer lazy ass out there and start plowing, we need those oats planted this week."

He told the jury that Grinnell was often drunk and had been on a bender that had started a few days before. "The boss liked his drink and women rough; he was ok when he was sober, but when he was liquored up, watch out! He had a riding quirt and he weren't a feared to use it when he'd get mad."

Mr. Linsen again raised his hand and said, "I'd like to know why he didn't have but socks, a shirt, and pants on when they brought him in. He sure smelled like whiskey as well. Do you know anything about that?"

Joe had a half smile on his face as he started another part of his story of that fateful day, "Well you know we all like to have a drink now and again. Well, some of the other men and me carried George's body to The Blind Pig and just set him on a chair in the corner and started having a wake to toast to his memory. Well, every third drink someone would pour a drink on George's head so he could enjoy it along with the rest of us. I guess at one point his hat was soaked through so someone took that off. Then his vest got soaked, and we were worried about his watch getting wet so that came off right after his vest. I guess the whiskey was pooling on the dirt floor around his boots so those came off next. Before we knew it we had drunk ourselves sober and the sun was rising. You fellows, (and he pointed at three members of the jury) came along with a wagon and a tarp around noon and found us still toasting George in the saloon. I guess that's about all I remember, until today of course."

Mr. Carpenter said, "Thanks Joe. I think that pretty well answers all the questions we have, does anyone else need to ask Joe something?" They all shook their heads as a collective no. Carpenter thumped his stick on the table and said, "You're excused Joe. You can go now, unless you're waiting to drive Mrs. Grinnell back with her children." Joe nodded and said, "Yup, I'm driving back with her. Can she go now to or should I just wait outside with the horses and wagon?"

Carpenter looked at him and said, "We'll come out and let

you know as soon as we're done here." Joe stood and lifted his hat to his head, nodded and went out the door.

Other members of the coroner's jury who had seen the body started talking amongst themselves. A jury member closed the door and they went into deliberation. After a short time, they wrote the verdict down:

"We, the coroner's jury, empaneled to inquire into the death of George W. Grinnell do find that he came to his death by an act of God, through His agent, Josephine. That George Grinnell came to his death on the 7th of May, 1888, between the hours of 1 and 2 o'clock p.m. by 'Act of God' aided and abetted by the hands of his wife, Josephine Grinnell." The jury went on to explain the verdict this way "George Grinnell was choked to death by his wife with the aid of a leather watch chain around his neck done accidentally in protecting her own life.

Years later when Buford Territory became part of the state the county officials went back into the records and removed the 'Act of God' statement, but still left Josephine acquitted of murdering her abusive husband. Josephine's troubles were not over at that time, she had much to do and learn over the next part of her life. George was buried with military honors and laid to rest in the military cemetery at Fort Buford.

Chapter Twenty-Seven
Water Rights

Swirls of dust surrounded the truck as she pulled into the campsite and she waited patiently for it to settle before cracking the window and opening the door to get out. She had arrived and thought about the upcoming meeting with Dr. Albert Fairland. Missy decided to keep her thoughts to herself about him and only discuss her ideas with Chuck. When she had talked to Chuck last night and told him about all the things her dad and Marian had lined up he had echoed her frustration over the entire situation.

"Apparently he is feeling better since he can't let us just have fun with this search. For Christ sakes honey, why didn't you just tell him to butt out?" Those exact words made her want to hang up the phone and not return today.

She just replied in kind, "You know I wouldn't dare speak to my dad like that. To tell you the truth I'm glad he felt well enough to want to be involved and try to protect us. Good grief Chuck, you know Dad meant this as protections for you and the company. Get off your high horse and realize what could we have done if we had found something anyway? If we sold it, we'd have to report it to the authorities. This way we'll have a rightful share of any items we uncover. Stop being a dumb ass, I'll see you tomorrow and I'll be there before Fairland shows up at the site. Apparently Dad told him the co-ordinates of where we're camped and he told Dad he would pull into the area mid-afternoon. I'll see you tomorrow, love you, hanging up now." As she ended the call without waiting to hear the response he always said, "Whatever happens remember I've always loved you Babe."

Missy climbed down from the driver's seat of the truck, the ground was dry and little swirls of gray dirt puffed around her boots as she headed with a load of food toward the trailer. She looked around and tried to imagine where Fairland would park his rig, depending on the size of it, and what was contained in it.

After Missy was done unloading the truck and making lunch she took a quick shower and changed into clean jeans, a button-down plaid shirt and her comfortable boots. Brushing her hair and braiding it she placed a baseball cap on her head and let the braid hang out the back of the hat. She felt ready to meet the Professor whenever he showed up. She had already decided to invite him in for lunch that first day and try to figure him out. She was really glad when Chuck showed up for lunch and they were able to eat together before the Professor arrived. They had time to talk things over between them. She was glad that Chuck had simmered down about the research her dad and Marian had done. When she explained all the time they had saved her on researching, he nodded and smiled at her, a good sign. Chuck stood up from the table and said, "I've got to head back Babe, we are really busy at the site today. Come here and let me give you some squeezes before I go." He reached for her and quickly unbuttoned the top three buttons of her shirt and nuzzled between her breasts. "Well tonight we'll have some time alone and then we can enjoy each other again." He turned and headed toward the door.

They both heard the noise of a motor pulling up into the area. Chuck swatted her on the rear and said, "Let's go meet this Prof and see what the dude is like. Maybe I'll have some fun with him."

Missy nodded and, winking at him said, "Just be nice, remember Dad has been talking to him for a while. I don't know what he is like, but hopefully he isn't arrogant. If he is I'll do my best to try and be polite, That's about all I can promise."

The motor home driven by the Professor pulled into the area, it was fully equipped for boon docking anywhere he went. A dark brown color with swirls of darker brown and red on the side. It contained a large holding tank for fresh water, a chemical toilet that he didn't need to have pumped, solar panels on the roof to provide electricity for heat and air conditioning as needed, and 4 slide outs that looked like contained more room in the living/kitchen area and expanded bedrooms. He sat in the driver's seat of the large motor home and proceeded to push buttons to level the motor home automatically. He was towing a jeep behind him and Chuck wondered if he needed help unhitching the vehicle. He didn't think so since this man looked prepared, at least from the outside appearances.

Professor Albert Fairland stepped down from his very large, very expensive motor home that contained his working field office, full satellite reception and most of the comforts of home when he was out on a dig. He was a non-descript man; neither large nor small, heavy nor thin with thick salt and pepper hair, clean shaven, leather tanned skin and thick bottle lens glasses. Chuck would come to find out soon that he was so self-absorbed in his own past success that he had forgotten the lessons of truly great minds, humility. He was dressed all in tan from his hat to his boots; the long-sleeved shirt was the thin material with UVF sunblock and looked like the fishing shirts Chuck himself wore. The hat had a large brim on it with a neck protector on the back and was only slightly darker than his shirt, pants and boots.

Making matters worse was the fact that he had not done his due diligence in this different portion of the West. His inflated ego was going to become a major stumbling block. Because of his work on his doctoral thesis in early pioneer building and trials traveled on he was considered an expert in the field. He had recently arrived in Dakota from the Southwest area of the country. After completing his research and being in charge of a major dig he had won national acclaim and attention. His co-workers in the capital city had only known Albert a few months and they were already happy to see him be placed at a dig site far away from where they worked on a daily basis. If a number had to be applied to the focus of his conversations it would be 98% about his work and his awards and the other 2% would be general small talk about the weather and any current funding others had received.

Immediately heading straight towards Chuck, the Professor held out his hand and with a firm grip, shook his hand and said, "Hello there, you must be the son-in-law Mort told me about. He said your name was Chuck, I hope I can call you that unless you prefer a different name?" The professor kept speaking and not waiting for an answer said, "You may call me Dr. Fairland or Professor, I really don't like to be called Albert since that was my father's name and I'm certainly not my father." Dropping Chuck's hand from his smaller hand he gave a little smirk meant to be a smile.

"That really was meant as a joke, you know." He quickly added when Chuck gave no response to him."

"Oh, I see that you have a sense of humor Professor, you'll certainly need it out here you know. I'm headed off to the work site; my wife will be out soon. You may call me Chuck if you prefer. It seems to have worked well for me all my life and works well for my crew and business partners." Chuck placed his hard hat on his head, smiled, nodded and turned to head towards the company truck. He shook his head as he left the yard making sure to spin his wheels when he went by the motor home to give it a good dusting of dirt and gravel.

He shook his head all the way back to the site as he thought of the obnoxious little man they would need to work with over the next month or so. It had Chuck thinking that it might be a blessing if nothing was found, he had a sense that he would lose the bet if he wagered on that thought. Oh well, at least the night would be theirs and he and Missy would enjoy themselves tonight. That thought chased away all thoughts of the dive, the Professor, and even work that afternoon. He was caught three times sitting in his truck and texting ideas to his wife at the camper about his plans for that evening. Each time when one of his men came to the truck they would have to tap on the window to get him to stop and answer the questions they had for him. His foreman finally said on the third time, "Just go back to the camper and bone the old lady and then come back with your head screwed on straight will you!"

The last comment surprised him only slightly, and he hoped none of the men had seen what he had sent his wife about his ideas. He relished the times of playing love games with her and didn't want anyone getting any ideas about how important she was to him. He reluctantly left the phone on the seat and got out to go see what the issue at the site was. He was in for a sweet surprise when he returned since Missy had responded to his last idea with a photo of her own in her maid outfit. Her lips were pouting, painted deep red, and she was sucking on her middle finger. The comment she sent was; "Oui Mousier, I hope you have something else to suck on." She followed that up with only one comment about Professor Fairland. "Our Prof is a self-absorbed little man. He's more interested in making more of a name for himself than anything else. I'll see you tonight, darling!"

Chuck would drive back to the campsite later that afternoon staring at the picture on his phone with his hormones raging. Part of him was delighted Missy had pegged the Professor right off the bat and it echoed his feelings entirely. He was in no mood for idle chit-chat with anyone other than his favorite "Kitty." As he spun gravel turning into the site there was the Professor on top of the motor home adjusting his satellite dish. He waved frantically for Chuck and yelled, "Could you help over here, Chuck?"

Chuck stayed on his side of the pickup and wanted to just go into the trailer and spend time with his wife, but good manners prevailed instead. "What seems to be the problem, Prof?" He left his hard hat on his head as he walked over to the large motor home.

Professor Fairland said, "I need someone to go inside and make sure the satellite signal is being received properly. Do you understand anything about these technical issues? Your wife, ah Missy, that is. She gave me permission to call her that, by the way. She said she had no idea how to set the dials and I was better off asking you when you got home. I do appreciate your help and please call me Professor if you will."

Chuck went into the motor home with a smile on his face. He knew what Missy had done since the Prof had probably come on to her and she had set him straight and left him to figure out his problem with setting the satellite dish himself. He decided right then to have some fun with dear old Prof. He set the co-ordinates perfectly, but they were all set backwards and read back to front instead of the correct order. He figured he would only need about half an hour to figure out what the problem was since he seemed to be struggling with doing the initial set up. That would give Missy and him time to eat alone and talk more about how to handle tomorrow's dive.

As they sat eating together and discussing the day Chuck finally asked, "Did the Prof put the moves on you? By the way, before you answer, you need to know he hates being called Prof and would prefer to be called 'Professor.' I wonder how many times he'll repeat that to me tomorrow on the dive?"

Missy finished chewing and swallowing her salad and finally answered, "Yes, he did. He didn't touch me at all but just gave me the eye-leering treatment and kindly offered his shower whenever I wanted a nice shower. I told him we were a fully equipped camper and we didn't need to use his. That's when I went back inside and locked the door and sent you that picture. It gave me a creepy feeling and I took a shower myself before I dressed up and sent you that picture. I thought it might make your day go faster. Did it work?"

Chuck started to unbutton his shirt and said, "Now, Kitty let's see how much it worked." No sooner was this said than a pounding started on their door and the Professor's voice outside was heard, "Say, Chuck and Missy, are you decent? May I come in?"

Chuck buttoned his shirt up and said, "Do we let him in?" Missy nodded yes and proceeded to clear the table to go wash up. Chuck got up and headed toward the door, saying, "Coming, Prof to let you in, hope everything is ok." Opening the door, Chuck said, "Come on in Prof, Missy will have coffee ready in a minute and I think we have some dessert tonight." Chuck turned to Missy as the Professor came inside. "Don't we have cookies or something Babe?"

Missy smiled from behind the counter and said, "Come on in and have a seat, Professor. Coffee will be ready in a minute and yes, I have some of our neighbor's homemade cookies. I hope you like oatmeal and raisin cookies."

The Professor smiled at her and said, "I love cookies and tea. May I have a cup of tea instead of coffee, please, if it's no bother?" he then dismissed her as if she were nothing more than hired help by turning his head to speak to Chuck instead. "Now Chuck, you know it took me a while to figure out what the problem was with the receiver inside, but I finally found it. You entered the numbers backwards. I know it's a newer model, but I thought I should let you know about the equipment I have so next time I ask for help you will be more comfortable with it."

Chuck immediately interrupted him by saying quite loudly to his wife, "Yes, Babe, I'll have some cream in my coffee with some of those delicious cookies Marian made. Thanks so much for getting that for us when you're busy doing the dishes." Turning back to Professor Chuck then said, "Ok Prof, what were you saying to me about your equipment?"

The Professor squirmed in his seat and said, "I prefer you call me Professor if you could please. It sounds so much better than 'Prof' don't you think?" In the background Missy held up one finger to let Chuck know she was counting the corrections starting now. Chuck just absently smiled at him and reached for the cup of coffee Missy handed to him and then she set the hot water in front of the Professor with three different kinds of tea bags to choose from. The plate of cookies followed and Missy sat down in between the men as she sipped on her own cup of coffee.

The Professor reached over and patted Missy on the knee and said, "Now, dear, this conversation might be very boring for you since we will be talking about technical items. If you need to do something else, please feel free to leave." He kept his hand on her knee and he rubbed it lightly. Missy was about to speak when Chuck took over.

"I'll have you know Prof that Missy is quite the expert at 'technical items' as the daughter of a rancher and the wife of a business owner and a CPA she can tell you just about everything you need to know on most subjects. By the way if you aren't careful where you lay your hands around here it's possible they could get broken. If you catch my drift *Prof*." The last was said with a snarl as Check reached for a cookie and bit it in half.

"Oh, my of course, no harm intended here." He stammered a little and lifted his hand off her knee. He grabbed his tea cup and it shook slightly as he raised his Earl Gray to his lips. "No harm at all intended or disrespect to either of you." Finally reaching for a cookie, he took a timid bite out of one edge and then his eyes widened behind his lenses and he said in surprise, "Oh my, this is delicious. I wasn't expecting this flavor!"

This sent the Professor on an entirely new bend in the conversation about his training at a Cordon Bleu school as a pastry chef before he decided to actually become an archeologist of the old western trails and historical data. Missy and Chuck let the Professor rattle on as he went from one story to another about himself. Chuck finally looked at his watch after an hour. Three cups of tea and half a dozen cookies were consumed by the Professor. "Well Prof, looks like it is time to call it a night. With the dive tomorrow you must need your sleep as much as my wife and I do. We'll see you bright and early tomorrow morning before the wind kicks up. Let me show you the door."

"Ah yes, it is getting late. It turned into an enjoyable evening; don't you think?" Not waiting for a response, he continued. "Yes, a most enjoyable evening. Do you mind if I take the cookies home with me? I really do enjoy them."

Missy went to the kitchen, got a sandwich bag and placed the three remaining cookies in the bag, zipped it shut and then handed it to Chuck to give to the Professor. "I'm going to wash up the cups so I don't have dirty dishes in the sink tonight. We'll see you in the morning Professor." She turned without the handshake he wanted and headed to the kitchen area.

"Here you go Prof, I even turned the outside light on for you. Don't stumble on your way home." Chuck smiled as he held the door open for the Professor.

"Now Chuck, you know I prefer Professor over the term 'Prof.' It just sounds so disrespectful to merely call me 'Prof,' don't you think? Missy held up two fingers behind the counter as she washed up the cups and cookie plate. She smiled and just shook her head as Chuck just patiently ignored the correction, he said again. "Good night Prof. See you in the morning bright and early." "He shut the door with a satisfied clunk and locked it.

Turning the lights off one by one as they headed to bed,

Chuck rubbed Missy's shoulders and said, "Funny how knocks on the door can interrupt a good mood, isn't it? I think I'll take a shower and then we both need to just crash tonight so we're fresh for the dive tomorrow."

Missy turned into his arms and, hugging him around the waist said, "No worries on my end. I think I know how to put him in his place now without even calling him Albert, or Prof or Dumb Ass. A good night's sleep sounds perfect to me. We'll catch up with alone time later, darling."

The next morning, they ate a light breakfast and packed sandwiches for lunch together in the kitchen and quietly talked about the dive to take more photos and grid off the area. They made enough lunch for the Professor since they had no idea if he would know enough to pack his own lunch. Cold chicken sandwiches were the order of the day, with containers of tomatoes and lettuce in case anyone wanted to have more on their sandwich. They headed out the door together right at 6:00 A.M. and locked the camper. Started up the truck and drove over to sit beside the motor home and wait, and wait, and wait. Finally, Chuck blasted on the horn and the Professor opened the door still in his robe. "Um, you said early but I thought you meant 9:00 A.M."

Chuck snorted and Missy placed her hand on his knee, "Just be nice, tell him we are headed out and we'll be back with pictures later on this afternoon. That way, he can get a look at the site without getting wet and cold. Apparently, he isn't an early riser." Chuck rolled down his window and informed the Professor they were headed out and would see him later on. Spinning the wheels and covering him in a cloud of dusty gray and gravel, they headed off without him.

The dive was peaceful that day on the lake. Even the river bed area below the surface played along by being calm. The pictures were excellent and when they floated slowly to the surface they both felt they had been given a reprieve by God. Having lunch together in the quiet, warming air with the lap of the water gently swaying the boat sent them both in memory back in time when they were a young married couple. The day without the Professor was perfect. The lunch was delicious, the pictures had turned out wonderfully and they both felt they didn't have a care in the world.

The quiet was soon interrupted by the sound of a fishing boat motor approaching them. The man at the motor was waving one hand and yelling "Ahoy mates, ahoy!" When Chuck realized it was the Professor and that he had rented a boat from the Marina across the lake he just flinched and turning to Missy said, "Well, there goes the neighborhood."

Chapter Twenty-Eight
Cooking Moon

The demand for payment of all George's outstanding loans came a few years after his death. When the law firm of Hedrick, Jordon and Leighton went through paper work and figured how to get some of the cattle, crops and land back. They needed to find a way to sell it off and have Josephine and her children move back to Fort Berthold Reservation Mission. The Mission had been opened in 1876 at 'Like A Fishhook Village' when the Arikara (Son of the Star), the Hidatsa (Crows Breast), and the Mandan (Red Cow) had given half a million acres of land for the Congregational Mission. The original Fort Berthold was established on May 9, 1876 because of that land gift. Finally, in 1897, nine years after George's death, Fort Berthold was moved about 20 miles over to Elbowoods. The mission built new buildings in that place and homes for the tribe to live in.

Seven years before his death George and the other ranchers in the area had a bad winter and lost a great deal of their herds. The crops were poor the following summer because of drought and two tough winters made it hard for all of them. George had borrowed heavily against his land, road house and the future. River travel was still good and the miners were still headed west to make their fortunes and possibly be fleeced by George. Outlaws hid in the areas around the river cliffs and all farmers and ranchers protected themselves with guns. Immigrant trains were coming into the area and dropping off sod busters by box car loads.

When the law firm took a look at the papers they held against George's place, they knew they could make some money from the sale. They waited a few months before they started to come and visit Josephine and offer to help her with the books. They figured she would never marry again, and maybe by convincing her to move back to Reservation lands, she would have tribal help raising her four children. Her sister Mary had already sold the homestead that she and her husband Frank Fleming were proving up and moved back to Fort Berthold. The law firm also thought it was their Christian duty to get Josephine away from the Road House and move the soiled doves out of the area.

Once the plan was put into motion they discovered a shrewd businesswoman in Josephine. She had discovered that as a widow of a Civil War Veteran she was entitled to a pension. When the lawyers first brought up selling the ranch, roadhouse and livestock she told them she would think about this if they would help write letters to the War Department that would allow her to receive her rightful pension as a widow. Mr. Hedrick was especially surprised at this since he was unaware of how shrewd a thinker Josephine was. As he left the ranch that day he stopped to shake her hand and said,

"Josephine, it might take a while, but we will do everything we can to get you that pension. Then we will talk about selling the ranch and business to us. Does this meet with your approval?"

Josephine calmly nodded yes as Ellen clutched at her mother's skirts and stared wide-eyed up at the man with the round-top derby hat. Josephine went back inside to check the funds left in George's pouch. Sitting at the table, she wrote down how much she would need for food for the next six months for her and the children, then the boots and clothes they would need as well. The boys would soon be going to the one-room schoolhouse a few miles from here. She had asked the foreman to make sure the two oldest, George and John, both had horses that were well-trained to get the boys there and home safely. Her head started to throb again, and she had to place the papers up on the shelf out of Ellen's reach since the toddler got into everything. She lifted Ellen up and went to the door and told George Jr. and John to watch Charley and play with him. George asked," Mother, are you sick?"

She said, "My head aches, I am going to lay down with Ellen. My head will not ache if I can rest." Those headaches would come back over the years because of the beatings she had endured. The stress only increased with worry over her children, money, the ranch, and the pension she was fighting to get.

After getting Ellen to rest with her and resting herself, Josephine took the coins from George's pouch, the oldest ones she took out and making sure that Ellen had dozed off soundly she separated them. Lifting each corner of the bedpost she grabbed the strings of the pouches she had made from strips of leather and placed the coins in each of the four pouches, one for each child. She slid the pouches back into place in the cool brass of each of the four posts and that made Josephine feel better. Finally, that task was done and Josephine lay down beside her sleeping daughter and closed her weary eyes for a much-needed nap.

Mr. Hedrick and partners Jordan and Leighton had considered George a good risk and loaned him money for a start. When he returned to town he had a short meeting with his partners; Jordan and Leighton. "Gentlemen, we are not getting the ranch and roadhouse this year. It will take a while, but Josephine will sell to us. We have to start letters to Washington, DC War Department to get Josephine her Civil War Widow Pension first. Then we can start talking sale price. I think we need to keep helping her with the books, she clearly is making good profit there and we want to make sure we keep getting our share plus a good interest rate." So, the work with Josephine and her family began with the first letter from the law firm of Hedrick, Jordan and Leighton being sent to the War Department in March of 1891 requesting she immediately be placed on the Civil War Widow Pension roll. Finally, in 1897 she was granted the sum of $8.00 per month plus $2.00 for each child.

George had settled bottom land along the Missouri River to Farm when he started out. He had a contract with the government to raise oats and was given the use of all the land he could get water on. The oats were taken by boat up river to Fort Buford to feed the government horses held there.

George farmed about 1200 acres and to provide water he dammed Beaver Creek and flooded his field with heavy black loam. George employed about sixteen men for work on the farm and ranch and the building on their place at 'Grinnell Flats,' that were all made of log. A large house, bunk house, small store, post office, saloon, barns, shed and corrals for the horses and mules made up the ranch area along the river. The boats that went up and down the Missouri brought provisions and also whiskey for his saloon and men changed horses when carrying mail across the prairie here. Miners would stop to get something to eat and drink at the saloon and were entertained by the 'soiled doves' in The Blind Pig when they had the money.

When Buford Territory became part of the new state of North Dakota things rapidly changed for many including Josephine and her children. The loans that Mr. Hedrick and his partners held were called in were being called in and were paid slowly with a high interest rate being charged after George's death. The tribes from the area were asked to move to the Berthold Reservation and many went, including Josephine's sister Mary and her children. With no charges against her, she and her family decided it was time to move to be closer to her sister Mary in Elbowoods.

As the family moved into the smaller house in Elbowoods, Josephine felt her spirit was finally set free. There would be no more beatings and threats, her children would be kept safe and she knew that both she and her sister would be treated better on Tribal lands. The first order was to get everything she had brought from Tobacco Garden to her new home here off the wagon and into the house. The two oldest boys could be of great help, Charley and Ellen were younger and would be needed to do the lighter loads and helping with making the beds and sweeping.

To the rescue came her beloved sister Mary and her two children. Mary said "Let the children carry boxes and I'll help while you tend Ellen and Charley. When I get tired you can carry things in and I'll play with Ellen and Charley." Josephine smiled as she hugged Ellen in one arm and hugged her sister with the other, "Oh Mary, we are back together here, with no husbands and these children you make me know we will be alright."

Slowly the items were brought inside; the pallets lay on the floor in the loft for the three boys to sleep on, the bed and horsehair mattress brought in to the only bedroom on the first floor and a little pallet laid on the floor for Ellen to sleep on. The dishes were moved into the kitchen area as Mary started a fire in the large stove. She said, "This is a big cooking stove. You can make bread here easily and good meals will come from here."

Josephine smiled as she took a cake of lye soap out and shaved some into a bucket of cool water as she waited for the water in the reservoir to heat up. "This will feel good to clean up this house for us. I'll start bread as soon as I wash the shelves off and stack the dishes on them. Today and tomorrow will be busy days for us all. Mary is your house bigger than this one?" Addressing her sister felt so wonderfully normal and safe that she paused every so often to smile a little smile that didn't make her face ache.

Chatting together as the children were in and out of the house, the older boys moved the horses into the little barn and unhitched the wagon and harnesses, rubbing down the horses and giving them feed and water without being told. They finally approached the house to see if anything had been made to eat. The little ones happily grabbed at their legs and said, "Give me a ride, give me a ride." Since they were both tall and strong they easily picked up the two younger boys and placed them on their shoulders and gave them a ride into the large kitchen area and set them down on chairs placed around the table.

"Mother, do we have something to eat now?" the eldest child of Mary and Frank said. Mary answered quietly "Yes, bring the basket from our wagon. We have meat, bread and some dried apple pie I made for this day. We will eat together."

And so, the first day at Elbowoods started for Josephine and Mary. Both widows with children to raise the best they know how. In 1900, Josephine was awarded 160 acres of homestead land in McLean County. After her sister Mary died in 1910, she inherited another 80 acres.

Josephine became a cook, while attempting to get her Civil War Widow's benefits from the Federal Government. She finally won the battle and started to receive her small pension as the widow of a Civil War Veteran. Her life settled down as she raised the children she adored.

She finally met a man to marry and in 1894, married Charles W. Moore a rancher from the Elbowoods area. Fortune did not smile on this marriage either and within a month Moore deserted her and disappeared. Whether he thought Josephine knew of hidden gold is not known. Josephine filed for divorce in Ward County District Court at Minot, the divorce was granted on September 14, 1897, and the defendant defaulted. She always seemed to have enough funds so her adored children did not go without. Josephine and George's daughter Ellen grew to be a wonderful young woman who would attend college in Minnesota and learn to walk in 'heels this much' (holding a span of two-three inches between your fingers) that her Mother would brag about later on. As Josephine aged and her children grew, married and had families of their own, Josephine moved in with her beloved daughter Ellen in Elbowoods, ND.

Her oldest son, George Grinnell Jr., was educated at Carlisle College and became a blacksmith. He was employed as a blacksmith and engineer by the government at Elbowoods for thirty years. The other two boys; John and Charley also attended school and worked hard all their lives. Their father's influence overshadowed them later on in life and they experienced many marriages over time. The truth is that they all loved their mother dearly. Josephine wisely kept her counsel about the hidden gold and paper funds in the bedpost until her children were older. Toward the end of her life, she had called the children to Ellen's house and told them of the gold and paper money she had kept hidden for years in the bed post.

She instructed her oldest two boys to go and get the pouches from the bottom of the brass bed. They followed their mother's directions and went into the bedroom and as one would lift the corner of the bedpost up the other would remove the cap on the end. One pouch slid out into their hands from each corner post, each pouch was made of strips of leather stitched together. The leather had not been worked or softened over time and was hard to the touch. The gold pieces made the pouches heavy to hold but they carried them into the front room and laid them on the marble top table beside the rocking chair where their Mother sat.

"These pieces are yours my children. I've tried not to spend them all and only took out a few when we needed funds to buy food and clothes. You all will receive the same gold pieces and paper left by me and your father." With that she proceeded to slowly open each bag and empty the contents onto the table. Twelve gold pieces and four bills were what were contained in the four bags. The gold pieces were ten-dollar gold eagles that George had always preferred. The paper money was different though, the largest bill was a fifty-dollar watermelon bill with President Grant's face on it, that bill would go to George Jr., the oldest. Josephine had thought about this for many years and wanted all four to know how much she loved them since they had all grown together keeping each other safe from an abusive man.

She smiled lovingly as she placed each gift in separate leather pouches and, starting with her oldest, gently placed them in their hands and spoke of her love for them. All four children bent and hugged their mother tightly and spoke of their love for her as well. Josephine would never speak of how she had gotten this money when asked. She would only say, "The money came from hard work on the ranch and saloon."

And then she would change the subject when her children tried to press her about the fact that their father had much gold.

The children learned later on that their father had left coins buried around 'Grinnell Flats' where the ranch, post office, bunk house, and saloon were located. When George Jr. passed away in 1948, three years after his beloved Mother passed away, he left his $50 Watermelon marked bill to his brother John Alfred. John sold it later that year at a private auction sale on the East coast.

Before the dam was built and Lake Sakakawea flooded the area in the early 50s, many people would go digging around Grinnell Flats and Tobacco Garden looking for anything below the surface that might be pouches of coins. To this date, nothing has been reported as being recovered.

George Grinnell's body was moved to another fort years later. Josephine passed away at Elbowoods Hospital on March 13, 1945 and was buried in the Catholic Cemetery there. Her oldest son, George Grinnell Jr. died three years later at Elbowoods on October 4th, 1948 and is also buried there. Surviving members of the family still live in the area and the elders retell loving stories of the spirit of Josephine and her love for her children.

Chapter Twenty-Nine
Golden Family

A week later another camping trailer was pulled into the area where the Professor's motor home and the fifth wheel trailer that belonged to Missy and Chuck was parked. The new trailer had two beds in the back, a smaller bath as well as a second bath with a shower and bedroom. This second fifth wheel was almost identical to Missy and Chuck's, but was almost two feet shorter in the back garage area. It contained a little surprise of two quads in the back with four helmets, attached seats for passengers and a rifle rack on the front of both. Chuck wanted to surprise his brother-in-law since he knew these items could be used on the ranch and it would be a great tax write off when used for herding and fencing.

Chuck was also secretly excited about having another man to talk to since speaking with 'Good Old Prof' had gotten increasingly annoying over the last three days of listening to his ideas and retelling stories about his personal importance. The professor had taken to giving mini lectures when spending evenings looking at the dive photos from the area where the original ranch, bunk house, post office and saloon were located.

His first "min-lecture" left Chuck snorting all the way back to the camper as the Prof displayed his total ignorance and lack of historical research about the outlines of what they were observing by stating:

"What you are seeing is the remains of a very early structure that was possibly a barn or a portion of a fort blockade structure."

Whenever Missy would try to stop and explain and show him the drawing Mort had quickly sketched he would interrupt her and state; "Thank you for your effort and that of your dad, but really let's remember who the expert on this really is after all." He would continue on by explaining, in multiple ways, about all the work he had done in the South West. He would add how many articles he had written and go on to explain that he was, in fact, the most knowledgeable man concerning the history of the western states in the nation.

Missy was not concerned about his need for self-aggrandization and would continue to interrupt him as many times as she could. Not only to provide a source of amusement for herself and her husband, but to also keep him from writing about their find to early on. She didn't want the area to be flooded with other treasure hunters right now. This seemed to me more of a family dig and she hoped they could keep other people being involved to the bare minimum.

The next day when they returned from their dive in the early afternoon the Prof announced it was time to start moving items slowly around the area to determine what lay underneath some of the raised areas he thought might be the site of where the buildings had been located. Much to the delight of both Missy and Chuck they saw a truck with another boat behind it parked beside the almost new fifth wheel trailer left for Jeth, Babs and the twins. Missy started waving excitedly from the bow of the boat and yelling, "Ahoy little brother, Ahoy Babes, Marlow and Nylee, Ahoy!" As soon as they got close enough to the little beach area she jumped out with the line and waded to shore as she pulled on the rope to anchor the boat to the iron ring they had pounded into a rock. "Oh, it is so good to see you all!" She exclaimed as she rushed up to hug her brother and his wife and then the twins in turn.

She neglected the items on the boat she normally would carry ashore and just figured this one time the Prof could handle all of his own equipment. She only hoped that Chuck would feel the same. After he lifted the motor up he got out and came up to greet the family. He surprised Missy even more when he said, "Let's all go into our trailer and just have some nice cold drinks and something to eat. I'm sure the Prof can figure out what to carry up to his motor home by himself."

One arm over Missy's shoulders and the other over Babs, he herded them all up the slope away from the little man left standing in the boat with all of his gear and a puzzled look of surprise on his face. Professor Fairland realized he would be in charge of lugging all of his own equipment back up to the motor home and taking care to rinse everything off by himself. He had just assumed that Chuck and Missy would always be doing this for him and was stunned to realize that it wasn't the case anymore. He would make sure to let his annoyance over this be known in a few hours when he was done.

It was more than a few hours later when Professor Fairland finally finished cleaning and drying off his diving gear and exhausted he fell asleep in the chair without having any supper. His brain swirled before he fell asleep with thoughts of making sure this family would never receive one penny of anything recovered. He couldn't believe how poorly he had been treated as a visiting and knowledgeable professor of fame. He would show them; he would show them were the last thoughts that swirled in his brain before he loudly began to snore.

The hilarity continued well past supper as Missy and Babs got burgers ready to throw on the grill while Chuck told stories about dear old 'Prof' and his thoughts and comments. When he stopped laughing, he finally said, "I probably shouldn't keep teasing him, but he is so pompous and annoying I can't seem to stop. Sure, he has degrees, but he has no social skills with other people at all. Sometimes, he acts like we are the village idiots." Then he made a prediction, "Just you wait you four, I can't imagine how he's going to be treating you guys!"

Missy kept shaking her head back and forth as she giggled, and finally when she stopped her lilting laughter, took a breath and said, "Chuck is right, and Babs, when he sees you he'll get all tongue-tied and try to put the move on you. Just wait and see."

Chuck came around the island and grabbed the platter the burgers were loaded on, "Missy's right you know, he'll start off by rubbing your arm above the wrist when he first meets you. Anyone want to make a bet with me on this? We'll be doing dishes for a week if you dare."

Babs said in almost a whisper, "No betting for me. I'm not wasting time or money on this anymore."

Chuck simply looked sad and said, "Sorry Babs forgot about that." He turned and with his free arm gave her a hug in response to her comment. "I kind of feel like an ass now, I really didn't mean to embarrass you."

Babs returned the one arm hug with her own and continued to stir the fresh salad dressing and said, "No apologies needed, things are slowly getting better with counseling and my sponsor keeps in touch. Plus, having a family that loves me as much as mine does makes me feel like I've already won the lottery." Chuck and Jeth went out the door to start barbequing and both men had big smiles on their faces at her comment.

The Professor was sound asleep in his motor home and missed out on a wonderful dinner of burgers, salad, chips and conversation. Missy thought he might show up later for dessert and coffee or tea, but she decided to not worry about the annoying man and just enjoy the time with family. When they had eaten their fill they went down and unloaded the boat. Chuck showed Jeth, Babs, and the twins how to rinse everything off from the water tank placed on metal stilts that they kept filled with potable well water. He gave specific instructions about what the water was like below the surface and what might likely happen when they would start to dig. He warned them again about the Professor's attitude, but gave him high marks for his diving expertise. The man knew what he was doing and avoided getting in the trace flow that might move him faster downstream than he could handle.

Missy decided tonight was perfect for S'mores beside the metal fire ring they had set up. The twins moved their bags into the family trailer and took quick showers as the older members started up the fire and got the items ready for making the treats. Wine for the women, cold beer for the men and soda for the twins filled the cooler they set beside the eight lawn chairs that circled the fire pit. The bag of marshmallows, chocolate bars and graham crackers were set on a small table opposite the cooler and the roasting sticks were stacked on top. Jeth whistled and called "Ready kids? Fire is going and you've got a perfect spot to roast those marshmallows!"

Someone with wet hair that smelled like shampoo dressed in flip flops and baggy sweats emerged from the camper and it was hard to tell if it was Marlow or Nylee who came out first. As she got closer to the fire it was easy to see the smile on Nylee's face in the dark. "Sorry it took so long; I made Marlow wait his turn by getting in there first!" Then she giggled and added, "I'll make it up to him by getting his S'mores done before mine!"

The first day ended on a pleasant note for the family with quiet stares into the flames, gooey fingers and a gentle feeling of satisfaction as one by one they headed into the camper and left Chuck and Missy fireside to clean up and take care that the embers were cooled and totally out by covering them with water. The two headed into their camper and mentally felt they were ready for the dig part of the dive tomorrow.

The Professor woke up before dawn with a stiff neck from sleeping in the chair with smelly clothes and hunger pains rumbling in his stomach. Running a hand over his face his first thought was for a cup of hot tea, a shower and then something filling for breakfast. He was still annoyed over the slight he received las night and was mentally preparing what he would say to the newcomers.

After cooking himself eggs, bacon and toast the Professor finished his third cup of Earl Gray tea and rinsed off his dishes as he talked in small comments to himself as if he was having a conversation with Chuck and Missy and was verbally smashing them with his expertise.

The Professor didn't believe that having such a heavy breakfast might give him stomach cramps when he dove later that morning, but he would soon discover the error of eating too much before a dive. When he finally emerged from his motor home he discovered both boats in the water and what appeared to be a group of people in swim suits going up and down the ramp as they carried items from the campers down to the boats.

Since he wasn't accustomed to more than two other people to deal with he realized immediately he would need to interrupt this constant flow of activity and get back into control on the spot. Clamping his hat on his head and pushing his sunglasses up on the bridge of his nose he set forth to do just that.

"Ahoy there!" Smiling and waving his clipboard he approached the young man headed up the ramp. "You must be Marlow, Chuck and Missy's nephew. Welcome to the dig young man, welcome. I'm so glad you decided to get involved in an archeological dig. What a welcome site it is to see young people interested in the past." The Professor barely stopped to take a breath when a whistle from the river stopped him.

Jeth was waving and yelling something, "Marlow, talk to the Prof later will you? We have to get the tanks and diving gear finished loading. No worries Prof, you can talk to Marlow later on, he's got a job to do so we can get going here."

The Professor realized once again the family was trying to steam roll past his position of command and he started to do a slow boil as he turned to grab his own tank and fins. He headed straight towards Missy and Chuck's boat as he started to mumble under his breathe, "Ingrates, worthless incompetent fools. Just who do you think you're dealing with here you idiots?" He kept the phony smile on his face as he proceeded to carry his items to the boat and load them in the spot that Chuck said would be best for him.

Chuck had been right, of course, but the Professor would not let him know that. After all what was he anyway? "Just a man who plays in the dirt." The Professor continued to mutter to himself as he had an imaginary conversation with himself.

"Oh yes, I'm going to stop this family from getting even a mention when I publish the results of this find. They all think they're so smart, well I'll show them what smart really is. These ingrates won't see a penny of anything. I'll have it all, yes I'll have it all." He kept repeating this litany over and over as he headed up to the motor home and got the rest of his diving gear. He had made his own lunch that day since he didn't think this family would bother to make him a sandwich anymore. By the time all was loaded and ready to go it was close to 9:00 A.M. and the Professor discovered his big breakfast wasn't sitting well with him.

I must apologize all. You'll need to wait for me, I ate too much this morning and now I have to go use the restroom." Blushing under his tan the Professor headed up the slope to his motor home and was almost too late using the bathroom inside. He needed to change out of his swimming trunks and shorts since he had left streaks in both of them.

His stomach was still miserably full and he decided to take stomach antacid tablets along with him in case he would need them. He changed clothes after spreading more suntan lotion on, headed out the door almost half of an hour later.

Everyone was waiting in the boats slightly off shore with the trolling motors holding the boats in place. "Come and wade out Prof." Chuck merrily waved at him, "water is nice and warm, you'll be fine."

"Sorry for the slight delay folks, you'll be glad to know I'm feeling better. Now with the man in charge aboard we can all set out for today's adventure." The Professor merrily, or at least with a phony smile on his face, waded out to the boat and after setting his ever-present waterproof clipboard on the seat, stepped up on the rear ladder and climbed aboard.

Chuck had warned Jeth and his family about the notes the Professor would write on the clipboard to inform them exactly what to do in each grid area. He also told them the Prof would start out being pleasant, but by the end of the day he would get very irritated and grouchy with all of them, but not himself. Arming themselves with smiles they headed out to the co-ordinates mapped the day before on the GPS unit attached to the dash board. Jeth followed to the side of their wake and when the motor slowed they could hear the excited voices of the twins talking.

With the boats anchored feet away from each other it created a quieter zone to enter the water and would provide some protection for them when they would slowly come to the surface. The Professor was in full academic control mode and acted as if none of them knew what to do at all.

Finally, Babs snapped at him and said, "For God's sake Professor, we aren't idiots you know. Stop treating us like we're all in school, you're being ridiculous, we are all certified divers here." With that statement hanging in the air between the boats and the Professors mouth hanging open Babs lowered her face mask, inserted her mouthpiece and slipped off the back of the boat into the water behind her husband.

"Well, I for one have just had it with this family!" he screamed as his face turned a bluish red. "You are all idiots and as far as I'm concerned I'll make sure none of you ever get..." and he stopped mid-sentence as he grabbed his lower belly and ran below deck to where the chemical toilet waited for him.

Chuck wanted to laugh, but secretly thought it was no laughing matter if the Prof was really sick. He just smiled and winked at his wife as he slipped his hood on, placed his face mask on, inserted his mouth piece and slipped off the back of the boat to be followed by Missy.

Using hand signals Chuck joined the other four and motioned with his hand what level to drop to and how many feet up ahead they needed to swim. They knew the Prof would join them in about an hour by the time his bout was done in the head.

Almost exactly forty-five minutes later the Professor showed up with his white clipboard and underwater pen to write on it. The first thing he wrote made them all stop and stare at him. On the clipboard in the gray green water, they read:

"I'm fine, as if you assholes care!"

He furiously rubbed that off and then wrote again, "Don't move anything until I tell you to. You're all a bunch of idiots and this dig is under my control, NOT YOURS!!!!!!"

He rubbed it off again and then wrote, "If you think your names will even be mentioned in my article think again you ingrates! I'll have you know you will not be getting one penny if we find anything and I'll make sure of that!"

He rubbed if off again and wish a swish of his flippers moved past them rapidly to the first grid area where he proceeded to raise a cloud of dust by rapidly swinging his arm inside the grid area before reaching down to lift up what looked like a silt covered piece of wood.

Marlow and Nylee swam closer to their parents and made circling motions on either side of their heads as if to say, "He is crazy."

Babs nodded yes and held onto Jeth's hand and refused to go closer to where the Professor was attempting to lift the board even though he was waving them over to him. The Professor was rapidly writing on the board again, "Can I have some help over here? Please? I'm sorry I lost my temper, but my stomach is upset and it is making me grouchy."

Chuck motioned for Missy to stay with Babs and the twins as he and Jeth swam over to the Professor to attempt to help him move some of the boards. After moving them around and taking more photos in the grid area they didn't even notice when Missy swam to the other side of the grid area about one hundred fifty feet away.

She gently reached down and slowly moved a plank that looked lit it was at the top of a depression area. It appeared to have been the covering for a well since it was away from the other structures they had outlined. She also remembered something her Dad had said to her about when he was younger. He and his Father had taken the ferry across to Grinnell Flats and his Dad said, "Mort, no drinking water from this well. No one knows for sure who or what was dropped down inside."

Missy decided since this was on the opposite side of where the men were working, she would slowly investigate this area over the next few days and let Chuck know what she had seen at night. She slowly and carefully moved things barely an inch at a time and it became easier to see that this had indeed been a well at one time. The center had caved in but on the edge she saw an angle shape covered in silt sticking up. She took a picture with her own underwater camera from three different angles then carefully and slowly replaced the boards to cover her tracks when the professor would swim by the grids before surfacing.

After his comments to the family, she felt no twinge of remorse or guilt at what she was doing. She also felt that if anyone deserved the credit it should be her Dad and not someone like Professor Fairland who was merely riding on the coat tails of others.

That night, after getting back to the campsite later than usual, Chuck announced that everyone was in charge of rinsing off their own dive suits. Missy had planned well and made crock-pot lasagna and had garlic toast ready for the oven for everyone, even the Professor was invited. His stomach was growling from hunger and he simply nodded 'yes' without a thank-you to anyone.

When he went back to his motor home to change out of his trunks Jeth turned and stuck out his tongue at his retreating back. "Dad!" Marlow and Nylee proclaimed simultaneously and then burst into laughter. "Just can't help it. That guy is a real jerk; you were right Chuck. Think his name is A Prof for Asshole Prof as far as I'm concerned." Jeth turned and walked with Babs to the camper followed by the twins, all were ready to change.

Missy motioned Chuck over and said in a very quiet whisper, "I've found something in the well. It looks like a metal rectangular box. It'll take me two or three more dives to keep uncovering it and trying to gently pry it out. Can you keep the Prof busy and away from me? I want to take it back to Dad and let him open it. The Prof can just go to hell as far as I'm concerned!"

Chuck smiled and his face beamed like sunlight as he grabbed his wife in a hug and said, "Perfect, just like you Kitty!" As he kissed her he said, "I'm not saying nothing to anyone, I'll just let Jeth think we are messing with him by screwing the grids up so he needs to redo what we are doing. That will give you more time. You need to try and figure out the size of it and what you estimate the weight of it is. That way we'll know if we need the net with the air floats attached to bring it up." When you're ready to move it give me a fist pump in the air. I'll see you and cover for you so we can get it to the boat somehow. We'll figure out if we can tow it far enough behind to keep it from the Prof."

It took her three days after painstakingly moving and recovering boards and stones Missy was finally able to determine the size of the metal box with rusted handles, it was approximately 12 inches by 10 inches by 7 inches. The handles on the outside looked like they might be pulled off if she tried to lift it up by them. It was all recovered every afternoon so when the Professor swam by all he saw was the same thing he had seen and took photos of the days before.

When she finally felt they could safely move it up out of the water she realized it was close to 200 pounds. She felt that this was something George would have done to hide his ill-gotten funds by lowering this strong box down the well by a rope, and lifting it up when he needed funds in a hurry. After hurriedly taking pictures of it with a tape beside it she started to recover it all, including the boards. She looked up to see a commotion beside her as she realized the Prof was headed towards her and she couldn't see Chuck nor Jeth anywhere.

As the Prof swam directly to her he was looking at the grids on the ground. He wrote on his white board, "What are you doing way over here?" and then handed her the board.

Missy wrote back, "Thought I'd swim over here and check this out. Startled me, sorry I kicked up the silt." She pointed down as she handed the board back to the Prof.

He read what she had written and nodded and then motioned for her to swim back with him to where the others were. Giving him a thumbs up, she swam in front of him back towards Chuck. When they both got their Chuck shrugged his shoulders and then winked behind his mask and pointed three fingers down at a grid. As soon as the Prof swam up to them, he swam around him and grabbed one of the grid markers and picket it up and shook it close to the bottom. The Prof wrote furiously on his board, "STOP!" Chuck kept on messing with the grid markers moving them all a foot away from where they were located, while stirring up the silt from the bottom.

They all headed towards the mooring line to begin their ascent leaving the Prof for last. Missy was first with Chuck right behind her. She figured she had about ten minutes on the surface to let Chuck know about the size and estimated weight and her thoughts about why it was hidden in the well area. She also needed to figure out with Chuck how to actually take the net with buoys down and hide it and then partially fill the buoys and tow behind the boat tomorrow.

Once on top she quickly explained to Chuck about the

rusted metal strong box with handles and the approximate weight. He came up with a plan immediately about the net and how to hide it right by the spot from the Professor. He planned on going out early the next morning, diving and taking the net with buoys down and covering it in silt right beside the well area. At the end of the dive tomorrow he would go and gently move the box into the net, then wait for the Professor to move up the mooring line first. His plan included disabling the chemical head and letting the Prof know he'd have to go back with Jeth and his family since the head hadn't been drained the day before and that he couldn't use it.

They would tow the net far enough and deep enough behind the boat and he would pretend the motor was acting up when they did this. That night he would bring the net to shore and take the wagon down and pull it in and place the strong box in the wagon and cover it with a tarp and place in the back of Missy's 'Betty Burb'. By hiding it in plain sight they would have no problem with her taking it back to the ranch for Mort to open.

The next day, just like planned, everything was in place, Jeth and Chuck had messed with the grids and the Prof was busy replacing grid lines and checking his camera constantly. At the end of the dive time the Prof swam over the site once again checking everything. He swam to the mooring line first and headed up. Chuck waited on the bottom and as soon as he saw Jeth getting close to the Prof on the line to block his view below Chuck headed over to the well and started his process.

Once all were up in the two boats Chuck went below and came back up and said, "Sorry Prof, looks like you have to go in the other boat if you need the head. This one is out of order until I drain it. Sorry, really."

The Prof just grunted and removed his googles, mouthpiece, tank, and head gear. "Great, just great. Now I have to swim over to the other boat! I've never seen such a stupid family in my life! Why didn't you drain the tank last night?"

Chuck started to respond and the Prof kept right on talking. "Never mind, what does a dirt digger know anyway? I'll just swim over to the other boat and go back with them. Can you at least throw my little cooler over to them so I have something to eat?"

Chuck nodded and smiled and turned to holler at Jeth, "Prof's gonna ride back to shore with you so he can use the head. Here's his lunch." As he threw the little lunch cooler over he made sure it landed beside the boat and not in it. "Oops, sorry can you can snag it Nylee?"

Nylee leaned over and simply grabbed the handle and lifted it aboard. "Got it Uncle Chuck!" and then she giggled.

The Professor had been swimming his way back to the other boat and started cussing when he saw what had happened. Climbing aboard the ladder he muttered all the way in, "Stupid, careless fools, never going to see a penny or any mention, I'll make sure of that!"

As Chuck gunned the motor he and Missy started slowly until they felt the tug on the line. Chuck hollered to Jeth, "Go ahead of us, the motor is acting up, I think I need to do a choke adjustment on the motor. We'll take our time going in slowly, just go ahead of us. No worries, we'll just take our time going back!"

Jeth drove the boat up onto the beach area and anchored it off the bow. As Chuck and Missy slowly moved closer to shore, Chuck fiddled with the ignition switch to make it sound and look like he was having problems. Missy watched him drop the anchor and then she proceeded to dive over into the water to swim ashore. Chuck followed after he had picked up the tow rope from the front and brought it to the beach to tie it to the ring they pounded into the rock.

The curious Prof came down to the beach even before he finished washing his gear off to see what the problem was. Chuck just said, "Like I hollered to you guys in the boat the motor was acting up. I'll swim back out later and work on it and then haul in our gear to rinse off. No worries Prof!"

The Prof simply turned and walked back up the ramp muttering to himself, "See if I care, bunch of ingrates. Stupid family, don't even know how important I am in this. I'll show them, no mention of who they even are. Damn fools the lot of them!"

As they settled back into camp they all met around the campfire ring following a tradition they had established the first day of diving. They would discuss what they had seen and review the photos and decide what to do the next day of diving. As they all took their seats with sodas and water in hand they passed around a container of homemade cookies that Babs had made at the ranch. The Professor helped himself to four of them while the others took only one each. The double chocolate chips were a special recipe that Babs had created and were rich and moist even after being frozen and thawed.

Talking around a mouthful of cookies the Professor immediately started in on Chuck. "Now you know I think you thought you were helping by moving the grids, but you might have set up back a day by your actions. Do you think you'll remember not to move anything from now on? If you don't, I might have to request you stay topside to avoid this problem from now on."

Chuck managed to look sorry and said, "Gee Prof, I thought they were placed wrong since you had them on a slope. I promise not to touch them and move them again."

The Prof nodded and said, "I'll make sure you don't since I'll be watching you closely."

Just then a cell phone rang and all seven people grabbed for their phones in their pockets to see who the lucky person was to be able to leave the mini lecture about to start. Luckily it was Missy's phone, she had called Marian right before she got in the shower and asked her to call her in about ninety minutes with a fake emergency call.

She got up from the campfire ring and proceeded to speak to Marian in quiet tones, "Yes, I understand. Ok, I'll leave tomorrow morning and be back around noon. Will that work? Yes, I did."

On the other end Marian was quietly asking if something had been found and recovered. With the quiet answers of 'yes'

Marian informed Missy she would let Mort know and they would be waiting for her return the next day with the item.

Missy went back to the campfire ring and told the family not to worry, but the current tests done on Mort had come back and she was headed back to the ranch for a few days to check on things. She assured them all that she would be back in no more than two days. She and Chuck headed to their camper for the night and discussed the plan.

Chuck waited for about fifteen minutes and then quietly headed down with the wagon to the beach in his trunks, swam out to the boat and pulled the net up to the boat. The strong box without anything inside would weigh about 50 pounds, this one weighed around 180 according to Chuck when he lifted it onto the boat. He deflated the air buoys and started the electric trolling motor to bring the boat to shore. He quietly moved the wagon close to the bow, jumped back in the boat and lifted the strong box onto it and moved it into the wagon. All lights were off in the motor home, the other trailer and in his. He pulled the wagon up the ramp slowly and moved to the back of the 'burb', lifted the tail gate and placed the strong box in the back and covered it with a tarp.

He headed into the trailer and gave Missy a hug and said quietly, "No worries, it's in the back covered. I'll miss you tomorrow on the dive, have fun with Dad when he opens this!" They headed to bed to wait for the sun.

The next day she headed directly home and when she arrived she waved Marian and Mort to come down from the porch to the back of the suburban as she opened the tailgate. Without ceremony, she flipped the tarp back and uncovered the strong box. "Dad, you need to open this here. It's close to 200 pounds and I can't lift this by myself. I think you and Marian get the privilege of opening this first. Then we'll talk about what to do next."

Marian said, "We'll let your dad do this by himself Missy. After all, this has been more a family dream than mine." She sipped her coffee and waited as Mort reached for the box and opened it slowly to the glitter of coins and nuggets reflecting the sun inside.

Epilogue

Stands of lush silvery green cottonwoods and gray-green elm trees towered on the river bend as they shadowed the thick underbrush of chokecherries, buffalo berries, and even wild sweet strawberries. Here in the shady cool river bend the bugs were thick, the dragonflies droned and hummed as they captured one mosquito after another. The river, Holes in Water, called the Missouri by others always ran into it, and in earlier times right by it. When she didn't, the problems seemed almost unbearable when they came.

Not if they came, but when they came. The problems that came to me last summer came when I was away from the river. It is true that some came when I was in it, and around it, but most of them came when I was away from it. I have a sense of deep moving with her wispy soul and a common link with the mud that clogs her sweet taste. I too have been wispy in thinking and clogged up with so many memories I feared I would never move again.

So, I'd like to start my story again for the umpteenth time. They say the more you share it the charm increases and I hope they are right. If they aren't I'm afraid this story will be lost for all time, I would be truly sad if that happened. So let me back this truck up and tell the story the way it was told to me, and how I got myself into this predicament in the first place.

Over one hundred years ago in this peaceful place of prairie beauty, a prairie queen of a town, grew. She was a landlocked beauty known by many names over the years. Before humans settled and stayed in her rolling hills she was home to many others. Wild horses with bits of sage in their manes and bite marks from fighting would cross over to get to her from the other side. The banks were full of ash, cottonwood, hickory and oak, while the draws were filled with wonderful berries. The area was lush and green in the spring and most of the summer.

The nations of the Hidatsa, Arikara, Mandan, Sanisch, Blackfoot, Lakota, Sioux and Hunk Papa would travel in migration to her area to find 'Kinnikinnick'. That wild tobacco was plucked, dried and was used as smoke and trade around the campfire. Many stories of brave hunting feats were told as the smoke would curl up into the cooling clear prairie sky. The tribes followed the migration paths of the animals they would hunt for survival. One day it would all change as others would journey into the area.

Trappers from the Hudson Bay Company were soon followed by explorers; the most well-known were Lewis and Clark. Perhaps that small curiosity from the eastern shores of this wild country is what eventually lead to her downfall. I can only speculate from where I sit now.

Tobacco Garden and Grinnell Flats became a wild area filled with a saloon, bunk house, post office, barns, corrals and a ranch house. They were swept under the water when the dam was built for the control of water traffic further south. They had lifted their skirts for anyone who came their way, and because of that, they would change the history of this country in ways almost unimaginable. And now, a year later, I am sitting here at the graveyard wondering what to do with the contents of the rusty old metal strong box. Now all of them are gone; Mom, Dad, and Marian and her husband.

I made a promise and intended to keep it to them for the next two years. Professor Fairland had written his paper and, as promised, didn't mention the family once. He never found anything but the remains of the place and hinted that more was buried deeper below the surface.

I would head out from the ranch tomorrow to stay with my husband, Chuck. Jeth, Babs and the twins had settled in well here. The ranch was slowly making progress towards paying off the land and staying in the business of raising cattle and doing some farming on the side.

Laying the wild roses on all four graves gave me a reason to move again. I hoisted myself into the saddle as I turned my horse back towards the barn once more, two aging women out for a ride to clear their heads.

Bibliography

North Dakota Lost Treasure

From:

https://www.metal-detecting-ghost-towns-of-the-east.com

Fort Abercrombie Ruins: Located east of Abercrombie on Route 81. Built in 1858, first Federal Fort in ND, abandoned in 1877.

Fort Dilts: Located on Route 12, between Rhame and Marmath built in 1864, everyone was massacred, fort was burned down.

Fort Bartlett: Located north of State Route 4 miles west of Lakota, a ghost town, many saloons and treasures large and small are located around ghost towns.

Belmont: A river port located 14 miles south of Grand Forks; destroyed in 1897 by a flood, several safes were swept into the river and never recovered.

Old Bottineau: On Oak Creek near the Canadian Border 1-mile north of Bottineau Star Route 218. Treasure hunters have located buried treasure here.

Pleasant Lake Ghost Town: Located 45 miles northwest of Devils Lake on Route 2, in the 1880's bank robbers buried several chest of gold bullion in town.

Big Butte Treasure (Sentinel Butte): Located near the town of Lignite State Route 52, $40,000.00 in gold and silver were stolen from a Hudson Bay Paymaster and the coins were buried near here. The robber was being interrogated by the Royal Canadian Mounted Police in Portal and died.

Fort Clark: Miners buried $90,000.00 in gold nuggets 1 mile east of Fort Clark in Oliver County. The miners were returning from MT gold fields and were attacked by Indians.

Knife and Missouri River Junction: Approximately $100,000.00 in gold dust and nuggets were buried by a miner, never recovered.

Sunset Butte: Treasure of gold coins was stolen from an Army Paymaster during the Civil War, buried here and never recovered.

Belli, Anthony M., ND: Gold Frontiers, pg. 28 December 2010, Lost Treasure

Slope County: Chalky Butte-East Highway 85, South of Amidon, 5 to 6 miles, 4 outlaws hid gold; Sioux man observed their actions and hid the treasure in another spot.

Sunset Butte: South of Amidon, around 1900, 3 revolvers were found, marked USrdquo and USDquo rusted wagon irons were also found, no gold recovered.

Stark County: Belfield area, gold discovered in a 'mountain' camp near Belfield in 1864 both gold and silver was hidden there, 150 years later no gold or silver has been recovered.

Burke County: Approximately 7 miles south of Lignite in the

hills a cave known as 'Robber's Cave' is located, a rock with 1877 carved on it was found in the cave, no gold or silver from the Hudson Bay Paymaster robbery has been recovered.

Rules and Regulations

From:

https://investusgoldbureau.com"What to do if you Find Treasure/U.S. Gold Bureau

Posted on February 9, 2017 by U.S. Gold Bureau

*Exactly how old an object must be to be considered treasure is unclear, but court rulings have defined it as both after a point that the original owner is unlikely to claim it or after at least a few decades (In 1991 both an Iowa court ruled that 35 to 59 years should be sufficient).

Treasure Trove Definition:

The items in a treasure trove must be gold or silver, gems, money or jewelry. These items revert to the finder if the owner is not known. The superior claim goes to the finder except for the following conditions; treasure hunting done on public lands.

Archaeological Resources Protection Act of 1979

States that any 'archaeological resources' found on these lands belongs to the government; this law has been extended to just about anything over 100 years old. If you find something and it can't be considered treasure you are legally obligated to take it to the police. It will go into their custody and be handled like any other case of lost property.

Reservoir Salvage Act of 1960

A historically valuable shipwreck can be treated as an archaeological or historical site instead of a commercial property. The term 'embedded' means any submerged object in the states submerged lands and they belong to the state under the embeddedness doctrine.

Newspaper/Magazine Resources

Mountrail County Promoter, Breeling, Lutie T., March 18, 1954, pg. 2 Killing on Grinnell Flats

North Dakota REC Magazine, Rolfsrud, Erling Nicolai, March 1984, pg. 45, An Agent of God

National Enquirer, Ruehl, Franklin R., February 10, 1987, pg. 23, 100 Years Ago This Battered Wife Was the First to Kill Her Hubby – And Walk Free

State Historical Society of ND, Fargo Forum Special, Williston, ND, August 22, staff writer, Musty Williams County Records Reveal 'Act of God' Murder.

Williams County Historical Society, Eide, Marlene, Coordinator, 1975, Vol. 1, pgs. 33-38.

Bismarck Daily Tribune, (Bismarck, Dakota [N.D.]} 1881-1916, March 22, 1902, image 2>>Chronicling America>>Library of Congress

About the Author

This is the first novel for this author. Matsie Non has written some short stories and poetry in the past. If you would like to comment to the author, please contact Matsie Non at email; matsienon@yahoo.com.

www.ingramcontent.com/pod-product-compliance
Lightning Source LLC
LaVergne TN
LVHW031536060526
838200LV00056B/4521